Jobs of Work

D. Scott Apel

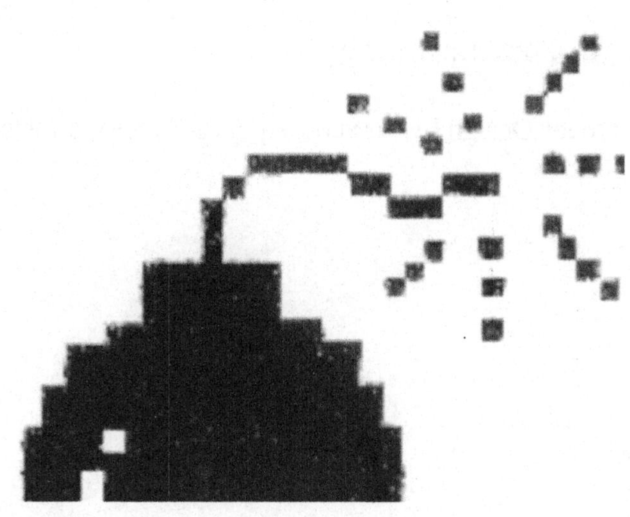

Jobs of Work
By D. Scott Apel
Published by The Impermanent Press

First Print Edition: 19 March 2023

v01.7

Publisher's Note: Names of actual persons or entities appearing in this work of fiction are included solely for purposes of verisimilitude.

ISBN 978-1-886404-47-2

Cover Design by D. Scott Apel & Catherine Inslee

CONTENTS

PART I:
BEFORE
1

PART II:
THE DURING TEST
15

PART III:
AFTER
239

Also Available from The Impermanent Press
255

DEDICATION

To Mike Malone

Preeminent journalist,
Peerless stylist,
Tireless booster of my career,
Friend

"Early in life I had to choose between honest arrogance and hypocritical humility.
I chose honest arrogance and have seen no occasion to change."
—Frank Lloyd Wright

"All I can do is be me, whoever that is."
—Bob Dylan

PART I:
BEFORE

"Every adventure requires a first step."
—The Cheshire Cat, *Alice's Adventures in Wonderland*

Chapter 1.0

April 1, 1977

I was on my seventh attempt to reach my answering service, but instead of getting my messages, all I got was my seventh busy signal. The irony did not escape me.

They answered on the eighth try, just as a scruffy hippie walked into my office. His long black hair was tousled as though he'd recently awakened from a year-long nap. His beard was sparse and scraggly. His T-shirt was sweat-stained and his blue jeans were ripped and soiled. He was barefoot, and his bare feet were dirty. He probably thought he looked like Jesus.

Oh boy—a client.

The operator at the answering service said "Please hold." I wasn't about to hang up after all that effort just to be polite to this gamy vagrant. I waved my free hand at him to shoo him back out the door, but instead, he took a seat in the wooden client chair in front of my desk. I'd only been in the private investigation biz a few months, but I'd scored a sweet corner office on the second floor of an iconic building in downtown Los Gatos. The single room was big enough for my desk, my chair, and me. A client chair was crowding it. An actual client was about all the excess space the room had to spare. Lucky for me clients were a rarity.

He sat. And he propped his feet up on my desk. His filthy, stinking feet.

I had my lunch on the desk—a veal parmesan sub from the All American Sandwich Shop on Moorpark. Breaded cutlets, tangy red sauce, mozzarella. Best sandwich in the Valley. I grabbed the wrapper and slid it to the other side of the desk, far away from his funky, fetid feet.

"Any calls?" I said to the answering service operator once she returned and I identified myself. As usual, the answer was no, so I hung up.

"Your office is a real shithole," my uninvited guest said.

I interlaced my fingers and placed my fists on my desk.

"Buddy," I said, "in a second or two I'm going to ask you what I can do for you. But first I'm going to tell you something: Get your filthy fucking feet off my desk."

"Or?" he challenged.

I opened the middle drawer of my scarred wooden desk. I withdrew a 12-inch wooden ruler and slapped it against my palm.

"Bastinado," I said.

He chuckled. But he removed his feet.

"Now: What can I do for you?"

"I'd like you to locate my father."

"How long has he been missing?"

"Since I was born."

"Would you care to elaborate?"

"I'm adopted," he stated.

"OK," I said. "So you want me to track down your birth parents?"

"Just my sperm donor."

"You don't want to know about your mother?"

He shook his head. "Time's not right."

"OK," I said trying to usher him out of my office gracefully. "I'll think about it and get back to you."

He remained seated.

"I'm not leaving until you agree to take my case," he said.

"Has that approach ever worked for you?"

"Ask Nolan Bushnell," he replied.

I had no idea who Nolan Bushleague was. But I don't like to advertise my ignorance. I have no budget for a billboard that size. He seemed cocksure that his abrasive nature had worked on this Nolan Bullshit guy, however, even if he was a homeless hobo.

What he didn't count on was that I could be as obstinate as the next guy. I wasn't about to let him force his business on me. Nonchalance was the prescribed response. So I picked up my sandwich and took a bite. He watched me intently.

"Would you like the other half?" I offered casually. It seemed like the right thing to do since he looked like his last supper had been sometime during the Ford administration.

"I can't eat that," he said. "I'm a fruitarian."

"I don't care if you're gay," I said.

"No, I only eat fruit. It keeps me naturally pure and odor-free, so I have no need to bathe."

"And how's that working out for you?" I said, swallowing. "And for the people around you?"

He stayed silent. And he stayed planted in the client chair.

Time to try a different approach.

"Have some wine?" I asked. "It's made from grapes. Which are fruit."

"I don't see any wine," he remarked.

"There isn't any."

"Then it wasn't very civil of you to offer it," he said angrily.

"It wasn't very civil of you to sit down without being invited."

I was getting tired of this mad tea party, so I played my ace. I told him my rates and my retainer. That'd get rid of this disgusting derelict, this reeking street freak. To my surprise, he reached into the pocket of his filthy jeans and retrieved a wad of cash. He peeled off a few Franklins and spread them on the desk.

"That cover it, you think?" he said.

The previous few months had not been great, workwise. Not only was California beginning a second year of drought, but my finances were suffering a severe dry spell as well. The parade of bald Bens looked mighty inviting.

"OK," I conceded. "Consider me hired. But I'll need some information. Your name and birthdate, for starters."

"Steven Paul Jobs," he said. "My adopted name. Born February twenty-fourth, 1955, in San Francisco."

So far, so good. The research could be done nearby. And he was a Pisces. Like me. I didn't care, but my girlfriend might consider it important. She was into that kind of mumbo-jumbo, bless her human potential movement-oriented heart.

And so it went for a few more minutes. I grilled him for details that were important to me but irrelevant to this narrative. And when I ran out of questions, I opened a desk drawer and retrieved the form I'd need authorizing me to access the necessary records. He read it and signed it and got up to leave.

"Oh," I said. "One more thing. How'd you pick me?"

"You doing market research?"

"Just curious."

"I saw you on some PBS show. KTEH. *Watching the Defective,* or something."

"You too, huh? Maybe I should just stop paying for an ad in the Yellow Pages."

"I'd keep buying the ad," he advised. "The show was a piece of shit."

I was beginning to wish bastinado was still an alternative.

"I'll call you when I've found something," I said. "How do I reach you?"

He pulled a card from a pocket in his jeans and handed it to me. A bum with a business card? That was unexpected. Across the top, in an odd font like something out of *Star Trek*, it read: *apple computer inc*. Beneath the name, in a simpler, sans serif font, was an address on Stevens Creek Boulevard in Cupertino and a phone number. And at the bottom, in the same unornamented font, it read: Steven Jobs, Vice President, Operations.

I took the card and he extended his hand. It was a little cleaner than his dirty, filthy, stinking, cheesy feet, so I shook it. But I'd go down the hall to the powder room and wash my hands before I picked up my sandwich again.

He left. I opened a window.

Chapter 1.1

April 4, 1977

Three days later…

Tracking down Jobs' birth parents could have been a bureaucratic nightmare, wrapped in apathy and neatly tied with bright red tape. Since it was a closed adoption, I knew that driving up to the San Francisco County Courthouse and requesting the files was a waste of time; those files could only be released by court order. Social Services likewise would likely stonewall me. Steve didn't know if there was an organization involved, so checking local adoption agencies was out. But even if it had been that difficult, there are few doors that can't be opened with a well-placed Grant or Franklin. Or a credit card. Not to charge a bribe, you understand, but by wedging it in a doorjamb to pop the lock after hours, when offices are empty and information is free.

As it turned out, however, luck was on my side. For a change.

I started by looking up Steve's adoptive parents in the phone book. Paul and Clara Jobs still lived in Cupertino, so I drove out to their house and simply asked them if they knew how the adoption had been arranged. They told me it had been orchestrated by a doctor, and gave me his name. Once I knew that, tracking him down was simple. I found him by employing the complicated methodology of looking him up in the phone book. Once again, my years of professional training paid off. Or I got lucky. Either way was OK by me.

The doctor was retired but still local. I drove to his house and explained Steve's request. I showed him the papers Steve had signed authorizing me to ask on his behalf and asked politely for his cooperation. He gave it, even though he said he'd expected to share that information only from his deathbed.

Turns out the "sperm donor" was a Syrian immigrant named John Jandali. Once again, my primary tool—the phone book—provided an address. Like the doctor, Jandali was still local, managing a Mediterranean restaurant right here in the Valley. I drove out to his eatery and had a meal. Who'd pass up a chance to have kabobs, or shwarma? Or baklava? Especially on someone else's dime? I left a big tip (which I'd add to my daily expense account, so why not) and asked to speak to the manager.

The resemblance between Steve and his birth father was not obvious but was unmistakable. Same hawklike profile, for one, and the same cold, penetrating brown eyes. I praised his food and said I'd spread the word about his place among my coworkers in the tech industry. He seemed pleased. "They come here all the time," he said. "Even Steve Jobs has eaten here a couple of times. Nice guy. Big tipper."

Jobs had already had a face-to-face encounter with his birth father and neither of them knew their relationship? That's the kind of coincidence you find only in bad novels and real life.

I called my client and told him I had his information.

Chapter 1.2

April 5, 1977

I was on the phone the following afternoon disputing a long-distance charge with an unsympathetic operator when a slick businessman walked into my office. He was wearing a sharp three-piece suit—Wilkes Bashford, if I knew my unaffordable fashions—and expensive shoes. He was immaculately groomed: his stylishly long dark hair was combed over his forehead and his beard and mustache were precisely trimmed.

I motioned him to have a seat in the client chair. He sat. And he propped his feet up on my desk, ankles crossed.

"I gonna have to call you back," I told the operator and hung up.

My visitor gave me a smartass smirk. An unmistakable smartass smirk.

"Jobs?" I said. "What the hell happened to you?"

"I have an industry event coming up in a couple of weeks," he said sourly. "West Coast Computer Faire in The City. My business partner and ethics guru, Mike Markkula, said I had to clean up my act and look professional for the industry bozos. I was a lot more comfortable in my T-shirts and Birkenstocks."

"Well, if it's any consolation," I said, "you clean up nice."

"*Nicely*," he corrected. "Grammar. Words are important."

"Well, I got two words for you," I said, pulling a manila envelope out of my desk drawer. "Your information."

I slid the envelope across the desktop. He did not pick it up.

"Don't you want to read it?"

Instead of answering, he reached inside his vest, pulled out his own manila envelope, and slid it across the desktop to me.

"What I want," he said, "is for you to open this and compare the results."

I picked up his envelope. It was sealed. Clearly never opened. I opened it. Inside was a two-page typed report on letterhead that read "Top Shelf Investigations, San Francisco." The report was dated a few months ago.

"'Client: Steven Paul Jobs,'" I read.

"No, no, not out loud," he protested. "Just read it to yourself and see how it compares to your results."

I skimmed through the report, which detailed a search for the client's biological father. The same assignment he'd given me—with results identical to mine: John Jandali.

"You had this done before?" I said, sliding the pages back into the envelope.

He nodded.

"And you had me do it again why?"

"To verify the results."

"Results you don't want to know," I said. "After you've had them researched twice."

"The time isn't right," he shrugged. "You just hang onto them."

Now it was my turn to shrug. "Well, it's your nickel," I said. "Speaking of which, there is at least one page of my report I'm going to have to insist that you read." I pulled out my invoice and handed it to him.

"How about a trade?" he suggested after scanning my bill. "I can get you a deal on the Apple II computer we'll be debuting at the Computer Faire."

"The hell would I do with a computer?" I scoffed.

"It's a bicycle of the mind," he said cryptically.

"I need a computer like a fish needs a bicycle of the mind," I replied. "Cash is fine."

"Your loss," he mumbled.

He wrote a check. I took it. We shook hands and said goodbye.

And that was the last time I ever saw Steve Jobs.

Chapter 2.0

June 1979

Until it wasn't.

I was hooking up a phone answering machine in my office—Rockford had one, so I had to have one—when who should walk in but Steven Paul Jobs.

The first thing I noticed is that he seemed to have split the difference between Dirty Hippie Jobs and Slick Businessman Jobs. This time he was just a skinny, angular guy in faded, beltless blue jeans and a long-sleeved dress shirt, untucked and unbuttoned at the neck. He still had the semi-satanic beard and mustache but they were neatly trimmed; his thick, glossy, dark hair was Beatle-length and still combed over his forehead.

"If you're looking for your adoption information," I said without preamble, "it'll take a few minutes to dig it out of my filing cabinet." I'd added the cabinet to my minimal décor sometime during the previous couple of years. It took up valuable space, but it had become a necessity, which I took as a sign of my success.

"Nope," he said. "Got a different assignment for you this time."

"Oh lucky me," I said, sitting in my same old squeaky wooden chair and motioning him to sit in the same old wooden client chair. Aside from the filing cabinet and the phone machine, nothing else in the office had been upgraded. "And how may I be of assistance?"

"Well," he began, "I'm the founder and CEO of Apple Computer in Cupertino. You might have heard of us?"

"Nope." Arrogant bastard. Maybe my ignorance would put him in his place.

"Oh. OK. But you have heard of Xerox, I assume."

"Yep."

"OK, it's a start. Xerox has an advanced research facility up in Palo Alto. Xerox PARC."

"What kind of park is it?" I said. "Swing sets, teeter-totters, that kind of thing? Frisbee on the lawn?"

"Ah…no. It's P-A-R-C. An acronym. Palo Alto Research Centre."

"And?"

"And I want you to get a job there."

I smiled and gestured at the magnificent splendor of my workspace.

"I already have a job."

"This would be different," he said. "I want you to get employed there and do some research for me. Snoop around the different departments and report back to me about what they're working on."

I felt the pit of my stomach drop.

"I think I can arrange to get you in there," he continued. "They only hire the best and the brightest, but I'm sure they need janitors, too."

Where was my gun when I needed it? Oh, in the bottom desk drawer. I employed my legendary self-control and did not retrieve it.

"Those Xerox PARC guys, they're a bunch of bozos," he continued emphatically. "I think they're sitting on some real technological breakthroughs, but they have no idea what to do with them. I do. They don't deserve them. I do."

"Mr. Jobs," I sighed wearily, shaking my head, "how old are you?"

"Twenty-four."

I outranked him by nearly half a decade, which I assumed made me both wiser and more experienced about the ways of the world than this brash asshole.

"Twenty-four," I repeated with a heavy sigh. "Kid, you've got a lot to learn about the business world. What you're proposing is called *industrial espionage*. I can't do that. Not only is it illegal, it's also unethical."

He did nothing but glare at me, as though he could intimidate me with the one-two punch of silence and the Evil Eye. I'm intimidated by guns. I'm intimidated by women. Clowns, of course. But silence? Not so much.

I figured his strategy was a variation of the old cop trick, based on the assumption that Nature abhors a vacuum. Stay silent long enough and your perp will feel compelled to keep talking and maybe inadvertently reveal something of importance. Clearly, this kid had no idea that I'd been trained in this same technique and could use it to my advantage.

"Hey," I continued talking. "Didn't you tell me long ago that you had some kind of guru?"

"Neem Karoli Baba," he said. "Maharaj-ji. In India. But he died before I could meet him."

"No, no, an ethics guru. Dracula?"

"Oh. Markkula," he said. "Yeah."

"Did you run this plan by him?"

He was silent until he wasn't.

"Yeah."

"And what did he have to say about it?"

"Same as you."

"So why ask me?"

"I thought," he said levelly, "you might be more… flexible."

"No amount of yoga in the world could make me that flexible."

He returned to staring-glaring at me. It was in fact becoming unnerving. The bastard.

"So here's an idea," I said, mainly to get rid of him. "You want to see what they're working on? Buy a ticket to the show."

His brow furrowed. "What do you mean?"

"Make 'em a deal," I suggested. "Buy a shitload of their stock. Or if you can't afford that, offer them a stake in your company. Sell 'em some stock. Cheap. Once they're investors, give them a tour of your facilities. Then ask for reciprocity. Ask them to open the kimono, give you a peek. No subterfuge necessary—you're invited. You go in, you look around, you go home and figure out what they've got that you can use."

His brow furrowed even further.

"Just call them up and ask for a tour?"

"Whattaya got to lose?"

He pondered this. Silently, of course.

And at length, he nodded to himself, rose, and left my office without so much as a by-your-leave, a ta-ta, or a toodle-oo. Or even a TTFN.

It was rude. But I was OK with that, as long as he left.

And that's the last time I ever saw Steve Jobs…

PART II:
THE DURING TEST

"I am not crazy. My reality is just different from yours."
—The Cheshire Cat, *Alice's Adventures in Wonderland*

"Leave the beaten path and dive into the woods."
—Alexander Graham Bell

Chapter 3.0

April 11, 1980

…until it wasn't.

I was scrutinizing the new Snoopy phone on my desk, trying to decide if it was appropriate for a professional office. It was a masterpiece of 3D plastic molding: a smiling, foot-high figure of the iconic character and his sidekick, Woodstock, standing on a telephone base. It was a playful personal phone, but was it a proper private eye phone? I worried it might send the wrong message to prospective clients, that I was silly and frivolous and that they could not take me seriously. I had a solution to that eventuality, if it ever occurred: I'd show them my gun.

I was interrupted when—once again—Steve Jobs entered my office.

He was still gangly and lanky, still awkwardly angular. He seemed to have settled on a wardrobe by now, however, as he was dressed in blue jeans and a long-sleeved dress shirt, just as I'd last seen him. He'd added round wireframe glasses since then. His thick hair was still long and still swooped over his forehead, but on this visit, he'd shaved the satanic beard and was sporting a Frank Zappa look: a mustache and a "jazz beard" under his bottom lip.

He didn't wait to be invited to sit. He just sat.

"Well well well, if it isn't Mr. Steven Jobs," I said in mock astonishment.

"Third time's the charm," he said with a knowing smirk.

"And what can I not do for you this time?"

"I think I'm being followed."

No polite amenities; no screwing around with small talk.

"By who?"

" 'By *whom*,' you illiterate idiot. You clearly don't know shit about grammar."

He'd been in my office thirty seconds and already I wanted to slap him. In my experience, however—and despite Sam Spade's typical *modus operandi*—many potential clients do not respond well to being slapped. So I stifled my instinct and played along.

"Don't you have your own security people to handle things like this?"

"I don't want to do this in-house."

"So you decided to come to my little outhouse?"

"I don't want to use corporate resources. For all I know, there might be a mole in my company. Who knows? I'm not sure who I can trust."

"So what makes you think you can trust me?"

He gave this some thought until he had a bullet-point argument to present.

"The first guys I hired took three weeks to track down my birth father," he said. "You did it in three days. That indicated to me that you were efficient. My next request? What you called 'industrial espionage'? You agreed with my ethics consultant—my own personal Jiminy Cricket—which indicated to me that you have integrity."

"Aw, shucks," I demurred. "I thought it was because I have a gun."

"No," he said. "It was because I decided you must be good at what you do to make a living as a detective in a small town like Los Gatos. But mostly it's because you work cheap."

Not today, I decided.

"Speaking of which..." I replied.

We talked fee. It was a pretty one-sided talk. I told him my rates—my new, improved rates—and he agreed.

"OK," I said, hitting the carriage return. "Who do you think might be following you?"

He shrugged and shook his head. "I don't know. We're going public in a few weeks—"

"Who's 'we'? And what does that mean, 'going public'?"

He looked at me as though he was assessing me for a spot in a Special Ed class.

"'We' is Apple Computer, the company I founded," he said slowly. "And 'going public' means we're going to start selling shares of stock to the public. So it might be the SEC following me."

"The Securities and Exchange Commission?"

He nodded. "Yeah. Doing some research on me. See if I'm legit. Trustworthy."

"Deep background by the stock market cops," I said. "Or…?"

"Or it could be the FTC."

"The Federal Trade Commission. Makes sense. Consumer protection. They'd want to make sure you were legit as well—no fraud or deception."

"Or it might be the FBI. Checking me out, see if I'm loyal."

"Right. Make sure you're not gonna sell American high-tech to the godless commies. Or trade it for the hostages in Iran."

"Or," he said, tugging absently at his soul patch, "somebody could just be plotting a simple, garden-variety kidnapping. I'm worth over a million dollars."

"Possible," I said. "That kind of thing happens in South America all the time."

"Could be the FCC," he continued.

I must have had a quizzical look on my face. I don't know—I was too busy being confused to pay attention to my expression.

"They set the standards for electronic devices," he explained. "Or it might be Xerox, although I don't know why they'd be after me since they're stockholders now. Might be HP… No, I know those guys. They're trustworthy. Too ethical."

"Xerox makes copy machines," I said. "And, uh, HP? What does that stand for?"

He stared at me like my middle name was Ed and my first name was Special. "I can't believe you live in Silicon Valley and don't know any of this shit," he growled. "What a bozo. I'm beginning to think you're not very bright."

Jesus. Even Gandhi would want to bitch-slap this crass asshole.

"All I know is what I read in the funny papers," I cracked back. "So what is it exactly that you want from me?"

"Three things," he replied. "One, I want to find out whether or not I'm actually being followed. Two, if I *am* being followed, I want you to find out who it is and what they want. And third, I want you to stop them. This is all very distracting, and I'm working on a lot of big things. I don't have the bandwidth for sidetracks like this. I just want it to end. You think you can accomplish any of that?"

I ignored the blunt insult and nodded. "One: yes. Two: yes. And three… Well, I do have a gun."

"That's a little mega-overreactive, I'd say," he said.

I'd tried to tease him but he was clearly dead serious about his troubles.

"All right," I said. "Consider me hired. Sleuth and bodyguard. We'll start with One: establishing whether or not you're being tailed. Do you think you were followed here?"

He nodded.

"Well, then let's find out," I suggested brightly.

"What are you thinking?"

Here's what I was thinking:

It's dinnertime. I'm hungry. Laurel is working swing in the ICU at Good Sam, so I can't show up at her house and talk her into cooking for me, which means I can stick with Steve. Or that I'm stuck with Steve. We've gotta go somewhere far enough away that we can be certain someone is in fact following us, and public enough that they can hide and watch us if they want but can't abduct us in front of witnesses. Pianto's on Stevens Creek? Best ravioli in the world. No—it's a deli; only three tables. Too small. And I'd just want to go next door to JJ's Blues Lounge to listen to some music after dinner anyway. Pedro's is here in town. Short walk down the street. Not far enough to establish a tail, though. If there even is one. But Mexican? Mmmm. Jalisco Taco Bar on Stevens Creek? Great food. Big enough, but never busy enough that the tail can hide from us, or crowded enough that they couldn't abduct us. Ah, but—

I knew exactly where we should go. I figured, what the hell. Maybe Jobs was just paranoid. At least I'd get a free meal out of this scruffy, irritating beatnik. Ex-beatnik.

"OK," I announced. "I have a plan. Let's go."

As he rose to leave, I opened a side drawer in my desk and brought out a small compact, which sounds redundant, but isn't.

"I know you were on TV," Steve said, "but do you really need makeup to do this job? A disguise?"

"You'll see," I said, slipping the compact into my pocket. I opened the bottom desk drawer and retrieved my gun.

Steve took one look at the piece and froze.

"You're bringing a gun?" he asked quietly.

"Don't worry about it," I said. "I'm licensed. And I've never had to use it off the firing range."

"Still, makes me nervous. I got robbed at gunpoint once, in the parking lot of a pizza joint in Sunnyvale. That's what motivated me to get out of the blue box business."

I had no idea what he was talking about, but it was irrelevant to his main concern: the gun.

"Think of it as an insurance policy," I said to him. "You have no idea who's after you." *If anyone,* I said to myself. "It's a safety net. And the safety's on. If they are in fact bad guys, this can level the playing field."

The gun was small and flat and fit nicely in the palm of my hand. I held it up like I was palming a card in some dangerous closeup magic trick. Now you don't see it, now you do. My gun is quick. Maybe not as quick as a card trick, but it has a lot more impact.

"Beretta Four-Eighteen," I said. "Semi-automatic pistol. Eight-round mag of twenty-five caliber bullets."

"Beautiful design," he said, his curiosity or sense of aesthetics apparently overcoming some of his trepidation. "Nice sleek lines. Sweet curves."

I tucked the piece into the waistband of my jeans and pulled the bottom of my black Moody Blues T-shirt over it.

"*Voila*," I gestured. "Invisible."

"Wait a minute," he said. "A Beretta? Isn't that the gun James Bond uses? Is that why you chose it?"

"No," I said, maybe a little too forcefully.

Chapter 3.1

I shrugged into the red Pendleton shirt I was currently using as a jacket and we left the office. As I locked the door, Steve headed down the hallway to the stairs. He was about to turn right and take the staircase that led to the rear entrance.

"No," I said. "Use the other staircase. On your left."

"But my car is parked out back."

"Yeah, so's mine. But we don't know if your tail is watching the back door or the front door. So we exit using the front door then walk around the building to the rear parking lot. That gives them plenty of time to spot you no matter which door they're watching."

We exited out onto E. Santa Cruz Avenue. I just stood there on the sidewalk for a minute, looking around.

"Are we going?" Steve asked.

"Yeah, soon. We need to give your tail a chance to wake up and spot us."

He didn't argue, so I didn't move. Instead, I pointed up the street.

"East Santa Cruz Avenue," I said. "The main drag. Pedro's Mexican restaurant is a couple of blocks that way. And the Chart House. Surf and turf; great steaks. The Gatos theater, a leftover from the Art Deco movie palaces of the twenties. Looks its age. And the Black Watch. It's a dive bar, but I'm honor bound to drink there occasionally since I'm Scottish."

He scrutinized me closely. "You don't look Scottish."

I shrugged. "Scottish on my mom's side. My dad was adopted. We don't know what he was. Various clues indicate an Italian, a Greek, or a Syrian as the leading contenders."

"Assyrian?" he said. "They still around?"

"Mountain Charley's bar," I said, continuing my stationary tour by pointing across the street. Then I aimed a finger in the opposite direction, toward the Post Office and the entrance to Highway 17 South. "Montebello Park. Nice view from my office." We began walking toward the park, past the Curious Bookshop that occupied the ground floor of my building. When we turned the corner onto Main, I pointed down the street. "Big antiques store in the old Opera House right there. Civic Center a few blocks down the road—police and public library. Farther down, Los Gatos High and the Jaguar and Ferrari dealership. And my dentist's office."

"Yeah, I know Los Gatos a little," he remarked. "Bought a house here last year. Up in the foothills." He looked back the way we'd come. "Did I see a place called 'Carrie Nation's'? Is that a bar?"

"Yeah. Why? You want a drink?"

"Nah. I don't drink. Much. A beer or a glass of wine occasionally. Looks like it might be a good place to have a business meeting is all. I just like the irony, naming a bar after a rabid temperance leader."

We took a left into the parking lot behind my building. This was the first time I'd stood next to the guy. He was, I'd estimate, about six-two. I'm six even, but he stooped a bit, like a bent straw, so we appeared almost even.

"Where's your car?" he asked.

I didn't want him to see the piece of shit I was driving. He might lose all respect for me. I know I would.

"We should take your car," I said. "That's what your tail will be looking for. It's familiar to them, and we don't want to throw them any curve balls. Don't want to confuse them. Or lose them."

He nodded and led me to his car: a silver Mercedes-Benz 450SL. The two-door coupe. Brand new.

"No license plates?" I noticed. I am a detective, after all, and trained in the fine art of observing the obvious.

He smiled a crooked smile and unlocked the car.

"Yeah, I know that trick," I said. "Lease a new one every six months so you never have to have permanent plates. Protects your privacy."

"How do you know about that?" he said.

Now it was my turn to smile. "You hired a detective," I said, climbing into the passenger seat. "Nice wheels. Elegant. Graceful. Classy."

"Yeah. It was this or a new Jaguar XJS. Love 'em both. Beautiful designs. All curves, no angles. Smooth, sleek, efficient."

"You know a lot about cars?"

"Not really," he said. "I'm more into design. My dad is the car guy. When I was a kid I used to help him do repairs in our garage. But I had no interest in cars. I just wanted to spend time with my dad."

"Your adopted dad?"

"My *dad*," he said, starting the car. It purred smoothly. "So where we going?"

I gestured behind us.

"Eventually, Campbell. But right now, just go back the way we walked. Right on Main, right on Santa Cruz. Whether your tail is out front or back here, they'll spot you. We'll give 'em redundant chances and multiple opportunities."

"Isn't that itself redundant?" he mumbled. Rhetorically, I assumed.

We headed down E. Santa Cruz. When we reached the Highway 9 intersection he turned on his clicker for a right turn.

"No, no," I directed. "Keep going straight."

"Campbell? We're not taking Seventeen?"

"No. The freeway's too fast. Too big a risk of losing them. We'll take the back way. Surface streets."

The street name changed to Winchester Boulevard, but we drove on as if the name didn't matter. Because it didn't.

I pulled out the compact, opened it, then held it between us.

"Oh," he said. "I get it. Your own little secret rearview mirror. You look for the tail, but they can't see you looking."

"You catch on," I said. It was too soon to tell if any specific car was following us. There was one candidate: a poop brown Pontiac Cutlass I might have seen earlier. It's difficult to mistake that ugly rectangular grill and those nasty square headlights for any other car. I'd keep checking.

"You mentioned your dad," I said, clipping the compact shut. "What's he do?"

"He's an engineer. Worked for International Harvester in the Midwest before he moved out here. Before I was born."

"No shit? My dad worked sales at IH in Illinois. Before we moved out here. What's he do now?"

"My dad? He works at Lockheed."

"Whose doesn't?" I chuckled. "Everybody I've ever known in the Valley has some relative who works for Lockheed."

"Or IBM."

"Yeah. Even Steven Spielberg's dad worked for IBM."

"Wow. Cool."

"Yeah, his family lived here a couple of years in the mid-sixties. He graduated from Saratoga High School. But yeah, Lockheed and IBM were the two anchors. Between the two of them, they jumpstarted the Valley into the twentieth century."

"Twenty-first," he said. With conviction.

"Feels that way, yeah. The New Florence. But all that… *progress* gets a little exhausting. One of the things I like about Los Gatos is how it never seems to change. Still looks and feels the same as when I first saw it in the early sixties."

"Yeah," he said. "Really incredible how much the Valley has changed in the last twenty years."

"Oh, for sure. Used to be called 'The Valley of Heart's Delight.'"

"And now it's Silicon Valley."

"All those orchards back then," I waxed nostalgic. "Orchards everywhere! Peaches, pears, Charlie Olson's cherry orchard..."

"Don't forget apples," Steve added. "And apricots. My high school girlfriend Chrisann and I used to cut class and hang out in the apricot orchards next to our school."

"I think that's pronounced 'apricots,'" I said.

"No, it's pronounced 'apricots,'" he insisted. "You must have grown up in the Midwest. We pronounce it 'apricots' here."

I wasn't going to argue about trivialities when we were on a conversational roll.

"Every spring the fields were bright yellow with those little flowers on the mustard plants..." I reminisced.

"And every summer they plowed them all under to fertilize the trees," he finished my thought.

"The only thing growing in most of those fields now are those ugly tilt-up buildings," I said. "Those huge pre-fab concrete slabs they toss up like toadstools along 101 to house all the new electronics companies."

"Sometimes I think the only remnants of those days are the wineries."

"Yeah," I said. "Novitiate up in the Los Gatos foothills. Mirassou."

"Paul Masson," he added.

I had to chuckle. "When I was a kid I used to live on a street off Blossom Hill Road, a block from the Masson vineyards," I said. "My friends and I would ride our bikes through the vineyards, eat some grapes, pee on the vines. I watched Lyndon Johnson's inauguration party on TV and when I saw they were drinking Paul Masson champagne, I thought, 'Ha! The President is drinking my pee!' We found the company dump once and thought we'd struck gold—empty champagne bottles to throw rocks at, huge piles of corks."

When we crossed an intersection I pointed at the street sign.

"There it is," I said. "Blossom Hill Road. What I've noticed is that around here they tend to name streets after what they've paved over and destroyed. You can drive along Blossom Hill Road from Los Gatos to IBM, way down there in South San Jose, for instance, and never once see a blossom or a hill."

"Yeah," he agreed. "You can drive Wolf Creek Road and never see a creek. Then again, the upside is, no wolves."

So maybe this guy did have a sense of humor.

"Where'd you say your office was?" I said.

"Stevens Creek Boulevard."

"So you can't see a creek," I said, "but you can see a Steven."

"Two, actually. Me and Steve Wozniak, my business partner."

"Well, where we're going, you won't see any prunes."

"Prunes don't grow on trees. They're dried plums."

"You'll see. Just drive."

"I don't really like looking back," he said. "And I for sure don't want to wallow in nostalgia. The times they are a-changin'. The future is where it's at."

"Well, it is where we're all going to spend the rest of our lives," I said.

"Cool," Steve said. "A Charles Kettering quote."

"I got that from Woody Allen," I said. "Who's Charles Kettering?"

Steve glanced over at me, but so quickly I couldn't tell whether he was shocked or disappointed. All I knew for sure was that it wasn't an admiring glance.

"Early twentieth-century engineer," he said. "An inventor of the caliber of Edison. Founded Delco, headed the research department at General Motors for over a quarter of a century, until after World War II. Worked at DuPont, developed freon. Held a hundred and eighty-six patents."

There was nothing much I could say to that. Thanks for the tutorial? We continued in silence for a bit. I took advantage of the lull in conversation to flip open the compact and check behind us again. The Cutlass I saw earlier was still there. But it might have been a different Cutlass. Fucking ugly things were ubiquitous.

"Shit!" Steve spat out of nowhere. "Shit shit shit!"

"What's wrong?"

"I need to call my office, tell 'em I won't be back until later. I should have called from your office. Now I need to find a pay phone."

"Yeah, sure. Just pull into the next gas station."

We were traveling through the industrial area of Campbell. There were few gas stations around here, but nowhere in the Valley was very far from a pump, and we spotted a Shell station less than a mile later.

He pulled off the road and stopped alongside the phone booth. I checked the station sign. Gas over a dollar a gallon? Surely the End Days were upon us.

I watched Steve in the booth. He was holding the handset up to his ear and clicking the hookswitch repeatedly. Eventually, he slammed the handset into the cradle and returned to the car.

"Broken."

"Ah, well, there'll be one at the next station."

We drove a block and pulled up to the phone booth at a Chevron station. Steve entered the booth, lifted the receiver, and held it up for me to see. The cable on the handset was torn off, exposing a few stray, frayed wires. He returned to the car. We drove on. But we didn't stop at another gas station.

"Never a phone when you need one," I commiserated. "Too bad we don't have one of those Dick Tracy wrist radio thingys."

"A what?

"You know. Dick Tracy. The comic strip detective?"

"I was never into the comics pages."

"Well, he used to wear a two-way wrist radio—a miniature communication device, so he could keep in touch with police HQ. They upgraded it in later strips to a two-way wrist TV. In case he needed visual communication. Real face-to-face time with his caller. Here… Make the next right."

Just before Campbell Ave., we made the turn.

"Orchard City Drive," I said, pointing around.

"And no orchards," he observed.

"I rest my case."

A minute later we took a left on Railway Avenue. Another right put us on Campbell Avenue, where we crossed under the Highway 17 overpass.

I checked the mirror again. That butt-ugly, shit-brown Cutlass was still behind us. This was starting to look like a non-coincidence.

"Right turn here," I pointed. The little street twisted a few blocks around some open space and a few generic buildings. "In here," I said and we pulled into a parking lot next to a hacienda-themed hotel.

"The Pruneyard?" he said.

"Aw, what gave it away?"

He pointed through the windshield.

"Well, the tower, for one."

There was indeed a tower—a multi-story black glass edifice, right behind the mall. The tallest building in the Valley outside of downtown San Jose.

We parked and walked along a covered sidewalk—Steve more loping than walking—through the Pruneyard, an upscale outdoor mall that had been around for a decade. California-style architecture, with covered walkways wrapping around and connecting the various stand-alone buildings.

"Why did we come in the back way?" Steve asked. "We could have gone down Bascom."

"Too much traffic," I said. "This way it's unlikely that anyone driving behind us through that maze of backroads is a coincidence."

We passed a Japanese restaurant tucked away in a corner.

"Great," he said. "I love sushi."

I continued walking.

"What," he protested. "This isn't the place?"

"Oh hell no," I said. "Too small, too quiet—no place for your tail to hide and observe us. Besides, they serve raw fish in there. I'll wait 'til that bait catches something. Hopefully a cow. Here—this is where we're going."

Chapter 3.2

I pointed toward the front doors of El Burro—not just my favorite Mexican restaurant, but my all-time favorite restaurant of any persuasion. Even though it was located in a mall, the owners did their level best to give the impression that you were eating inside a hacienda in some rural Mexican town. The entryway was a pair of tall, arched wooden doors set in a brick wall; the floors were bright tile, patterned with colorful images; the seats, high-backed wooden chairs and lacquered wooden benches. The ceiling was lined with massive exposed wood beams. The beige walls were spotted with stucco swooshes to give them the feel of an adobe casa, punctuated by *trompe l'oeil* paintings of wood-shuttered windows that looked out into scenes of a local zocalo in a small villa. Intricate wrought ironwork decorated every door, window, and lighting fixture. But even while the management spared no expense to create an authentic atmosphere, they refrained from including strolling Mariachis—yet another detail for which I would be eternally grateful. Who can converse over the Tijuana Brassholes?

It was too early in the year for the outdoor patio to be open, but the inside was cavernous. The ground floor contained several large, separate dining rooms, and the second floor had two huge rooms—each with its own bar—at the top of a wide wooden staircase.

The one fly on our plate was that it was dinnertime Friday, and El Burro was one of the most popular and therefore most frequented eateries in the area. Already a couple dozen diners cooled their heels in the small lobby, waiting for a table. I knew we might have a long wait before we were seated. But there are always workarounds…

"I'm going to get us a table," I whispered to Steve. Speaking in a normal voice over the din of diners and lobby conversations was the ambient equivalent of whispering. "But I don't want to use our real names, in case she writes them down and those guys outside come in and know we're here."

"They could do that anyway, just look around for us."

"Yeah," I said. "But why make it easy for them? Do you have a pseudonym you like?"

He nodded. "Oaf Tobark," he said. "My alias from my phone phreak days."

I wasn't about to waste time asking him what the hell a "phone freak" was.

I retrieved my wallet and flipped through the selection of fake business cards I always carried. A clusterfuck of this magnitude required an impactful appearance. I chose a card and fished a twenty-dollar bill from my pocket, then shouldered my way through the thick crowd and approached the young woman at the rough wooden lectern-like reservation station.

"Excuse me," I said over the noise of milling and chatting. "How long a wait for two?"

She checked her list.

"About one hour, sir."

"Well, that's a problem," I said gravely. "You see that man over there? Do you know who that is?"

She looked over at Steve and shook her head. Of course she didn't know who he was. And she didn't look like the kind of person who watched PBS regularly, so there was little chance she knew who I was, either.

"That man is Oaf Tobark," I said. "He's a special envoy to the State Department from Sweden, and I have to put him on an airplane two hours from now." I handed her a business card that read simply "G. Marx" and "U.S. Department of State" and sported a very official-looking foil seal that I'd picked up at a crafts store. A sheet of twelve cost me less than a dollar. I had the twenty folded over twice behind the card and passed them both to the hostess. "But he really wanted to taste the best Mexican food in the Valley, so of course I brought him here. Is there anything you can do to perhaps speed things along? In the interests of cordial international relations?" I looked her in the eyes intently and held her gaze, partly so she wouldn't notice that I was dressed more like a college student than a government official, and partly to mind-control her into believing my silly, silly story.

Eventually, she broke free of my hypno-gaze. She looked at the card. She frowned and hesitated. She shifted from one foot to another. Then she slipped the twenty into her apron pocket.

"I'll see what I can do, sir."

I peered around her into the small bar area.

"That table there," I said, pointing to one of only two small tables in an alcove across the aisle from the five-seat bar. The young couple at the table was standing by their chairs. "That party is just leaving. That's perfect. We can take that table and be out of your way in a jiff."

She turned and looked into the dimly lit room. The busboy was already clearing and cleaning the table. For us.

"Right this way, sir," she said, smiling at me.

I motioned to Steve to come over and he slithered his way through the crowd. The hostess led us to the table and we took seats in wicker chairs with enormous, fan-like leather backs. Like sitting in a clam shell. I thanked the hostess and she returned to her station.

"How'd you do that?" Steve asked. "There's gotta be a hundred people out there waiting for a table."

I shrugged and grinned widely. "It helps to be on TV." He'd buy it. That's how he discovered me, after all. And as for the bribe, it would go on his invoice under "Miscellaneous."

Our waitress—a dark-haired, middle-aged woman wearing the El Burro uniform of frilly peasant skirt and white blouse with puffy sleeves—dropped off a basket of warm tortilla chips and a small bowl of salsa, then handed us menus.

Each menu was the size of a tabloid newspaper, printed on what appeared to be ancient parchment, although I doubt if the Early Californians had lamination. On the front, beneath the name "Mario's El Burro," was a pencil sketch of a burro head. And inside was a veritable wonderland of food. Delicious, hearty, filling Mexican food. Who couldn't love this? Another thing I loved about this place: the menu never changed.

"I've tried literally everything on the menu," I said, "and it's all good. I'd suggest one of the three sampler plates. La Niña, for instance. Taco, enchilada, chili relleno. Plus rice and beans.

Of course. And portions that practically dare you to clear your plate."

"There's nothing I can eat here," he declared. "I'm a vegetarian."

"You won't be after you taste their enchiladas."

He shook his head. "No. I won't eat anything that has a face. Or anything that can have kids."

Jesus, this guy was a pain in the patoot.

"OK," I challenged. "Does cheese have a face? Do eggs have a face? Can chilis have children?"

"Uhh…no."

"Then try the chili rellenos."

I saw the waitress approaching us carrying two bowls. And I saw a golden opportunity to stick it to a guy who'd rather eat a raw fish than a beefy, cheesy, gravy-drenched enchilada.

"I'll tell you what," I said, magnanimously. "I'll get you a salad."

The salad came with the meal. Yeah, I'd been here before.

The waitress placed the small wooden bowls in front of us. The dish barely qualified as a salad—some shredded iceberg lettuce topped with a couple slices of pickled beet, swimming in a vinaigrette so sour it pulled your asscheeks together.

Steve just glared at his bowl. Gotcha. Then he turned his glare on me.

"What?" I said, smiling sweetly. "You want my beets?"

I credit the presence of the waitress for preventing him from throwing a tantrum.

"Would you like to start with a margarita?" she asked. I did. A triple. But I couldn't. I was working, and while a triple would enhance the food and my mood, it might impinge on my judgment and sharply-honed skills of observation, so I reluctantly declined. Steve also declined, but he kept his reasons to himself. He said he didn't drink much, and now I realized he might actually be telling the truth. If ever there was a legitimate reason to drink, it was with Mexican food. Another reason to love it.

"We're ready to order," I announced.

"I understand you're in a bit of a rush," the waitress said with a smile. "There might be something I could do to speed your order along."

Word travels fast, I guess. I pulled another Jackson from my pocket and handed it to her. The bribes were costing me more than the dinner. Ah, what the hell. It's Steve's money.

As for dinner: I knew what I wanted. I always knew what I wanted here: La Niña. Steve ordered the chili rellenos without protest or further discussion.

There were those who claimed they wouldn't eat at El Burro because the food was not "authentic." These are people I refer to as "idiots." I'd spent time in Mexico. I'd had "authentic." And I can state categorically that El Burro's food was much, much better than authentic. Mexican food was never *haute cuisine*, and when it tastes this good, words like "authentic" and "gourmet" are irrelevant.

"I chose this seat on purpose," I said before Steve could express how much he hated me at the moment. "It's the most private table in the place."

"What about them?" he said, pointing across the aisle to the few people sitting at the small bar.

"The El Burro bar is not a place where people come to drink. It's a place where people come to wait. They'll all be gone soon. It's the location that's important." I pointed behind him, towards the lobby. "We can't be seen by anyone here unless they walk right by our table. But I can see into the lobby and can keep an eye on anyone who might look like they're looking for us."

"This salad dressing has too much vinegar," Steve said acidly. Clearly, he'd been paying rapt attention to my explanatory rap.

"Vegetarian, huh?" I said while I dug into my bowl. "Never had a Big Mac? You should try a Mac. You'd love a Mac."

He had no response. He just continued picking at his salad. I realized that if I was going to get any conversation out of him, I'd have to try a new tack.

"So, you think it might be the SEC or the FCC or the FTC or the FBI," I said. I'd been paying attention, and this caught his attention. "If it had to be a three-letter acronym, too bad it couldn't be LSD."

"You drop?"

"Ever heard of Captain Trips?"

"Jerry Garcia was Captain Trips," Steve said acidly. "You were not Captain Trips."

"No sir I was not. I was his superior officer, Major Trips."

He just shook his head. "And I suppose your father was Intrepid Trips and your mother was Mary Prankster."

"No, but I was on the bus. I'll tell you one thing I learned on acid," I continued. "Don't trust anyone who hasn't dropped acid."

This made him smile. Almost.

"You know who John Lilly is?" I asked around a mouthful of lettuce, determined to jumpstart a conversation.

"The guy who talks to dolphins?"

"Well, the guy who wants to, anyway. Also a notorious acid-head. He published a book a couple of years ago called *The Center of the Cyclone*, where he talks about his acid experiences. At one point during his first trip, for instance, he recalled pounding on the top of a file cabinet, declaring that 'Every psychiatrist, every psychoanalyst, should be forced to take LSD in order to know what is over here.' Then in the next paragraph he backpeddles, and says something like, 'What I meant was that anybody who has anything to do with the human mind and its care should be trained in these spaces.' I read that and I thought, 'I know what you really meant, you lying sack of shit. What you really meant is *Everybody should be forced to take LSD in order to know what is over here*."

Steve laughed out loud. "Feed your head."

"Yup. What the Dormouse said."

Ice breaker: accomplished. But I'd learned that it's good business sense to get to know your clientele, so I forged ahead, determined to keep the conversational streak going.

"So," I said. "You grow up around here?"

"Los Altos," he said. "Homestead High."

"Really? I rode my bike out there every Saturday morning one summer to take a lifeguard class."

"I was a swimmer," he said. "You were a swimmer?"

"In, uh, in a manner of speaking. My friends, the two guys I hung out with, they were swimmers. Good swimmers, too. But I sucked."

He gave me a chagrined grin. "I was a runt," he admitted. "The other guys bullied me. Snapping towels in the locker room, mocking me when I lost a race and cried. I suspect they all called me a crybaby behind my back."

"Oh, I'm sure that's not true."

"All I know for sure is I fucking hated it."

"I think that's probably an appropriate attitude toward high school in general."

"Well, yeah, if only because I was bullied in general," he confessed. "I even got beat up after Confirmation class one time. Some thug named Curtis Brown. You imagine that? A white guy named 'Curtis Brown'? Jesus. I'm just glad I had a girlfriend the last couple of years. And pot. The only things that took the edge off."

"You smoke?"

He sighed. "Not anymore. Don't have much time for that anymore. But sometimes I wish I could just lay back and light up a joint," Steve said bluntly.

"Tell you what I hated most about high school," I confessed. "Being in the marching band."

"Oh, God," he groaned. "Fucking marching band."

"You too?"

"Yeah," he said, shaking his head. "Trumpet. I sucked. It sucked."

"Clarinet," I admitted. "I sucked."

"So where was this?"

"Leigh."

He looked at me, one eyebrow raised, Spock-like.

"We were arch rivals," he said.

"Yeah! Every Thanksgiving, the big football game. Bitter enemies, *grrrr*."

He shook his head. "I never gave a shit about high school sports. Or rivalries."

"Amen, brother," I said. "Adolescent waste of time."

"Immature," he agreed. "Petty competition."

Our waitress arrived carrying our dinner plates with thick pot holders. It does not do the flatware justice to call what she was carrying "plates," however. They were more like platters. Platters the size of hubcaps. Truck hubcaps.

"Very hot," she warned, setting the dishes on the table. The sauces were still bubbling.

"*Bon appetit*," I said to Steve, picking up a chip and scooping up some rice and beans.

He stared at me and once again raised an eyebrow.

"Three years of high school French," I said. "Leigh rules."

"It's Mexican food, so I think you mean *buen provecho*," he stated. "Four years of high school Spanish. Homestead rules. Leigh drools."

For some time after that, we didn't talk. We just ate. And ate.

"These…" he said at one point, waving his fork at the chili rellenos, "these are pretty damn good."

I win this round.

At length, the waitress brought the check. She hesitated as to which of us she should hand it to. I motioned toward Steve and she placed *la cuenta* in front of him.

"You're picking up the check," I said with a smile.

"Maybe I don't want to pick up the check," he said with a touch of petulance.

I shrugged. "So I'll get it. But I'll just add it to my expenses on your invoice. With a generous tip."

He scowled but retrieved his wallet and dropped some cash on the tray. Before he could make some gratuitous sarcastic comment I leapt into an analysis of our present situation.

"So here's where we stand," I said. "I didn't see anyone enter who might be our tail. Couples, families, the usual. But no solo guys. No teams. This makes sense—if there is a tail and if they're pros, they wouldn't risk coming in for dinner. They might miss us leaving, or have to bolt if we left before they were finished eating. If there is a tail, they're waiting in the parking lot and they plan to pick us up there. If they exist. I'm gonna give 'em one last chance to prove they exist."

"What do you have in mind?"

"We're going record shopping!"

Chapter 4.0

"My life is in danger and you want to go fucking *record shopping*?" Steve growled. "Jesus, you're an asshole."

"An asshole with a plan," I replied, rising. "C'mon, *vamos*."

We worked our way through the crowded lobby. I was sure I recognized a few people that had already been there waiting when we arrived. Peons.

We stepped outside through the arched portal and walked around the patio. There was a small parking lot between this building and the next. I stopped at the curb and looked around the lot. And I noticed a shit-brown Cutlass parked in the next row. Time to generate some actual evidence.

"OK," I said. "If *I* were tailing us, I'd park here, near the entrance, and wait for us to leave. So first we give them an opportunity to spot us. And then we head over there…"

I pointed down the sidewalk and across Bascom Avenue to a large, low-slung, faux adobe brick building. Near the roof, an enormous lighted sign, red letters against a yellow backdrop, read TOWER RECORDS & VIDEO.

We set off down the mall sidewalk towards Bascom. There was no light or crosswalk here, so we waited for a break in traffic then jaywalked across the four-lane street.

"We do this," I explained to Steve as we trotted across the busy boulevard, "and they can't follow us in their car. They'll have to follow us on foot. And that's how we'll spot them."

We entered the store and stepped to one side, where I peered between posters on the poster-plastered windows. It was dusk, and getting darker by the minute. Most of the passing cars had their headlights on. But between the streetlights and the mall lighting, I could see two guys standing on the curb of the Pruneyard mall, checking for traffic before they could jaywalk across Bascom like we did. They were dressed in short-sleeved white shirts, thin ties, and chinos. Jesus Christ—we were being followed by fucking Jehovah's Witnesses.

I pointed them out to Steve.

"So there ya go," I announced. "Good news and bad news."

"What's the good news?"

"The first of your three requests has been fulfilled. We've determined that you are definitely being followed."

"And the bad news?"

"You are definitely being followed."

Our tail was trapped by cross traffic, buying us a minute or two.

We worked our way around the perimeter of the store, in no hurry so we didn't attract attention, even though most of the patrons were too busy flipping through the bins of records to notice anything. I kept my attention on the front door, but Steve was looking around at the numerous bins.

"I guess we don't have time to check for Dylan bootlegs," he said.

"Nah. This is a legit business anyway. They wouldn't carry bootlegs."

Even though we were in a hurry, I couldn't help but get caught up by a display of the new Pretenders album.

"Look at this," I said to Steve as we passed by the cardboard cutout. "Now, I like that song 'Brass in Pocket,' OK? But why should I have to buy the entire album just to get the one song I like? We should be able to purchase individual songs, like the 45s we grew up with. *Any* song, not just the ones released on 45s. I'd pay a dollar a song if they made it convenient enough."

We moved along the back wall and crossed over into the video rental side of the massive store. The New Releases shelves stretched the length of the back wall and were as bare as Mother Hubbard's cupboard. Friday night at the movies in homes around the Valley.

"That's another thing that really frosts my ass," I groused. "Half the time you go to a video store, every copy of the new release movie you want is rented out. What's up with that? And I hate having to make two trips to rent a tape. Major waste of time."

Even though Steve seemed to be paying attention to my kvetching, he apparently had no opinion, or at least no response.

We reached an unmarked back door. I knocked and entered. The backroom of Tower was a storeroom, but it looked more like a storeroom that had suffered a recent earthquake. Boxes were strewn everywhere and stacked randomly; bubble wrap and shrink wrap littered the floor; carts of new merchandise, loaded and ready to roll out to the floor, were parked around the room like abandoned bumper cars. But in the midst of this sea of madness rested an island of tranquility: the desk of Barbara "Babs" Fahrney, the world's most beautiful record store manager. Babs was a brunette, but that word is far too weak to do her thick, glossy, raven hair justice. She had luxurious beesting lips, the cheekbones of a supermodel, and a lush figure no anorexic supermodel would ever attain. What's more, she was sweet, smart, and street smart. Every time I saw Babs I suspected she might qualify as perfect. And every time I saw her I had to remind myself how much I loved Laurel.

Babs had hired me a few months earlier to go undercover as a "new employee" and determine why so much store stock was disappearing. "Loss," they called it, and her corporate masters were disturbed by the increasing amount of missing inventory. I worked the back room for weeks, chatting up the employees, a ragtag band of purple-haired, pierced, and multiply-tattooed misfits who'd have difficulty finding gainful employment anywhere less tolerant of the punk rock aesthetic than Babs. Meaning virtually everywhere.

At length I was able to set her mind at ease: despite their social status as outsiders, the employees were honest, mostly, and not to blame for the disappearance of the sizeable amount of stock a recent inventory listed as MIA.

On a hunch, I asked her to provide me detailed invoices for the next several shipments of merch. A pallet or two of forty-plus boxes arrived at the receiving bay daily. They were promptly sorted onto carts and brought to the floor for filing. But no one ever checked the actual contents against the invoices—until I did. The task was simply too time-consuming to be profitable—it would have required an additional full-time employee dedicated to this one tedious task, and that would cut into profits, so Upper Management in their infinite wisdom deemed this step unnecessary.

Everyone simply assumed there was a one-to-one correspondence between the invoice list and the physical contents—until I discovered that each box was short by one or two videotapes or three or four albums. This was too few to notice in a box too full to count by a staff that was too short-handed to account for each individual item. It became apparent to me that this was not, in fact, a store problem, but a scheme originating in the central warehouse: some picker or packer simply removed a few items from each box before shipping, then smuggled the ill-gotten goods out of the warehouse and no doubt sold them to used record stores or at shady flea markets. How that happened was not my business, not my assignment…and not my problem.

Babs handed my report to her corporate masters. And—surprise, surprise—a couple of months later, she phoned my office to report that every single item on every single invoice was now being shipped in every single box. She got a raise and a promotion and, as a bonus for my exemplary efforts, she offered me free movie rentals for life, or at least for as long as she was managing the store. I graciously accepted…and always made a point of saying hi whenever I stopped in. I mean, as much as I love Laurel, I knew the obstacle course of a relationship could send even the best one south at any time…and I do love a good backup plan.

Babs looked up when we entered. And she smiled a smile that outshone the bright lights overhead like the sun outshines a flashlight.

"Oh my," she mock gasped as she approached us, adjusting her one affectation—a personal adornment of dozens of costume jewelry bangles on each arm. "Look what the Cheshire cat dragged in."

I gave her a quick hug. I thought of Laurel so I didn't think *I could get used to this…*

"Who's your friend?" she asked when we disengaged.

"This is Steve. He's my client."

"And to what do I owe this exceptional honor?"

"Babs, my darling, we need your help."

"Sure. What can I do for you boys?"

"Steve is being followed. The guys are in your store. Can you sneak us out the back way so we can ditch them?"

She raised her eyebrows and pursed her delicious lips. Then she smiled and retrieved a ring of keys from her belt.

"Ooooh, cloak and dagger stuff," she whispered. "This way, Mr. Solo, Mr. Kuryakin."

She led us to a wide metal door and inserted a key.

"This locks automatically when it closes," she warned. "So once you're out, you're out."

"Got it," I said. And in a mock Scottish accent—the voice of my people—I added, "Thank you, Mish Moneypenny."

"Call me Emma, please, Mr. Steed," she said with a wink.

"I can do no less for one so lovely," I cooed.

"Jesus, you two," a peeved Steve snarled. "Get a room."

Chapter 4.1

We exited and found ourselves in a paved area behind the store wide enough for delivery trucks to maneuver. Overhead lights attached to the building made bright pools on the black asphalt. Very film noir.

And no sooner did we exit the store than a car pulled into this enclosed alley, pinning us in its high beams. We couldn't get back in through the locked rear door, and the perimeter of the area was surrounded by a high cyclone fence. We were effectively trapped. Cornered.

Two guys got out of the car and sauntered towards us casually. I felt my belt and made sure the Beretta was there and easy to draw if need be, then stepped in front of Steve to offer some kind of protection. And resistance.

The guys who approached us were wearing short-sleeved white shirts, skinny ties, and dark chinos—as I'd noticed earlier, when they were crossing the street to get into Tower. Both sported crew cuts and black-rimmed glasses. Christ, we were being kidnapped by Mormons.

They didn't flash badges. Then again, they didn't flash guns, either. I was so focused on those immediate potential threats that it took a moment to register something odd: the guys I'd seen following us, the guys I'd seen crossing the street, were dressed similarly but were both about the same height. These guys were a mismatched duo, one tall and thin, the other, short and stout.

"Hey, wait a minute," I said. "I saw the guys tailing us. You're not the guys tailing us."

They looked at each other and smiled.

"Nah," the tall one said. "We're the guys tailing the guys tailing you."

The short one looked around me and waved.

"Hi, Steve," he said.

Steve stepped forward and scrutinized the pair closely.

"Larry?" he said. "Jerry?"

They nodded in unison. Synchronized unison.

"What's going on, Steve?" I whispered.

"These guys," he scoffed. "These fuckin' guys. We used to be in the Homebrew Computer Club together a few years ago."

The pair nodded in tandem. Again.

"And we're here to save your ass," the tall one announced.

"Get in the car," the short one said. It sounded more like an invitation than an order, but who really knew?

I turned my back on the Doublemint twins. With my left hand I gestured at them behind me to distract them, while with my right hand I raised my shirt enough that Steve could see the butt of the Beretta.

"I don't think they're a threat," I said to Steve. "I think we'll be OK."

"Who's this guy?" tall boy asked. "Friend of yours?"

"He works for me," Steve replied.

"I'm his bodyguard," I growled. Maybe that would intimidate them. Sure.

"Well, he can come along too, then, if you want," one of the Gold Dust twins said.

"I don't know if we want to do that," I challenged. How far were they willing to go to get us in the car? My hand hovered over my beltline.

Steve's tall clubmate shrugged.

"Hey, suit yourself, man," he said. "You can trust us and come along with us or you can stay here and deal with those other guys. But we can tell you who they are and what they want without you having to tangle with them. If you want."

"It's a simple binary decision," the short one added. Fucking nerds.

I looked at Steve, raised my eyebrows and shrugged. *Whaddaya wanna do, boss?*

He frowned and thought it over for a second.

"Yeah, OK," he said. "Let's go, turkeys."

Chapter 5

So we got in the car—Abbott and Costello in front; Steve and me in the back. It was too dark to see what kind of car it was. But it wasn't a Cutlass.

They drove us through the Tower parking lot and out onto Bascom. The driver took a left onto Hamilton and swung onto the freeway a couple of blocks later. 17 South. Back toward Los Gatos.

"Where are you taking us?" I asked.

The short one, the non-driver, turned around and smiled. "You'll see."

"How long till we get there?" I said. If I knew that, I could at least make an educated guess about where we were headed.

"Twenty minutes, honey," he said in a voice Mommy would use with a restless three-year-old.

We drove along at a good clip, past the green freeway sign reading "Los Gatos 6; Scotts Valley 21; Santa Cruz 26"; past the Winchester Drive-In; past the Camden and Lark exits. The roadside was mostly scrub brush and low trees punctuated by the occasional beige brick noise abatement wall.

When we reached Los Gatos and circled around the Highway 9 exit, I had a twinge of concern that they were driving us back to my office, which would make no sense at all. But then again, very little of what I'd been through today made any sense at all, so even more nonsense could perhaps make a 180 and turn into something sensible. But instead of heading into downtown Los Gatos, the driver turned onto Highway 85, Saratoga-Los Gatos Road. I breathed a sigh of relief.

He took a left on Los Gatos Boulevard and a quick right onto Kennedy Road and headed up into the foothills. Again, I had a momentary pang of discomfort thinking this time that they might be heading to my house. I was still living in the mother-in-law unit of a rich friend's mini-mansion up here in the foothills. Maybe Steve and I were neighbors and never knew it. But once again I breathed a quiet sigh of relief when he continued along Kennedy.

The winding road threaded through the forested foothills. It was quite a scenic drive—during the day, at least. I made a mental note that the next time I get abducted, I should do it while the sun was still out.

The tall dweeb at the wheel took the hairpin turns with graceful ease. It was clear that he'd been down this road before. The drive, I mean. Not kidnapping. As far as I knew, anyway.

A few miles later Kennedy became Hicks. This was rural. Really rural. A lot of open space, a few farmhouses, nothing much except trees and scrub for a few miles until you got to Almaden Quicksilver County Park.

Going to the park made little sense. There was nothing there but open space since the cinnabar mines closed decades ago. There was, however, one other landmark out here. I doubted they knew I knew about it, but all at once I knew where we were headed and who these geeks were.

My suspicions were confirmed when we pulled into the parking lot of a series of low-slung octagonal buildings that reminded me of my grade school. There was no sign identifying the facility.

The driver parked and we all climbed out of the car.

"Sorry about the cloak and dagger," the tall one apologized. "We need to keep this under wraps."

"Mystery's over guys," I said. "This is the IBM Advanced Research campus. I used to ride my bike out here years ago."

They looked crestfallen, like I'd spoiled the surprise party they'd planned. Good.

"And one more thing," I continued, intent on kicking them when they were down. "If you're planning to fold, spindle, or mutilate us, before you do that…think. Think different."

" 'Differently,'" Steve grumbled. "Jesus. Grammar."

Our IBM captors said nothing. They led us to one of the buildings and punched a code on a keypad to open the door. They ushered us in and I got my first good look at these dorks: square black glasses frames, short-sleeved white shirts, pocket protectors, high-waisted slacks that rode up to the top of their socks. Floods. I stifled the urge to ask them what time they were due back at Mission Control.

What did Steve call them? Barry and Cary? Gary and Harry? Jerry and Larry? Mary and Perry? Terry and The Pirate? It was too late to ask their names again without embarrassing myself. They didn't matter to me, anyway, and only Steve mattered to them. Since they were such an odd couple, however, I could probably refer to them as Oscar and Felix, just to keep them straight. But since they were so mismatched—one tall and lanky; the other a little teapot, short and stout—I had other options to identify them. The tall guy was clearly the Dominant Gene in their relationship, so shorty was Recessive Jean. Nah, those names won't stick. I'll have to keep workshopping them.

Goofus and Gallant (better, but not there yet) led us through the small building, which was mostly just cubicles, vacant at this late hour, and mostly dark aside from a few desk lamps some absent-minded professors had forgotten to switch off.

They led us to an enclosed room in the center of the building. One of them slid a key card through a reader. The door opened and they ushered us in.

The room was small and windowless. The walls and ceiling were covered with charcoal gray hand-sized wedges in an alternating vertical/horizontal pattern. I squeezed one. It felt like foam rubber.

"The hell is this?" I said. Oddly, my voice was dead in the air—no reverb whatsoever. Muffled, like talking in a snowstorm.

"It's baffling," the short nerd answered.

"Really?" I said into the thick air. "I thought you'd know."

"It's a series of baffles," he explained. "Sound absorbing foam. This whole room is totally soundproof—an acoustic dead zone. We use it for testing."

The baffling on the floor had been rolled up like sod, exposing polished concrete. The IBMers rolled in four desk chairs and we all sat. Four guys and four chairs just about filled up the room.

"You'll notice one more thing," Clyde Crashcup, the tall one, said. "No electronics. No computers, no telephones. We can't be bugged."

"And nothing said in this room can be overheard outside this room," Leonardo, the short one, added.

Steve broke out laughing. “It’s the Cone of Silence, Max,” he said to me. Then, to Willy and Nilly, “Guys, you should check and make sure he’s not wearing a shoe phone.”

“Uhh…” said tall Willy Wonka. “I don’t think those exist in real life.”

“And I don’t think they could build one into a running shoe like he’s wearing,” the Oompa Loompa added. Is it possible all engineers are born without a humor gland?

“OK,” Steve announced with an edge. “Fun time’s over, guys. Why’d you bring me here? Why all the secrecy? The fuck is all this about?”

The beanpole assumed a serious demeanor: lips pursed, brow furrowed.

“We want to warn you that your company,” he intoned gravely “—and maybe even your life—are in danger. We’ve recently become aware of a corporate giant that wants to take control of Apple Computer.”

“Who?” Steve demanded. “You? IBM’s a dinosaur. You don’t even have a consumer computer.”

“We’re working on a home computer now,” Bullwinkle said defensively.

“Oh, really?” Steve snarled. “So what do you expect me to do, take out a full-page ad in the trades welcoming you to the party? Seriously?”

“We’re calling it a PC—a personal computer,” short Rocky said.

Steve scoffed. “You have no idea what you’re doing. You guys are all shit-for-brains copycats. It’ll take you years to go to market with your machine.”

“Not years,” Bullwinkle protested. “We’re probably gonna release our PC in about six months.”

“And it will suck,” Steve sneered. “‘PC’ will stand for ‘Piece of Crap.’ Our computers will blow yours away. And we’ll out-market you. We’ve got our shit together. You assholes have no idea what people want.”

“Oh, and I suppose you do?” Rocky said in a tone dripping with sarcasm. “What did your market research tell you about what people want?”

"*Market research?*" Steve exploded. He was almost apoplectic. "Did Edison do 'market research' before he invented the phonograph? Did Alexander Graham Bell do 'market research' before he invented the telephone? People don't know what they want until you show it to them. People will want what I *tell* them to want!"

This was getting us nowhere.

"Guys," I said, "let's focus here. I think we should—"

Steve turned to me and turned on me.

"If I want your opinion," he spat, "I'll give it to you!"

I suddenly saw the advantage of being sequestered in a soundproof room: If I beat the living shit out of this arrogant little prick no one would hear him scream.

"The point," said tall Thing 1, "is that we're not interested in you. You're small potatoes."

"How do you like *them* apples?" added short Thing 2.

"Small potatoes, huh?" Steve grumbled. "Don't forget IBM blew a chance to buy Xerox in '58, when they were 'small potatoes.' Maybe they decided they couldn't let that happen again, and they want to devour Apple."

"We already told you," Thing 1 said, "it's not us."

Steve sat bolt upright. "Is it Xerox? They still pissed that I…recreated their graphical interface? They had no idea what to do with it. They're even more clueless than you turkeys. If that's even possible."

"It's not Xerox, you dumb son of a bitch," Thing 2 spat. "Why don't you go f—"

"*Focus*," I demanded. "All of you calm the fuck down. Who's going after Steve? Who's the threat to Apple?"

The trio took a few deep breaths and calmed the fuck down.

And at length, Thing 1 spoke.

"Does the word 'monopoly' ring a…" he prompted.

"Bell?" Steve said, clearly surprised. "AT&T?"

"The phone company?" I said.

Punch and Judy nodded. In unison. Jesus.

"Shit," Steve muttered, gobsmacked. "Biggest fucking company in the world. Shit. Fuck."

We all sat in silence for a bit, trying to digest and assimilate this incredible revelation.

At length, Steve—now considerably calmer than mere moments ago—spoke.

"All right," he said soberly. "Let's be linear and logical. First of all, how did you guys find out about this?"

"Well," tall Natasha said, "as research employees, we have a very high clearance."

"Which gives us access to virtually everything in the company," short Boris added.

"Authorized access?" I asked.

"Well…access," tall Helter said. "Perhaps an illustrative example is in order. You use Xerox copiers, right?"

Steve nodded warily.

"And you know that Xerox doesn't sell those machines, right? They only lease them?"

"Yeah… So?"

"So maintenance and repairs can only be done by authorized Xerox employees," short Skelter added.

"Can you get to the point?" Steve asked.

"The point," tall Punch said, "is that every time a Xerox maintenance man services a leased machine, he also switches out a little black box hidden away inside…a box that takes a photo of every document copied on the machine."

"Then they take those boxes back to HQ," short Judy added, "and develop the microfilm. There's a whole clandestine department devoted to nothing but evaluating every document every company ever copies on their Xerox machines. I've heard about ten percent are butt or breast pics—"

"Industrial espionage," I groaned.

"At the highest levels," Judy agreed.

"What's that got to do with how you know what Bell is up to?" Steve said.

"As I indicated, it's just an example. In our case, who do you think sold AT&T its computers?"

Steve nodded and continued this train of thought.

"And you built backdoors into every one of them, giving you access to every phone call ever made over an AT&T line."

"Well," tall Wally rationalized, "when we discovered AT&T was tapping *our* phones, IBM's phones, we just borrowed a page from their playbook. You know, turnabout is fair play."

"Guys," I said. "None of this qualifies as fair play."

"So, go on," Steve encouraged. "What did you do? And what did you find out?"

"Well…" The Beav shrugged, "We don't really have a lot to do around here. It's a think tank. Like Bell Labs. No immediate results are expected from our research, so we, uh, well, we…"

"Goof off a lot," I finished for him. "Fuck around. Flog the dolphin, spank the monkey."

Laverne and Shirley nodded. But not in unison, which is a good thing, since I was already beginning to suspect they were audio-animatronic.

"Once we discovered the backdoor to the AT&T computers," tall Mork continued, now that that was cleared up, "we started hacking them. As a lark. For the fun of it."

"You know how it is," short Mindy said with an apologetic shrug. "Once a phone phreak, always a phone phreak."

"Now just hold the phone," I protested. "The sheer number of calls would make it nearly impossible to monitor every call ever made."

"OK," tall Sonny sighed. "Two things. One, you're right. We don't do that. We're very selective. Two, Uncle Sam *does* do that. The federal government has the money and the manpower to accomplish that."

"The NSA has eighteen acres of mainframe computers under their HQ," short Cher added. "They tap every phone in the land of the free."

"Jesus Christ," I growled. "Is nothing private anymore?"

All three of them had a good laugh at that. I felt naïve. And pissed.

"Answer the question," Steve demanded once they were done laughing. "How do you guys know all this?"

"Well, like I said, Who do you think sold them their computers?" tall Officer Muldoon chuckled. "AT&T *and* NSA."

Steve nodded. "And your backdoors gave you access to information that revealed..." he encouraged.

Sawed-off Officer Toody took the bait and continued. "The NSA screens by keywords," he said. "They listen for words like 'bomb,' 'information,' 'infrastructure,' 'hijack,' 'smuggle,' 'secret,' 'plutonium,' 'assassinate,' and flag the calls for further attention."

"Oh, and you'll love this one," tall Joliet Jake added. "One of the key phrases they screen for is 'Bill Gates.'"

"Do they filter for my name?" Steve asked.

"Um..." Jake said. "Sorry. No."

"Fuck," Steve muttered.

"But," squat Elwood continued, more upbeat, "we built a filter to monitor a few lines in AT&T's headquarters in New York. And we included keywords like 'Steve Jobs' and 'Apple Computer.' And what we discovered was... Well, believe me, no one was more shocked than we were."

"What?" Steve demanded. "What'd you find out?"

"They want you to build a phone into your next computer."

Steve shook his head, possibly in disbelief. "We already did that," he said. "Two, three years ago, Woz hired John Draper—Captain Crunch—and they built an add-in circuit board they called the 'Charley board' for the Apple II. They told me it was a modem that connected the computer to the phone system and turned the computer into an automatic telephone dialer. Like we needed that. But then I discovered it was actually the ultimate phone phreak device. It did everything every other phreak device did—blue box, red box, black box, beige box—all of them. As if that wasn't bad enough, I realized that if they had a dozen computers with these Charley boards installed and linked them in a network, they could theoretically crash the whole phone system. The entire network—national, maybe even world-wide. And I said no. Absolutely not. I ordered them to take the board out. I tried to explain that we were legit now—a real company. We couldn't risk a potential trillion-dollar valuation by including illegal shit like that."

A trillion-dollar valuation? My, someone was certainly full of himself. Or of something.

"You hired Draper?" Dobie said. "Knowing he's nothing but trouble?"

"Well," Steve shrugged, "he's less trouble than he is bad luck. Always in the wrong place at the wrong time, with the wrong explanation—and the wrong attitude toward the authorities."

"I'll say," Maynard added. "Only phone phreak who ever did time. Twice."

"He's like that bad luck guy in the L'il Abner comics," Dr. Jekyll said. "Always hunched over, always all dressed in black, always with a black storm cloud hovering over his head."

"Joe Btfsplk," I said. "The world's worst jinx." They weren't the only ones who knew things. I knew things. Maybe not what a phone freak was, but…things. They just looked at me. "Steve doesn't read the comics pages," I said.

They returned to their conversation without comment.

"Anyway," Mr. Heckle said, "apparently Bell knew about that Charley board."

"How'd they know?" Steve demanded. "Do I have a mole?"

"Do you have a phone?"

"Of course."

Short Shields shrugged. "There ya go."

"But there are a lot of details I don't discuss on the phone," Steve protested.

"Doesn't matter," tall Yarnell said. "They have methods of turning any telephone into a microphone. Whether you're making a call or not. Anything you discuss in any room with a phone can be eavesdropped on. Ears everywhere."

Steve was ignoring them, looking off into the distance and screwing up his face, apparently lost in thought.

I picked up the slack. "You guys have any of those recordings? So we can hear this for ourselves?"

They shook their heads.

"That would be illegal," Boo Boo said.

"We don't want to leave any physical evidence," Yogi added. "You're gonna have to take our word for it. But, y'know, we've put our jobs on the line to alert you about this, so…" he trailed off and shrugged.

"Oh shit," Steve said at length. "I know how they know. Fucking Draper. A few months after I refused to let them add the

Charley board into the Apple II, Draper was arrested. Security guys from Pennsylvania Bell had been keeping an eye on him and when they caught him making illegal calls, they had the local authorities arrest him. And confiscate his Apple II."

"With this Charley board thing in it, no doubt," I speculated.

"Oh, for sure," Steve agreed. "And they shipped his Apple II to Bell Labs for analysis. Probably dissected the board and reverse-engineered it."

"So they know you can do what they want you to do," tall Spock said.

"They seemed pretty adamant about getting you to add a phone modem to your next computer," short Kirk added.

"How adamant?" Steve insisted.

"They discussed several options of increasing, uh, adamancy. They abandoned the idea of approaching you directly with their request when they discovered you'd already nixed adding a modem in the Apple II. Or in the Apple III. Which we know you're working on, by the way."

"That's when they started discussing what leverage they might have against you," Chip added.

"Like what?" Steve balked. "Like if I have an illegitimate child, they can blackmail me? Something like that?" The dorky duo remained silent. "What, then? Hacking Wall Street switchboards to manipulate Apple's stock price when we go public? Ousting me from my own company? That's never gonna happen."

"It goes deeper than that," Dale said gravely.

"A hostile takeover?" Steve howled. "Over my dead body!"

The two IBMers exchanged a grim glance.

"That's the plan, basically, yeah," Amos said quietly.

"Do not ask for whom Ma Bell tolls," Andy added.

"What?" Steve muttered, clearly flabbergasted.

"They even quoted *Apocalypse Now* in one of their conversations," C3PO said.

" 'Terminate with extreme prejudice'?" I speculated.

"That's the one," R2D2 verified.

Steve sank in his chair, put his face in his hands, and burst into tears.

"Oh my God oh my God," he wailed, his body racked by sobs, his voice rising. Even the sound baffling didn't muffle his increased volume. "Everything I've worked for! Everything I ever wanted to do to make a dent in the universe! I feel like John Fucking Kennedy."

I turned to the IBM guys. "Should we be worried?" I whispered.

"Nah," Fred whispered back. "He used to do this all the time in meetings. We all knew he was a big crybaby."

Then, after a beat, watching Steve blubber into his hands, Barney said to me: "You'll take care of our boy, right?"

"Somebody has to," I sighed.

"Are you gonna go to the cops?" Spaghetti asked.

"What could the cops do?"

"Good," Meatball said, clearly relieved. " 'Cause then you'd have to tell them—"

"Don't worry. I'm not gonna rat you out."

Gilligan and the Skipper both breathed a sigh of relief. After that the three of us just sat, embarrassed, waiting for Steve to compose himself, which he did. Eventually. Einstein was right—time is relative. The corollary is that the more embarrassing the moment, the longer time seems to stretch out. And in my book, there's little more embarassing than other peoples' emotions.

"Why don't they just buy us out?" Steve said after sniffling and pulling himself together. "Not that I'd sell."

"Well," tall Rowan shrugged, "we don't know. They never discussed that, that we heard."

"It's a mystery," short Martin added.

Steve looked at me.

"I think that's your cue," he said sharply.

"What?"

"It's a *mystery*, dumbass," he repeated. "A mystery I've hired you to solve."

I nodded slowly. "Yup." And to the IBM boys I said, "Why now? Why'd you wait until now to alert Steve?"

"We only overheard them discussing their plans about Apple a few days ago," KC said. "But when they decided to start following Steve we realized they were escalating their plan, so we decided to follow them. To protect him. You know…the veiled death threat and all."

"Not so veiled," the Sunshine Band corrected his coworker. "Pretty darn clear, actually."

"But now you've got this guy," tall George said to Steve, aiming a thumb at me, "I guess we've done all we can. Warning you."

"We felt like we had to tell you now," small Gracie added, "since we're gonna have to pull the plug on this operation. We can't allocate any additional resources to our unauthorized little project here. It puts IBM at risk if it gets discovered."

"Not to mention our jobs," Bert added. Ernie nodded in agreement.

"Speaking of your jobs," Steve said, now slightly calmed, "if I remember, you guys are pretty good engineers. Not Woz good, but who is? Why didn't you come to work for me at Apple?"

The Captain and Tennille looked at one another with mirrored furrowed brows.

"You," the Captain said. "You suggested we go to work for IBM and report to you on what they're doing—you know, if they had plans to create a personal computer. You don't remember?"

"Oh, uh, yeah," he replied. "Sure."

"Weren't you warned about industrial espionage?" I whispered.

"It's not industrial espionage if they're volunteering the information."

I just shook my head.

"Besides," Steve continued, "it's not industrial espionage. It's strategy. I tell them to get jobs at IBM. Then when they're ready to jump ship and come to work for me, I can brag that I've poached a couple of prime engineers from IBM. Just like we do with National Semiconductor and Intel. It's a coup."

He said this with such conviction that I almost bought it. Almost. I didn't bother to point out that this explanation was the direct opposite of his earlier explanation. Apparently to Steve Jobs, truth is not just fluid, it's whatever you can get away with.

We dithered around for a moment or two. It appeared as though our secret meeting of the He-Man Woman Haters Club was over, but Spanky and Alfalfa seemed at a loss as to how to end it, until one of them said, "C'mon—we'll take you guys back to your car."

"That's the least you could do," I said, "seeing as how you kidnapped us."

"It's not kidnapping if you came voluntarily," Tweedle-Dum said. "We'll drop you off when we pass through Los Gatos on our way back to Steve's car."

"No," I said. "I stick with Steve."

"So we'll drive you back to Los Gatos after we drop him off?" asked Tweedle-Dumber.

"Here's how we're gonna do this," I said. "We're all going back to the Pruneyard. You're gonna drop me and Steve off at his car. My guess is that his tail, the AT&T guys, are still sitting in the parking lot watching his car, waiting for him to finish shopping or whatever the fuck they think he was doing when we ditched them. And since they know he picked me up in Los Gatos and drove me to the Pruneyard, it'll look suspicious if they see him leaving the mall without me."

"But won't they just start following him again?" Tweedle-Dumbass asked.

"Yeah," I said. "But that's exactly what we want at this point. We need to act like everything is normal and that we don't have a clue that they're tailing him. Since we came to the Pruneyard in his car, it would look suspicious if I disappeared at the mall and he went straight home. So he drives me back to my office in Los Gatos, and you guys get lost."

"Won't they know who you are, then?" asked Tweedle-Dumbfuck.

"They already know Steve went to Los Gatos and picked me up 'for dinner.' It's not likely they know who I am or what I do or what our relationship is. The bottom line is they don't give a flying fuck about me. So Steve drives home and they follow him. Steve and I will take it from there." *Once I come up with a plan,* I said, but not out loud.

"Well, in case it's of any use to you," tall Donny said, "we gave the two guys tailing you code names."

"Mad Hatter and White Rabbit," little Marie detailed.

This was getting curiouser and curiouser.

"Why those names?" I asked.

"Better than calling them 'the AT&T guys.'"

Couldn't argue with that.

We were all pretty quiet on the ride back. Laurel and Hardy had delivered their warning, so they had nothing more to say. Steve didn't get hysterical or express any fear. Or thanks. Heaven forbid. I stifled myself from making some kind of lame joke about Jobs going from blue box to Big Blue, mostly because there was no joke there. Or it was still in R&D.

The ride back seemed shorter. Maybe because we knew where we were going. Maybe because we all had a lot on our minds.

Mutt and Jeff dropped us off at the Pruneyard.

"See you in the funny papers," I said.

Chapter 6.0

Steve and I got in his Mercedes and headed back to Los Gatos.

Within a few blocks of leaving the Pruneyard, I noticed we'd picked up our tail again. Good.

We drove along in silence for a while. The IBM guys had opened up a big can of worms for us, but I was still full from dinner. It was impossible to ignore the urgency of the situation. But I had other plans for the weekend, and deflecting Steve could prove a tough sell. Maybe, if I was lucky and kept quiet—

"We need to do something," Steve said.

"Yeah, sure," I replied. "Let's pick it up again Monday."

"You fucking kidding me? You think you're taking the weekend off?"

"I have plans."

"My life is at risk and *you* have *plans*?"

There was no denying the accuracy of his assessment of the situation…and no ignoring his response to it, damn him anyway. But what could I do? I tried to parse it out, out loud.

"We need to discuss this situation," I said.

"Duh."

"And then come up with a plan of action."

"Oh, you think?"

"But," I continued, "we need to discuss it somewhere where there's no chance of being overheard. Somewhere where there are no phones."

"Good luck with that," he scoffed.

"I might know a place," I sighed. "But it's gonna cost you."

"I don't care. I'm not in this for the money."

"Easy to say when you're worth a million dollars."

"I'm telling you," he insisted, "I'm not doing this for the money. I'm doing it to push Humanity forward."

"Uh-huh. The Great Humanitarian."

"You of all people should understand that," he chided. "You work so cheap you can't be in it for the money."

Jesus. Even Mother Teresa would want to slap this guy.

By the time we reached Los Gatos, I'd come up with a rudimentary plan. It was a Polaroid plan: developed in sixty seconds. It meant sacrifice for me. But it fit the bill perfectly, and Laurel would never know about the sacrifice, since I'd kept the weekend treat I was going to spring on her a secret.

"You planning on going to work tomorrow?" I asked.

"On a Saturday?" he said. "Of course."

"OK, good. You noticed we've picked up your tail again, right?"

"Yeah. I saw you checking."

"They'll expect you to go home now," I continued. "So go home. Let them follow you."

"You *want* them to follow me?"

"Man, we just discussed this. *Yeah*, we want them to follow you. We don't want to risk them suspecting we know they're there. That might force their hand to act before we can counteract. So yeah, let them follow you home tonight. Even if they didn't follow you now, they know where you live, and they'd no doubt be waiting outside your house in the morning."

"But what if they—"

"You'll be OK. Look, we have no indication that you're in any immediate danger from them. As long as you keep acting like you don't know they're there, at any rate."

"Then what?"

"Tomorrow morning, go to work. As usual. On your way in, make sure you're being followed. Subtly. Here—I'll give you the compact. Your building is on Stevens Creek, right? The address on your business card?"

"Well, that's the old building. We've—"

"Don't complicate things, man. I don't need to know your whole company history. Just park in back of that building so they know you're there and they'll watch your car. At noon, come out the front door. I'll be waiting to pick you up."

"Then we can ditch them again," he said, nodding.

"That's the plan."

"Well that's the stupidest fucking plan I've ever heard," he growled. "You're plan's a total piece of shit. What we should do is, I go to work tomorrow morning and sneak out the front door at noon and you pick me up, and we lose them."

So that's how it was going to be with Mr. Steve Jobs. Fine.

"Fine," I said. "Good plan, Steve. We'll do it your way. Oh, and one more thing—pack a ditty bag."

"A what?"

"An overnight bag. Necessities. Your meds, if you take any, a change of underwear, toiletries—toothbrush, mouthwash, deodorant. That kind of thing." If he even knew what those last two were. "And bring a jacket or a sweater."

"Where we going?"

"It's a surprise."

"I hate fucking surprises."

"Oh, don't get your bowels in an uproar, as my Scottish grandfather used to say. You know what Vonnegut says, 'Peculiar travel suggestions are dancing lessons from God.'"

"I don't read Vonnegut," he snapped. "Fuck Vonnegut. Fuck you. Fuck Mother's Day and Christmas, too."

"Oh, so you *have* read *Cat's Cradle*."

"What?"

"Nevermind. Is there anyone who'll miss you if you disappear overnight tomorrow night?"

"No."

Now that was just sad.

"Look," I said. "You're aware now that you're being tracked. And you've already been kidnapped. What could I have in mind that's worse than that?"

"What *do* you have in mind?"

I absolutely was not going to go into detail about my plan. It would be a piece of shit, and his verbatim repetition would be the most brilliant plan ever. That juvenile game would get old real quick. I chose to respond with another juvenile game.

"That's for me to know and you to find out, sweetheart."

"Christ," he spat. "You're as big an asshole as those Homebrew IBM guys. I feel like I've spent the last two days doing nothing but being abducted."

"It's not kidnapping if you go willingly," I said. "Trust me."

"Fuck you," he said as he dropped me off.

There are only two types of people that it's fun to tease. One type isn't upset by anything. The other overreacts to everything. Mr. Jobs was clearly a type 2. And I wasn't above tweaking his weakness.

I poked my head back inside the car.

"You know how they say 'fuck you' in Hollywood?" I asked. " 'Trust me!' "

Chapter 6.1

At noon the next day, I was waiting in front of the Apple offices on Stevens Creek, next door to the Good Earth restaurant, motor running. About ten after, Steve came shambling out the door. He was carrying a small leather valise. He tossed it in the back seat and got in the car. I pulled away from the curb and headed toward the freeway. I saw no cars pull out behind us.

"Your car is a piece of shit," Steve proclaimed. Always the politician.

"It's a classic," I rebutted.

"It's old enough to vote," he argued.

"Vote? Hell, it's old enough to drink!"

His dad was a car guy, like mine, so I thought I'd enlighten him.

"This, my friend," I said, "is a 1959 Plymouth Sport Fury Coupe. Two-sixty horses, three-eighteen cubic inch V-eight four-barrel. Hundred and eighteen-inch wheelbase. A quintessential example of Chrysler's 'Forward Look' of the fifties—low slung; side spears. And the biggest tail fins of any car of the era short of the Cadillac. It's a classic."

"It's a piece of shit," he insisted.

"OK," I conceded. "It *would* be a classic if it had been maintained. But this one… Well, let's just say I'm between cars at the moment. This here is your classic, legendary, hundred-dollar car. Got it from a junkyard, threw a few bucks at it to get it running, ran it through the car wash, and here we are."

I wasn't sure he was paying any attention to me, but he was looking around the vehicle.

"Dash-mounted rearview mirror," he observed. "Fabric seats. Is that a push-button transmission?"

"Yep."

"And those tail fins? Wow. Cool."

"You begin to see its unique virtues," I said.

"Man, my dad would have loved working on this."

"Yeah, mine, too."

"I think he'd call it—"

"—a *lead sled*," we said in unison.

And then a miracle occurred: Steve Jobs laughed.

As we approached Highway 85 he said, "Before we leave, I need to make a quick stop in Menlo Park."

"Forget something?"

"No, it's… I just need to… Just drive, OK?"

I was planning on taking 85 to 280 anyway—in the other direction. Given his new destination, I skipped the 280 interchange and headed north on 85.

"Take the Bayshore north," he gestured as we approached the interchange.

"101," I said. "The digital highway."

A couple of minutes later he instructed me to take Willow, then Bay. We snaked around the Menlo Park Veteran's Medical Center.

"Birthplace of the counterculture," I said, pointing to the hospital building.

"How's that?"

"Twenty years ago, it was here at the Menlo Park VA hospital that Ken Kesey volunteered as a guinea pig in the CIA's MK Ultra experiments with LSD," I recited. "He went on to write *One Flew—*"

"Yeah, I know. Take a left here on Ringwood. He started the Merry Pranksters, too. Stewart Brand was part of that gang."

"*The Whole Earth Catalog* Stewart Brand?"

"Yeah. That catalog had a profound influence on me. Putting power in the hands of people. One reason I'm so focused on Apple."

"Wild. Kesey had a profound influence on me, too. 'You're either on the bus or off the bus.' I was on the bus. And I mean literally."

"Wow," he said. "Cool. OK, take a right on Edge, then a left on Oak Grove."

I made the turns. A few blocks down Oak Grove, Steve pointed to the curb.

"Here. Pull over and park."

I did.

We were sitting in the middle of a suburban block. The houses had been here a while—maybe even pre-war. But they were well-maintained, which figures in an upscale town like Menlo Park.

Steve didn't get out of the car. I didn't know what he had in mind until I saw him watching a young woman a few houses up the street sitting on the grass and playing with a toddler in diapers. The kid was maybe two. Curly blonde hair. Cute.

The toddler toddled a few steps, fell on her butt, struggled back to her feet, wobbled a few steps, and fell again. Story of our lives.

I didn't figure this guy for a pederast, but I did have a hunch.

"Yours?"

He nodded. "Turns two next month," he said quietly. "I named a computer after her. Lisa."

I was surprised to see a tear running down his cheek. His eyes never left the baby.

"I missed her first steps," he whispered. "I missed her birth. Time wasn't right."

I refrained from reminding him that that was the same excuse he'd given me about finding out about his parents. *The time isn't right.* I didn't know his policy about touching, so I refrained from putting a hand on his shoulder. But I couldn't refrain from commenting.

"Buddy," I said, "you better find the right time or you're gonna miss everything."

We sat in silence, watching the Menlo Park Madonna and child until they went back in the house.

"OK," Steve said, a hitch in his voice. "Let's go."

I started the car and headed back to 101. I checked to make sure we were not being followed. We were not.

It wasn't until we got back on 101 that Steve seemed composed enough to be his usual obnoxious self.

"So where we going?" he insisted.

"We're lighting out for the Territory."

"The fuck is that supposed to mean? And why do I need an overnight bag? What're we, camping? I don't camp. I slept on enough dirt floors in India to last a lifetime."

I was getting a bit irritated, and not just because this guy who claims he read the classics didn't catch the reference.

"Steve," I said, "the entire history of civilization is about finding better places to live than outdoors. Shelter from the storm. Comfort. I don't camp either. I don't understand why anyone would voluntarily sleep outdoors."

This did not seem to mollify him.

"Then where are we going?" he insisted.

"We're going somewhere where there are no phones. We are going to sequester ourselves somewhere where we can talk and analyze and plan without anyone eavesdropping. Or interrupting."

"A retreat."

"Right. In order to advance, we must retreat."

"Your plan is shit," he said.

"You have a better one?"

He thought about this for a few minutes as we zoomed past all the little towns that made up the Peninsula: Redwood City, Belmont, San Carlos, San Mateo.

"Yeah," he said at length. "We need to sequester ourselves somewhere we can talk and analyze and plan without interruption or eavesdropping."

"Great idea, boss," I mumbled.

We drove along in silence for a while. I got us on 92 and aimed us toward the San Mateo-Hayward Bridge.

"I get it," I said, once I got it.

"Get what?"

"The little girl. You took advantage of the fact you're not being followed and used it as an opportunity to see Lisa without your tail discovering her."

He was silent for a while, maybe debating how much he wanted to reveal to me, his employee. His hired gun. At length, however, he seemed to make up his mind and sighed.

"We're so close to going public," he said. "I'm afraid if those guys found out about her they might use her existence as leverage against me."

"Or put her at risk," I said.

"Well, yeah, that too."

Once we'd traversed the inordinately long bridge over the Bay and hit Hayward, I turned onto 88 North.

"How much longer?"

"Not much. An hour's drive from the Valley." I didn't think I could take any more of his questioning about our destination, or his impatience, so I pointed to the glove box. "I have some tapes in there," I said. "Why don't you—"

"You put a tape deck in this crapmobile?"

"Just pick out some tunes, OK?"

He pulled a rectangular valise from the glove box and looked through the cassettes.

"This all you got? The Moody Blues? 'Dark Side of the Moon'? The Who? Do you have anything besides long-haired English groups? Prog rock?"

"I have," I said. "Yes."

"You mean you have something other than long-haired English groups, or that you have a tape by Yes, a long-haired English prog rock group?"

"Yes," I said with a smile. "Pick a tape. Who's on first?"

"Do you mean I should put The Who on first?"

"Yes," I said.

"Will you make up your mind? Yes or The Who?"

"Yes," I said. "Who's next?"

"Yes," he said, selecting *Relayer*. But then he hesitated. "Or do you mean put on *Who's Next*?"

"Yes," I said.

"OK, then. I'll put Who on second."

"No, Who's on first," I said. "What's on second."

"I just told you—Who's on second."

"No, Who's on first," I said.

"Who's on first?"

"Yes," I said.

"Jesus Christ," he grumbled. "Caught in an infinite loop. Are you pranking me?"

I could have said *yes*, but I let him off the hook. "There should be some Grateful Dead in there. Ronstadt. Johnny Cash."

"No Dylan?"

"I have no love for that pretentious, humorless, arrogant asshole."

"He's the voice of our generation!" he protested. He sounded personally offended.

"If by that you mean irritating and incomprehensible, I agree."

He gave me a look that suggested that if he was driving instead of me I'd be standing on the side of the road right now.

"You ask me who's the go-to voice of our generation," I continued, "I have to go to the Johns."

"You should have thought about that before we left."

"No, I mean the Johns—John Lennon and Johnny Cash. Maybe Dylan is the voice of some of our generation, but Johnny Cash is the Voice of America." *And a Pisces, like us,* I refrained from saying. "One thing Cash and Dylan have in common is that neither one of them could act worth a damn," I added, hoping to divert us from an argument. "Cash was in a couple of really bad movies. And an episode of *Columbo*."

He nodded, his irritation diminishing a bit. "Yeah, they both sucked as actors. They were no Elvis. But I did like Dylan in *Pat Garrett and Billy the Kid*."

I knew this one. " 'What's yer name, boy?'" I said in a thick cowboy accent, quoting the film.

" 'Alias,'" Steve croaked in reply.

" "Alias what?'"

" 'Alias anything you please.'"

"Yeah," I added. "Like 'Oaf Tobark.'"

We both laughed. Apparently, that patched up our little tiff, since he settled for Jerry Garcia's first solo album and popped the tape in the underdash deck.

And for a while, we just listened to "Deal," "Sugaree," "To Lay Me Down" (my personal favorite), "The Wheel," and all the other classics on that album. Sure it was a decade old. But it was worth every year. And how can you beat lyrics like "Since it costs a lot to win and even more to lose, you and me better spend some time wonderin' what to choose"?

Meanwhile, we drove on, passing by or passing through landmark East Bay cities like San Lorenzo, San Leandro, and my birthplace, Alameda. Still waiting for the shrine to be erected.

North of Oakland, 880 became 580, the road to Berkeley and the Bay Bridge. Before we got to Berkeley, however, we passed through Emeryville. Steve seemed intrigued, waving his head around to peer out the windows even though the area was little more than an industrial wasteland.

"You looking for the old Del Monte cannery?" I asked.

"No, I was thinking about how cheap industrial floorspace must be way out here," he said. "And what a great place to sequester a startup so no one could find it or bother the workers. That'd protect them from industrial spies, too. This could be an awesome secret location," he said with uncharacteristic enthusiasm. It was, in fact, the most animated I'd ever seen him.

North of Berkeley we began to see an increasingly rustic and increasingly lovely landscape of rolling green and golden foothills.

"Now, this is California," I said, gesturing around us. "Silicon Valley isn't California. I've been telling people new to the Valley that if they want to see the real California, they should just drive an hour in any direction."

"Except west," Steve observed. Couldn't argue with that.

And so we drove along, enjoying the scenery and the tunes. Until Jerry's voice started warbling. More than usual, I mean.

"Shit," I said. "Pull that tape, will you?"

He pressed Eject and the cassette popped out—trailing a length of brown audiotape along with it.

"There's a pencil in the glove box," I sighed.

I didn't need to tell him what to do. He knew about high tech. He retrieved the pencil, stuck it in the cassette spool, and respooled the unraveled tape.

"Piece of shit," he mumbled. "You should get a Sony Walkman."

"You can't wear headphones in the car," I grumbled.

"Your tapes suck," he opined.

Oh, this was gonna be a fun weekend.

Chapter 6.2

We passed the Richmond refinery and the Richmond Bridge heading north on Stenmark Road. The rows of tiny white military-looking houses trailed off and the road became lined with trees. The scenery was lovely but the pavement was in terrible disrepair. When I reached an intersection with a dirt road and a street sign that read "Western," I pulled over and retrieved a map from the glove compartment. I had about twenty, so it took a moment to locate the right one. And once I unfolded it, it took up half the front seat.

"Fucking maps," I grumbled while Steve leaned over against the door to avoid being covered by the tablecloth-sized document. "You find some way to replace maps, you'll have earned your million dollars," I growled while I refolded the accordion to show only the immediate area. I consulted my handwritten notes about how to get where we were going, checked them against the map, and checked both against the view out the windshield. The map is not the territory, after all—and we weren't lighting out for the map.

"Well, this has gotta be it," I shrugged and tossed the map in the back seat rather than spending ten minutes attempting to refold it correctly. I took a right onto Western. It twisted away from the Bay and headed east, over potholes, bumps, and cracked asphalt.

"You aren't taking me out to the middle of nowhere to dump me off and leave me to die, are you?" Steve asked. He tried to sound jocular but there was a hint of a quiver in his voice.

If only, I thought. But instead, I pointed to a sign that read "Point San Pablo Yacht Harbor."

"We're going yachting?"

I parked and grabbed my bag. "C'mon."

He retrieved his valise and followed me to the dock. There were a few weathered, low-slung buildings and a few small, weather-beaten trailers surrounded by a lot of open space, mostly dirt, puddles, and scrub brush. A handful of ancient fishing boats and other small craft bobbed silently in the water. I had to admire the sense of humor of whoever named this shithole the "Yacht Harbor."

I spotted what must be our boat: an open craft with the only other person on the dock standing next to it. The skipper was in his late 30s, maybe, but with salt and pepper hair and beard. He was wearing jeans and a windbreaker over a T-shirt, deck shoes, and a jauntily nautical white cap with a patch featuring a life preserver and an anchor. He should really make up his mind.

He checked his watch when he saw us approach.

"You're early," he said, but not in an accusatory voice. "You want to wait for the others or should I run you out now?"

"Let's go," I said.

"May I see your reservations?" he said. I pulled an envelope from my pocket and handed it to him. He took out the letter and perused it.

"It says 'Laurel' on the reservation," he said in an accusatory voice, looking at Steve. "He doesn't look like a Laurel to me."

"What?" I said forcefully. "It should say *Loren*. They must have misheard me when I made the reservations on the phone."

He shrugged. "Ah, close enough. You're here now." He handed the confirmation letter back to me and held out his clipboard. "All I need now is for you both to sign the insurance waiver."

I signed and handed the clipboard to Steve. He looked it over but didn't pick up the pen.

"C'mon, man, just sign it," I said. "Nobody ever reads those things anyway."

He signed but looked at the small boat with some apprehension. "We're getting into that and going out on the Bay?"

"Don't get your panties in a bunch," I said. "You're a Pisces. And a swimmer."

"He's got a legitimate concern," the captain noted. This was not helping. "Nobody could make it to shore through these frigid waters."

"Jack LaLanne," I said. "Frank Morris." They looked at me like I was the one who didn't know what he was talking about.

Steve still looked wary and skeptical.

"You're either on the boat or you're off the boat," I threatened.

Eventually, he climbed into the small craft. I followed. The captain cast off and we headed out into the Bay.

We sat back in the upholstered seats, trying to ignore the cold, the stinging sea spray, and the roar of the boat motor.

"Is this it?" Steve yelled over the noise. "This is your plan? Take me out on the Bay for a fucking fishing trip?"

"You see any fishing gear?" I yelled back. "Or any chains and cinder blocks to make you sleep with the fishes?"

"Where, then?"

I pointed directly in front of us.

"Alcatraz?"

"Jesus, Jobs," I said. "You gotta get out more. The tourist ferries to Alcatraz leave from San Francisco, not Richmond. This is the East Brother Lighthouse. A bed and breakfast."

"And we're here why?" he pestered.

"Because they have no phones. Can't run lines out here to the middle of the Bay."

This seemed to mollify him. "So no chance of being eavesdropped on," he nodded.

"Or discovered. None whatsoever. Completely isolated."

Our voyage only took about ten minutes. The water was calm, but we still had to clean our glasses twice to wipe away the frigid sea spray. Neither of us suffered. Quite the opposite, apparently.

"This is actually kind of invigorating," Steve announced as we approached the dock.

"Well, hell," I said. "You're rich. Why don't you buy a yacht?"

"I'm not *that* rich," he replied.

"Maybe a motorcycle, then," I suggested. "Same rush, but on dry land." I couldn't resist adding a little dig. "The yacht can wait until you're super-duper rich."

The Skipper pulled alongside a ladder that led up to a landing with a boat house. Steve and I scrambled up carrying our little luggage, then headed up a long ramp to the island floor. And once past a row of trees that blocked our view, we found ourselves in a stunning Wonderland set like a jewel in the middle of the Bay. San Francisco has a famous row of houses known as the "Painted Ladies"—a series of Victorian, Edwardian, and Queen Anne-style homes ornamented in gingerbread trim and pastel colors that slopes down Steiner Street. The East Brother Lighthouse building could easily have been a transplant from that iconic area.

The house itself was a three-story box with the light tower set in the middle—not the standard column, but instead a four-story square topped by a circular light fixture surrounded by a widow's walk.

We stopped for a moment to take in the sight.

"Wow," said Steve. "Cool."

We crossed the small cement courtyard and walked through the open front door of the house. The entry hall was lined with photos documenting the history of the island, most in black and white and featuring men in old-style coats and bowlers.

What was originally a living room, I guessed, had been converted to the front desk of the B&B. An attractive blonde, mid-30s maybe, looked up from behind the desk, smiled, and greeted us. I handed her our reservations. She didn't question "Laurel" as the Skipper had.

"Oh," she said. "You're in the cottage. The original Fog Station building." She looked from Steve to me and smiled at us. "We always love having San Francisco couples enjoy our romantic little hideaway."

"But we're not—" Steve started.

"We're not from San Francisco," I said, drowning him out. "We're from Silicon Valley."

She gave me a handprinted menu. "We serve dinner at six," she said. "Would you like to join the rest of us in the dining room or would you prefer to be served in your cottage?"

"If we could take our meals in the cottage, that would be great," I said, handing the menu back. I couldn't help smiling, and was glad that Steve was behind me where he couldn't see the menu or the smile. Oh yeah, I was going to have fun with this.

I leaned in close to the lovely blonde innkeeper. "Is it possible…" I began, and whispered my special request, cocking my head toward Steve.

"Oh, of course," she said quietly. "Not a problem at all."

"So you live here full time?" I asked while she updated our reservation card.

"Oh, yeah," she said with a smile. "My husband Jack and I. You met him on the boat. We run the B-and-B Thursday through Sunday nights, and do upkeep on the island and the lighthouse the rest of the time."

"Sounds idyllic."

Her smile remained but a shadow moved between it and sincerity. "This place requires constant maintenance," she said softly. "The foghorn alone is over a hundred years old and is very touchy. The windows need to be washed daily from the sea spray. Rust eats everything. We get all our water from a rainwater catchment and all our electricity from a generator—both of which are temperamental and require daily attention. The sea wind whips us constantly. It's a ten-minute boat trip to the shore, then half an hour on that miserable excuse for a road to get to the nearest supermarket. And the guests… Well, they expect the best—gourmet meals, rooms that are clean and dry and warm." She smiled wanly at me. "It's a handful."

"Then again," I encouraged, "you've got that view."

"Yeah. Once I clean the windows enough to see it."

"Do you have a phone?" Steve chimed in from the front hall.

"No, sir. No phone on the island. The office in Richmond handles all our telephone communications. We've got a marine radio for emergencies."

She pointed toward the front door. "Your cabin is that standalone building just outside and to the left. You can't miss it. It's unlocked. Make yourself comfortable. We offer a tour at four, and we'd love to have you join us."

"Thank you," I said. And to Steve, I said, sweetly, "Can you get the bags, honey-bunny?"

He stewed but followed me out the front door.

"I'm not gay," he grumbled.

"Ah, well, it's early," I replied gayly.

Our hostess wasn't kidding—our lodging was a small rectangular cabin with a steeply angled roof, mere steps from the house. If we'd taken any more steps, we'd be swimming.

The Fog Station building was a single room, no bigger than the average studio apartment. There was a half-bath—toilet and sink; no shower—on one end and a small round table set between two deep brown leather easy chairs at the other. Between the sitting area and the powder room, filling most of the room, was a pair of queen-sized beds.

"Oh, look, sweetheart!" I gushed. "Two queens!"

"Don't even start," Steve snarled.

I dropped my bag on one of the beds and began unpacking. Not that there was all that much to unpack: a sweater, a change of underwear, my shaving kit, a paperback copy of *Sand Dollars*, my mini-TV.

"What's that," Steve said, pointing at my stuff.

"A paperback book," I said. "Greatest invention of the twentieth century—cheap and easy access to knowledge, literature, and entertainment. Keep your media portable is what I always say."

"I know what a fucking paperback is," Steve snapped. "I mean that gray cube. The hell is that? A Rubik's Cube?"

"What the hell is a Rubik's Cube?"

"A new toy. A puzzle box. But what the hell is *that* thing?"

I picked it up and tossed it the hell to him. Gently. It was, as he'd observed, a gray plastic cube, no bigger than an apple. He turned it around in his hands and examined it.

"It's a TV," I said. "Full color. Runs on batteries."

"This is a television?"

"Yeah. Japs built it. Antenna telescopes from the top there. Buttons are on the sides."

He seemed entranced by the little device. "Compact," he muttered. "Love the cube shape—perfect and simple. Beveled edges, nice. A screen that's only about an inch square. Only three buttons?"

"Yeah. On/off, channel up and down, and volume."

"Hm," he grunted. "I wonder if there's a way to reduce it to just two? Or even one?" He wasn't talking to me.

"Remember when we were kids and TVs were furniture?" I said. "Huge consoles? They keep getting smaller and smaller until this—a miracle of micro-miniaturization. You got the whole world right there in the palm of your hand. Keep your media portable."

"If we could apply this to computers…" he mumbled. "Flatter, though. Bigger screen. Slip it in your pocket… So let me get this straight," he said, once again addressing me. "I drive a German car, you carry an Italian gun and own a Japanese mini-TV. Makes you wonder who actually won the war."

"*Jawohl,*" I replied. "Although I wouldn't mention that to either of our dads. Oh… It's almost four. Let's go back to the main house for the tour."

We set off across the cement courtyard just in time to run into another pair of guests, a man and woman in their 30s in casual dress pulling their luggage toward the main house. When they saw us the man changed direction and headed our way.

"Hey!" he exclaimed. "I know you. You're that detective on TV."

I didn't feel like insulting a guy I'd be stuck on an island with for the next day, so I refrained from my usual smart-ass, wish-fulfilling retort to that statement, "Yeah, I'm Jim Rockford." Instead, I leaned in close to Steve and whispered, "Haha, I'm famous."

The tourist glanced at Steve then said to me, quietly, "I didn't know you were gay."

Steve leaned into me. "Haha," he whispered.

"You guys should go check in," I suggested to the couple with a big smile. "Tour starts in a few minutes."

They moved on. As they entered, a second couple exited the house. Fortyish, stylishly dressed. No luggage. Probably just checked in. Deductive reasoning at its finest. They walked toward us.

"Hey, I know you!" the man said.

The price of fame, I thought. "Yeah, you probably saw me on TV."

"No, not you," the guy balked. "Him. Steve Jobs. I recognize you from your photo in one of the computer magazines."

Steve leaned in to me. “Haha, I’m famous,” he whispered.

“I didn’t know you were gay,” the tourist said quietly.

I leaned into Steve. “Haha,” I whispered.

By this time the first couple and Jack had exited the house. The lighthouse keeper motioned us to gather together.

“Welcome to East Brother Light Station,” he said. “Are you ready for the nickel tour?”

We all nodded.

“All righty then. We’re standing on a one-acre island,” he began his well-rehearsed and frequently repeated spiel, “located in the strait that separates the San Francisco and San Pablo Bays. The East Brother Light station was established here in 1873, and served as a guide to ships until 1976, when the Coast Guard decided to decommission the facility. Residents of nearby Richmond objected to the loss of this iconic attraction, and last year they formed a non-profit that leased the entire island from the Coast Guard and converted it to the Bed and Breakfast venue you’re enjoying today. We upgraded the house and all the facilities to accommodate guests.” He pointed to the perimeter. “And we surrounded the entire island with a classic white picket fence, which serves not only as an attractive decoration but also prevents you all from walking off the edge of the world and falling into the Bay.”

He got his chuckles.

“Let’s take a look inside,” he continued, leading us to the front door. “The house is a Victorian, designed in the American Stick style,” he said and launched into details about the architecture. He walked us past the front desk and into a formal dining room. A long table was set as formally and ornately as the fanciest restaurant I’d ever been to. The lighthousekeeper’s wife entered carrying a bottle of champagne and proceeded to pour a glass for each of us while Jack lectured about the furniture. Everyone seemed to pay attention, but whether out of genuine interest or simple courtesy, who could say?

Jack then led us, champagne in hand, back outside and up an outer staircase to the second floor, where he let us peek into the various guest bedrooms. (“Oh, that’s ours!”) Each was small but plush and cozy, and every one of them had a million-dollar view: big ships, little seals, wheeling gulls, the stringy, spine-like Richmond-San Rafael bridge.

From there he took us upstairs to point out the Common Room on the third floor, then, single-file, up a spiral staircase into the lantern room itself. The actual beacon was remarkably small, but the wraparound windows provided a panoramic view of the entire Bay. A billion-dollar view. We all spent a few minutes sipping our wine and admiring the scenery from the lamp room or the widow's walk surrounding it. Eventually, Jack suggested we head back down.

"Kind of like the Winchester Mystery House," Steve commented as we wound down the narrow staircase.

"Don't remind me," I mumbled.

Once again outside, Jack the tour guide led us across the cement patio.

"What's that other little island?" one of the wives inquired. "That one right out there all covered with, uh…seagulls?"

"And guano?" Jack teased. "That's Turd Island, which was the inspiration for a series of books by an author whose name has been all but forgotten in the annals of literary history." Since he pronounced it "anals," I assumed he was joking. "*Escape from Turd Island* is one. *Return to Turd Island. The Little House on Turd Island, Turd Island Confidential, Dorothy and the Wizard on Turd Island*…and so on. Come on over this way and we'll take a look at the fog horn."

Jack led us all the way to the other side of the island—a lengthy trek of perhaps twenty paces—and into a shed that looked like the inside of a waterworks or sewage treatment plant. Large, thick pipes, ancient but clean and all freshly painted, crisscrossed the little room.

"This is one of the original diaphone fog horns," Jack said, patting a piece of equipment. "Shall I fire her up?"

We all nodded. He took the cover off a diesel engine in the middle of the room and started it up. Steam-powered pistons hissed and beat out a rapid, deafeningly loud rhythm. The air was thick with the bus fart smell of diesel exhaust. He twisted wheels on some pipes and checked the needles on a couple of gauges.

"The diesel engine is attached to this air compressor," he said loudly, pointing to another series of pipes and valves and then to a pair of tall cylinders, like giant water heaters. "When these tanks are filled with compressed air, I open the valves." He pulled on a chain loop that disappeared into the ceiling, then stepped over to an antique electrical panel where he threw a small switch. "That's the timer. You all have about fifteen seconds to step outside and cover your ears," he warned, shooing us out of the machinery shed.

The horn mechanism on the roof was conical, bright red, and looked like one of Goddard's early experiments in rocketry.

"And thar she blows!" Jack bellowed.

The fog horn blasted a thunderous bass *BEEEE-OOOOOH.* I could feel it in my intestines. When it was finished the machinery returned to blessed silence, but the gulls continued squawking their complaint. You'd think they'd learn. We all applauded.

Jack the mechanic emerged from the fog horn shack, wiping his hands on an oily rag and nodding his approval of our enthusiastic approval.

"And that, ladies and gentlemen," he announced, "is the tour. Dinner's at six, so feel free to wander the island or relax in your rooms and enjoy the luxury—and the view—until then. Don't get lost!"

Chapter 6.3

We all thanked Jack—a true Jack of all trades—then split into couples and went our separate ways: the others back to their plush rooms; Steve and me back to our Fog Station cabin.

We each took a turn freshening up in the powder room—it had been a long drive and a kidney-bumping boat ride, after all. I washed the salt off my wireframe glasses and felt a twinge of sympathy for the lighthousekeeper's overworked wife.

A few minutes after six, there was a knock on our door.

"I'll bet it's telemarketers," I said to Steve.

"Did you bring your gun?" he said.

"Didn't think I'd need it," I replied. "Until now."

But it wasn't a door-to-door or island-to-island salesman; it was the much more welcome Jack, our skipper, tour guide, and now our maître d' —or at least our waiter. He rolled a serving cart into our little room and parked it at the table.

"Ready for dinner, ladies?" he thought he'd joked. We each took a chair and he proceeded to spread out a linen tablecloth, lay out silverware, uncork a bottle of red wine and pour us each a glass. He then served our plates, protected under silver domes on the cart. Spinach salad with strawberries. Italian Wedding soup. And the entrée: a slab of prime rib with mashed potatoes and asparagus. He was about to remove the cover from the final dish but I shook my head to stop him.

"Everything look OK?" he asked.

"Just too-too fabu!" I gushed. Steve the straight vegetarian just sat glaring at me and at the dead cow on his plate.

"I'll be back later with dessert and collect the dishes," Jack said as he left.

"What's the trouble, Steve?" I teased.

"Prime rib," he growled. "I can't eat this."

"Well, then," I offered, "how about I trade you my asparagus for your prime rib?"

"And your potatoes."

"No, I want my potatoes. But I did get you this instead." I uncovered the final plate—the secret second salad and extra side of mashed potatoes I'd requested, anticipating this negotiation.

He scowled at me with his unblinking stare, then nodded curtly and gestured for me to hand him my plate. I held it out while he transferred my veggies to his plate and his slab of beef to mine.

"You're welcome," I said with a smile.

He aimed a fork at my pile of prime rib. "Didn't anyone ever tell you about cholesterol?"

I grabbed the salt shaker and began salting my meat. Steve watched with a furrowed brow. "Or warn you about too much salt?"

I put down the shaker and smiled at him. "Tell you what," I said. "I'll make you a deal—you stop trying to save my life and I'll keep trying to save yours."

He gave me that unblinking stare but then broke it off and dug into his soup. I took his silence as agreement.

After that, we didn't talk. We just ate. And ate. And ate.

Apparently, I was correct in my assessment that two side salads, two helpings of asparagus, and a double portion of potatoes would be acceptable to my picky, prickly, food freak client. Two slabs of prime rib were just about the right amount for me. Fuck cholesterol.

Chapter 6.4

An hour or so later, Jack returned with crème brûlée and cleared the table. And once he left, Steve began pacing around the little room like a caged cat in a circus wagon.

"Look," he accused, clearly irritated, "we came here to discuss my situation. It's been all day and we haven't discussed a single goddamn thing."

"To work, then," I suggested.

"I think better when I'm mobile," he said. "Let's walk and talk."

"Did you bring a jacket or sweater like I suggested?" I said. "It gets pretty cold and windy out here at night."

He opened his overnight case and pulled out a sweatshirt. I slipped a long-sleeved black turtleneck sweater over my T-shirt, to accompany my blue jeans and gray suede New Balance sneakers.

I caught Steve assessing me critically while I dressed. Oh God I hope I was just kidding about him being gay…

"That looks pretty comfortable," he remarked.

"It's from the Illya Kuryaken collection," I said.

We stepped outside and were immediately greeted by a chill wind that whipped across the Bay and swept across the island. I was afraid I'd underestimated the weather and began to wish I'd packed even warmer wear.

We walked the perimeter of the tiny island, stopping occasionally to view the sights. Even in the dark of night we could make out the silhouette of Mt. Tamalpias in Marin. From the other side of the island we could see the Bay Bridge, and stood transfixed by a magical and unique view of the nighttime skyline of San Francisco's financial district. The twinkling lights spread across the landscape like a fallen Christmas tree. I was transfixed, at any rate. All Steve could do was mumble something about that "ugly" Bank of America skyscraper. Maybe he was right. The Transamerica pyramid was much more attractive, not to mention more easily identifiable.

We walked the perimeter twice before I stopped us.

"Steve, it's a one-acre island. Where are we gonna walk to?"

He just stood contemplating The City.

"You want to walk, try walking there," I challenged, pointing toward Baghdad-by-the-Bay.

"Maybe I could," he said, looking at me with that irritating know-it-all smirk.

I almost believed that he almost believed that he could.

"Jesus Christ," I muttered.

"Exactly!" he laughed. "Y'know, a few months ago I dressed up as Jesus for the Apple Halloween party. Back when I had a beard."

"You don't come across as a guy who would embrace costumes," I ventured.

Again, the smirk of superiority.

"About a decade ago," he said, "when I'd just graduated high school, so it would have been '72—Woz and my girlfriend at the time and I got a gig dressing up as Alice in Wonderland characters doing skits at the Westgate mall."

I was gobsmacked. "That was *you*?"

Now it was his turn to be flabbergasted. "What, you saw us?"

I chuckled at the uncanny coincidence. "Well, first of all, we lived close to Westgate. When I was a kid I used to ride my bike there and watch them construct it. And when I was in college working for my Police Science degree, we had to do internships for credit. I took a job that summer as a security guard trainee at Westgate. We were specifically warned about you guys. My boss thought you might be troublemakers."

"We never caused any problems," he recalled. "But I'll tell you one thing, we wanted to. Those costumes weighed a ton. And they were hot and sweaty. After a couple hours, we just wanted to wipe out some kids."

"Which one were you, the Mad Hatter or the March Hare?" Either, I thought, could be considered appropriate.

"Woz and I switched off. But I always wondered if that experience played any role in him marrying a girl named Alice."

Chapter 6.5

We stood quietly for a while, simply appreciating the beauty of the Bay and the twinkling wonderland of The City.

"Small world," I reflected.

"Small island, anyway," Steve said. "And cold."

"Friggin' cold," I agreed, jamming my hands into my pockets. "Look, we're not gonna walk anywhere here and we're not gonna think straight while our nads are freezing. Let's go back to the room. I've got something that'll warm us up."

He didn't argue or even bother to agree. He just headed back to the room.

Once inside our warm, cozy cottage, I went to my over-nighter and pulled out a bottle of Jameson. Don't leave home without it.

We sat back down at the dinner table and I poured us a couple of stiff shots.

"I don't usually drink," Steve said.

"You will after you taste this."

"Didn't you tell me you were Scottish? This is Irish whiskey."

"We're currently at peace with our retarded bastard Celtic cousins. Drink up."

He ventured a sip and nodded. "Smooth."

"The great thing about Jameson is that it not only warms you up, it also makes you more intelligent. I call it Smart Juice."

"You would," he sighed.

I slapped my palms on the table. "All right. To work, then. Let's assess what we know, what we don't know, and what we suspect. The Socratic method. Dialogue to stimulate critical thinking. And Jameson to stimulate creative thinking."

"Right," he nodded. "Like a flow chart or a logic tree."

"Sure," I said. I had no idea what he was talking about.

"I like to use a three-part strategy to solve problems," he began.

"OK," I said. "Let's hear it."

"First, you zoom out—look at the Big Picture."

"I think we got that from the IBM guys," I said. "Then what?"

"Next you focus in—gather facts, consider various scenarios."

I nodded. "I think we're there now. And the final stage is…?"

"Disconnect. Take a Zen approach. Go back to look at the Big Picture again, this time as objectively as possible, once you've removed as much misinformation and as many suppositions and assumptions as you've been able to discover."

"I don't think we're there yet. But we can focus on possible scenarios, given the facts at hand."

He nodded. "Fact one is that AT&T is out to get me. And Apple."

"No," I said. "That is not a fact."

"But they said—"

"I know what they said. But we don't know if it's accurate. We don't *know* that. We're assuming their information and analysis is accurate. But what if it's not? We can't make any assumptions. We need to question everything, including that."

His silence expressed his agreement. I assumed.

"Well," he said, "we *do* know *someone* is following me."

"Yeah. That we know. But it might not be AT&T. Do your IBM friends have anything to gain by lying about this? Revenge over some petty slight? Jealousy that you've gotten so much farther in the industry than they have?"

He considered this. "No. I know those guys. They're engineers. Pretty straightforward nerds."

"So we have no reason to disbelieve them," I said.

"No."

"All right, then let's consider that they were honest and accurate—which means that it is in fact AT&T that's after you. The question then becomes: Why?"

"They didn't know."

"You have any ideas? Maybe they're still pissed at you for abusing their phone lines during your—what did you call it?—your phone freak days?"

He shook his head. "I find it difficult to believe they'd go to such great lengths to avenge such inconsequential…pranks."

"They did send people to jail," I reminded him. "You said so yourself."

He nodded. "But my, uh…offenses were years ago. We've gone legit. I can't believe they'd carry a grudge of this magnitude—following me, planning a hostile takeover of Apple. Threatening my—" He shook his head. "No. It's gotta be something else. Something much bigger. Or why would they bother?"

"OK. Let's move on. The IBM guys were convinced AT&T wants you to build a phone into your computers, right?" He nodded. "Let's assume for the moment that they were honest and accurate about that information as well. Any idea why they'd want you to do that? And be so insistent about it?"

He pondered this and let out a deep breath. "One of the guys at Xerox has been experimenting with a system that allows computers to talk to one another. To exchange data. Alan Kay, I think. They call it the ARPAnet, which stands for the Advanced Research Project Agency Network, if I remember what Woz told me. He's been fucking around with that for years. It connects academic and research computers into a network. Through the phone lines. Woz wanted to build a modem into the Apple II so it could connect to the phone lines and to those other computers—any other computers that were on that network."

I had no idea what he was talking about, but he was on a roll, so I wasn't about to interrupt him.

"But he wanted to do that for pranking and hacking," he continued, "not to advance the Apple II—or the ARPAnet, for that matter—which is the main reason I said no. Someday all computers will be connected. And probably through the phone lines."

"Yeah, but this is today."

"Oh, it's inevitable," he said, lost in thought. "But right now it doesn't make any sense to network personal computers. They should be standalones, for individual use. That's the whole philosophy behind Apple's products—one person, one computer. Adding a modem would be premature. It's unsupported by any current infrastructure."

"Well," I said, "you're trying to wrest control of computers from evil behemoths like IBM and give them to the masses, right? This ARPAnet might expand to take control away from AT&T and give it to consumers unless AT&T builds it first."

Steve shook his head. “No, that can’t happen anytime soon. Ten, fifteen years, maybe.”

“Bell has been around for a hundred years,” I said. “They’ve gotta be good at advance planning. Playing the long game.”

He nodded slowly. “Yeah. You’re right. But at this point the hardware isn’t there, the software isn’t there, the algorithms just aren’t there.”

“The al gore who?”

“Algorithms. Mathematical directions that tell the computer what to do, and in what sequence.”

“Like a recipe?”

“Exactly. Computers are going to need a lot more processing power than they have now, not to mention better, more sophisticated algorithms—programs—to create or use a network like that.”

“But you know that this ARPAnet is already building a network of connected computers,” I protested. “So maybe this is AT&T pushing back at them through you. They want to ensure that a network like that uses their phone lines, so they’re trying to make your computers access-ready. It stands to reason the more the phone lines are used, the more money AT&T makes.”

He nodded slowly. “But… Jesus Christ. I mean, AT&T is the biggest corporation in the world. They own Bell Labs, for Christ’s sake. Why don’t they just build their own damn computer? Why are they targeting Apple?”

“That was another question your IBM friends couldn’t answer. And neither can you, apparently. So let’s put the ‘Why?’ on hold for the moment and discuss ‘How.’ *How* could AT&T convince you to add a… What’d you call it?”

“A modem.”

“Yeah. You said you already rejected your partner’s plan to build a modem into your computers. So how could AT&T persuade you if you’re so adamantly opposed to that happening?”

Again, he mulled this over while I sat silently sipping my Jameson. I had the better half of that deal.

“They couldn’t,” he said with conviction. “It’ll never happen until the infrastructure is in place, as long as I’m in charge.”

“What if you weren’t in charge?”

He furrowed his brow. "Like, how? I'd never leave voluntarily. Apple is my child."

"Could they force you out?"

He scoffed. "You fucking kidding me? That could never happen. Not in a million years. I'm the founder. I *am* Apple. They kick me out, it's suicide."

"OK," I said. "The IBM guys didn't mention them kicking you out," I continued, gently. "But they did mention *taking* you out."

His head snapped bolt upright. "What would anyone gain by murdering me?"

"Well, you said yourself you'd never sell and you'd never quit. And that you'd never agree to their plan to make your computers compatible with the phone lines. That's a lot of nevers. So maybe getting you out of the way is their only path to get out of Never-Never Land."

"Still…" he said. But he squirmed in his seat a bit and took another sip of his whiskey. If he thought of any objections, he didn't act like he'd convinced himself.

"Well, in any eventuality," I said, "who'd succeed you? Someone more open to AT&T's influence, maybe?"

"We don't have a succession plan in place. That comes much later."

"How about your partner? What did you call him? The Wiz?"

" 'The Wiz,'" he chuckled. "He'd love that. No, *Woz*. Short for Wozniak. He'd never agree to run the company. Woz hates management responsibilities. He's one hundred percent engineer. He'd rather quit than take a management position." He gave this a bit more thought. "But maybe Woz. He *is* the other founder, after all. The board might install him as a figurehead, to show our investors some continuity and stability—as long as they could convince him he doesn't have to actually do anything except tinker with computers. They could probably get away with that. He's easily manipulated."

"And he already wanted to build a phone modem into your computers," I prompted. "So he'd be open to AT&T's request."

"He'd have no idea how they were going to abuse the tech, though. He's a bit simple that way. Trusting." He made that sound like it was a character defect.

"How about your ethics guy, Markulla?"

He shook his head. "Nah. He wants to retire and enjoy his money, not run a major company. And he's so into his whole corporate ethics thing that if he ever became aware of AT&T's conspiracy against me—and Apple—he'd oppose them just on ethical principles. You know, 'the moral high ground.'" He made that sound like it was a character defect.

"Anybody else at that level?"

"Mike Scott. But there's no way they'd appoint him the crown prince. We're always at each others' throats. Sometimes I suspect they hired him just to be a burr in my butt—the 'Anti-Steve.' He's the only one at that level who has no hesitation arguing with me. Such an asshole."

"So he might be open to a move you've opposed—like adding a modem to your computers?"

"If I even thought he was complicit I'd can his ass," Steve growled. "I'd get the Board of Directors to toss him out."

"Any other candidates?"

He shook his head decisively. "I'm the only one who should be CEO. I'm the only one who can run Apple."

Even for Steve, this seemed a bit, oh, let's say, *overconfident*. But perhaps he had a point. I considered his vast managerial experience. I reflected on his world-class diplomatic skills, his saint-like patience, his humble humility. I ruminated on his infinite sympathy for the human condition, informed by the deep wisdom of a guiding philosophy drawn from '60s rock lyrics and Bobhisattva Dylan.

"A tip of advice, Steve?" I offered.

"What's that?"

"Don't believe everything you think."

We spent the next several hours sipping our whiskey and ping-ponging these same ideas back and forth, looking for an insight or an epiphany. Alas, none ever came. We parsed what little data we had six ways to Sunday that Saturday night to no avail. Eventually, we found ourselves doing little more than repeating ourselves and our analyses based on our few facts… and occasionally slurring our words while doing it. By midnight we were halfway through the bottle, half in the bag, and still miles away from any solid conclusions.

"This is fruitless," Steve sighed. "We simply don't have enough information to deduce what AT&T is planning, and without knowing that we can't develop an oppositional strategy. We can't clearcut the forest because we can't see the trees."

"Well, you're right," I agreed. "We're standing in an orchard of fruitless apple trees. The information we have is like this island—very little, and we only end up walking around in circles. You're gonna need a bigger island. Let's sleep on it and start fresh in the morning."

"And just what is it you think we're gonna do in the morning?" he said sharply. "You didn't accomplish shit tonight. I'm starting to think you're nothing more than a shithead. A shithead who sucks." He seemed steamed that I'd give up so easily, even though it was obvious that we were in agreement and correct in our assessment that we lacked raw data.

"Let me worry about that. You just follow my lead."

"I've been following your lead," he snarled, "but you've led us nowhere. The only place you've led us is to a tiny island in the middle of the fucking Bay. To Elba. I'm a leader, not a follower, goddamn it."

"Well, you're going to have to delegate that leadership role to me, no matter how difficult that is for your delicate fucking ego."

"You lead me on a wild goose chase then insult me on top of it?" he wailed indignantly. "I'm fed up. I've about had it with you, and just about ready to fucking fire you."

"Fire *me*?" I shot back. "Listen, asshole: You're in *my* wheelhouse now. We do things *my* way. It's my way or you can go back to Highway Sixty-one. Don't make me fire *you*."

"I expect my employees to give a hundred and fifty percent!" he howled.

"You can't sprint a marathon!" I countered.

"You're not doing your job!" he yelled.

"Not doing my— Sweetheart, I've been on the job since the minute you hired me. This island where there are no phones? This was supposed to be a romantic weekend getaway with my girlfriend. I even sacrificed *that* to save your miserable fucking pathetic selfish life. So just can the shit and can the shit fit."

He stood drop-jawed, perhaps in disbelief that anyone would dare talk to him this way, or talk back to him at all. But some part of my irate response clearly derailed his outrage train. I assumed it was the logic until he said quietly, "You have a girlfriend?"

I nodded.

"You have a picture?"

I pulled out my wallet and showed him my favorite photo of Laurel—a candid snapshot of her sitting in my car, head thrown back, laughing. A vision of red-headed ecstasy.

"How about you?" I said. "You have a picture of your loved one?"

He pulled out his wallet and withdrew a photo.

It was a marketing shot of the Apple II computer with the Apple logo prominently displayed.

"Good night, Steve," I said.

Chapter 6.6

I woke the following morning to the sweet sounds of someone screaming, "Jane! Stop this crazy thing!" in a tiny, tinny voice. When I opened my eyes, I could see Steve, fully dressed, sitting on the end of his bed, watching "The Jetsons" on my tiny television and spooning something out of a bowl. Like living with a fucking three-year-old, tantrums and all.

I sat up in bed, not the least bit bleary. If only the room would just stop spinning.

"They brought coffee and breakfast a while ago," Steve said, waving his spoon toward the table without looking away from the TV.

I grunted my understanding—basically the only communication I was capable of before mainlining the coffee. I rolled out of bed, slipped into my jeans and T-shirt—screw the change of underwear—and went off to the powder room, where I proceeded to do what people do in the morning in a powder room. Except shave. Thank you, beard.

I put on my shoes and socks then walked past Steve and sat down at the little table. Jack or his wife had delivered a tray of cut fruit, granola, and a carafe of blessed, life-restoring coffee. I poured myself a cup and added some cream from a miniature pitcher. Real cream. This place was first cabin all the way. I just hoped it wasn't first cabin on the *Titanic*. No, wait… In that metaphor, Apple would be the ship and AT&T would be the iceberg. A destructive but passive force. So that wasn't quite right. A more appropriate metaphor would be the *Lusitania*. Yeah. Apple would be the ship and AT&T the sub trying to sink them.

Oh God I needed that coffee badly.

"Watching a little TV, are we?" I joked to Steve. I had to hope the coffee would enhance the quality of the jokes, even though I knew there were those who would argue that not even Juan Valdez could supply the necessary amount.

On the teeny screen, I saw Jane Jetson sitting at her home computer terminal. The front was all screen, the body, all curved lines that tapered gracefully to a blunt end. I waggled a finger at the TV.

"Now, there," I said. "You should build a computer that looks like that. Very futuristic."

"What, that teardrop shape?"

"Yeah. Looks like half a lozenge."

"It looks like a suppository," he objected.

"Well, there's your ad campaign: 'Hey IBM—shove *this* up your ass!'"

He turned off the small set. "So did you come up with any brilliant ideas?"

"Matter of fact, I did," I said. "In my sleep."

"In your dreams," he scoffed.

"Seems impossible, I know," I replied. "But sometimes I've believed as many as six impossible things before breakfast."

He tossed the tiny TV to me.

"Crap," was his analysis. "Jetsons, Flintstones, Scooby-Doo… They all suck. Those assholes Hanna and Barbera ruined animation. Dumbed it down. Kiddie'd it up. Hard to believe they're the same guys who won Oscars for their Tom and Jerry shorts in the forties."

"Well, there is another side to that coin," I said. "You could make a case that they rescued animation from becoming an extinct art form."

"How do you figure?"

Now we were talking about something I knew something about—and more than he did, apparently.

"Most of the major film studios shuttered their animation divisions about 1955," I said. "Disney made its last short that year, for instance; Warner closed up shop on theatrical animation then; and when MGM stopped production in '56, their two producers, Hanna and Barbera, were laid off. Hundreds of people whose careers and lives were dedicated to animation were out on the street, unemployed. Hanna and Barbera opened their own shop in '57 and hired a lot of talented artists who had nowhere else to go. Michael Maltese, for instance, the guy responsible for writing most of the best Bugs Bunny cartoons at Warner."

The coffee was kicking in, and Steve seemed to be paying attention—and not interrupting to argue—so I continued stating my case for TV toons.

"Bill and Joe knew the golden age of theatrical animation was over," I said, "and realized the only way the industry could survive was on television…and working on a minimal budget and a quick turnaround was essential to TV. So they simplified everything and aimed the new toons at kids, who weren't used to lush theatrical animation anyway. They recycled simple backgrounds, emphasized dialogue over action to limit the amount of animation, reused shots and backgrounds over and over, and essentially did everything they could to keep costs low and production times down. And it worked—at one point a few years ago they were producing two-thirds of all Saturday morning TV cartoons."

"But it's all kid's stuff," he protested. "Nothing with any artistic value, like *Pinocchio* or *Sleeping Beauty*. Nothing of consequence. They're like the McDonald's of animation. Except they serve up Crappy Meals."

"Can't argue with that," I shrugged. "But they were very smart to concentrate on characters and dialogue. One side effect is that they saved—or started—the careers of any number of voice actors. June Foray, Daws Butler, Gary Owens, not to mention the king of cartoon voices, Mel Blanc. And my God, look at what they created over the past quarter of a century: The Flintstones—animation in prime time. The Jetsons. Yogi Bear. Huckleberry Hound. Quickdraw McGraw. Top Cat. Snagglepuss. Wally Gator. Magilla Gorilla. Jonny Quest, also in prime time. Space Ghost. Josie and the Pussycats. Super Friends. Tons of memorable characters."

"But nothing for adults," Steve insisted persistently.

"I have to think that adults are simply not interested in animation anymore," I said. "What have we had lately? *Yellow Submarine* was cool, but that was the Beatles, for Christ's sake. Other than that, what? *The Rescuers. Fritz the* fucking *Cat. Winnie the* fucking *Pooh.* Maybe, if we're lucky, this whole animation industry goes in cycles, and we're just at a low point now. I mean, before Disney and synchronized sound and that high point of animation in the thirties and forties, cartoons were black and white and silent. Did you ever see any of those early silent cartoons? No dialogue, no music. They were basically just eye toons."

"Hand-drawn animation is too time-consuming and labor-intensive," he said. "Computers will do all the animation in the future."

"I've seen computer animation," I balked. "Neon green skeletons on a black background. Garbage."

"Those are just wireframes," he protested. "But they get better every year, as computers get faster and more powerful."

"Man, is that your answer to everything? 'There's a computer application for that'? You ought to try thinking different."

"*Differently*. Jeez. Grammar." He shook his head. "Even Disney's dropped the ball. There may be no future for animation."

"I don't think anyone will ever top Disney in animation," I said. "But, hell, if you're so interested, you've got money. Why don't you invest in Disney and force them back into animation?"

He seemed a bit chagrined. "Even *I* don't have that kind of money," he admitted.

"Well, their stock's in the crapper right now. You could probably snap up a bundle for cheap." He had no reply, so I kept the pressure on. "C'mon, you're so smart, what would you do if you had some say over what Disney does with animation?"

He actually seemed to give this some thought. "I think I'd redo *Alice in Wonderland*," he determined.

"Why? Because of your costume character experience?"

"No, because it sucks. Even Walt didn't like it. Said it had no heart."

"He should know," I said. "He knew how much success depended on the quality of the product and on storytelling—not just in the animated films, either, and not just in Disneyland, but even in the mythology he created around himself and his company. There was only one creator at Disney Studios, for instance; only one name associated with it: *Walt Disney*. He was the only one in the public eye. Everybody else was anonymous. And he kept his biggest plans, like DisneyWorld, a total secret until the big reveal. And his marketing—my god, he was a master of marketing. You could learn a thing or two from Disney."

He nodded. “I’ve actually tried to emulate his career. To build something lasting, something of high quality, something people will love.”

“Well then don’t overlook that he also had a wife and a family. Not to mention a jet and a yacht.”

“Cut me some slack,” Steve said. “I’m only twenty-four. It took him a lifetime to build something lasting.”

“He also died young. Relatively young, anyway. Sixty-five.”

Steve was oddly silent for a moment or two.

“That’s the one part of his legacy I’ve always felt I’d live up to,” he said quietly. But he shook off the momentary introspection to ask, “How do you know all this?”

“When I was a kid,” I replied, “my parents bought me a couple of shares of Disney stock. Trying to teach me about capitalism or something, which I guess it did, since the stock tanked once Walt died. Doesn’t matter—I didn’t give a shit about the business side of things, but I was intrigued by the process of animation, so I dug in and did some research, and... Hey, what time is it getting to be?”

He checked his digital watch. “Ten-thirty.”

“The boat back to Richmond leaves at eleven. We need to get a move on.”

“What we need,” he reminded me as he began packing, “is information.”

“I might know a guy,” I said.

“So where are we going?”

“To brunch!”

Chapter 7

We pulled into San Jose about half past noon. Perfect timing, if my information was correct. The boat from East Brother brought us back to the Richmond dock and the drive back was pretty much like the drive up, except in reverse, and minus the conversation. We'd pretty much exhausted our limited store of information the previous evening, and Steve apparently had had no brilliant insights since last night. But I had.

Just because he was quiet doesn't mean he was passive, however. When I parked on Fourth Street in downtown San Jose and walked us up to E. Santa Clara, he finally couldn't contain himself.

"Where are we going to do this research?" he demanded. "The San Jose Public Library? We're not even close—that's blocks from here."

"No," I said. "The San Jose Public Library won't do us any good. I've been there. All the dots have already been connected in both books."

About halfway up the block, I stopped in front of the Quality Café and looked in through the picture windows.

"You're kidding, right?" he said darkly.

"Nope," I said. "The guy we're looking for has brunch here every Sunday with a bunch of Silicon Valley elite. So this is where we'll find him." I refrained from adding, *I hope*.

A couple too well-dressed to be eating in this greasy spoon exited, which made me more confident I was on the right track. We entered the rundown storefront, which seemed more like a soup kitchen than a café. Mismatched tables left over from the '50s and wooden chairs from even earlier eras dotted the scarred linoleum floor. Many seats were occupied by—judging solely from their appearance—a variety of street people and homeless downtown drifters. One long table was covered with an array of finished dishes—the detritus of a dozen long-gone diners. An old guy with a trim white beard and glasses and a young guy, about my age, were the only people left at the brunch table.

"Your mom is expecting you and Carol for dinner tonight, Mike," I heard the older guy say. "Wouldn't miss it, dad," the younger one replied. They stood to leave and I stepped up to the younger man. He had a baby face and dark, curly hair.

"Mr. Malone?" I said.

He looked at me, then past me, saw Steve and scowled.

Behind me, Steve spat, "Fucking *Malone*? *This* is the guy you were talking about?"

"Good to see you, too, Steve," Malone drawled.

"You guys know each other?" I said, unable to keep the surprise out of my voice.

"Yeah, we know each other," they grumbled in unison.

"Malone works the tech beat for the San Jose *Mercury News*," Steve informed me. "Writes a lot of shit about Apple. A real shithead."

"We go way back," Malone said to me. "And I've interviewed him enough times to know he's a fucking sociopath."

I had to salvage this situation, and quickly.

"Maybe he is a sociopath," I conceded to Malone. "But he's a sociopath who needs your help."

The tech reporter raised an eyebrow. But was he curious or skeptical?

"What're you," he challenged, "his shrink or something? His handler?"

I handed him my business card. My real card.

"Mr. Jobs is my client," I said. "He's in trouble, and he needs information…information that could save his company, possibly even his life. Information that you and perhaps you alone are likely to possess, in your position as the premier tech reporter in the Valley." He couldn't tell whether I meant "premiere," meaning the first, or "premier," meaning the best. Either way worked. There are those who say that imitation is the sincerest form of flattery. I believe that sincere flattery is the sincerest form of flattery.

Malone scowled at my card. He scowled at me. He scowled at Steve. I prayed that for once in his obnoxious life Jobs would keep his smart-ass mouth shut. He did. Maybe there is a God.

"Five minutes," Malone said and sat back down. We sat down at the table as well and I proceeded to give him the executive summary: How Steve suspected he was being followed and hired me to prove it. How we were voluntarily abducted by his former cohorts, now at IBM, and how we were informed about their illegal taps that exposed AT&T's plot to subvert Apple, even if it meant terminating Steve. How we'd discussed and analyzed the situation only to realize we lacked enough information to understand why they'd targeted Apple—and Steve—so intently, which prevented us from formulating a strategy to oppose their plans.

"So we've kind of reached a cul-de-sac," I admitted. "At this point, we're just spinning our wheels. It's taken all the running we can do just to stay in one place. We're gonna need more data if we're gonna make any headway, understand what's going on."

Malone listened intently. And when I was done, he sat quietly, apparently deep in thought. At length, he said, "Why don't you guys order some lunch?"

We were in.

He motioned for a man in an apron to come over to the table. "More coffee, please, Tom?" he asked politely. "And whatever these guys want." He turned to me. "They make a killer chili cheese omelet," he said, then addressed Steve. "Unless you're still eating nothing but fruit," he drawled.

"I'm a vegan," Steve replied.

"Yeah, this week," Malone mumbled, mostly to himself. But to Steve, he said, "You wouldn't be if you ever tasted one of these omelets."

"They sound good," I said. And to Tom: "One chili cheese omelet, please. And coffee."

Steve looked around the place like it was a sewer.

"I'm not gonna get anything," he said, curling his lip.

"Oh, you're gonna get *some*thing," Malone said with a sly smile. "The check." He picked up the bill from his brunch party and handed it to Steve.

"Hey…" Jobs protested, glancing at the tab. "This is a check for a dozen people."

"Information doesn't want to be free," Malone chuckled.

Steve perused the receipt more closely. "A dozen people had lunch and this is the total?"

"This is a great place," Malone said. "Clean, good food, fair prices for the less fortunate among us. Just out of curiosity," he said to me, "how'd you know I'd be here?"

I smiled. "Well, I am a detective."

"Yeah, right. C'mon, really."

"Yeah, alright. I read about your Sunday brunches in Leigh Weimers' column. What I'm curious about is why…here?"

Now it was his turn to smile.

"My dad, Pat, started this," he said. "You just missed him. We invite the movers and shakers of Silicon Valley to brunch here mostly because we like the irony of bringing the Valley's best and brightest to this transient hangout filled with the wretched refuse of San Jose."

"Hey, fuck you," a toothless old guy at a nearby table yelled, taking a pause from gumming his oatmeal.

"Fuck you too, Eddy," Malone yelled back cheerfully. "Your lunch is on me. Again."

"Thank you, Mike," the grizzled guy replied.

"So," Malone stated. "What is it exactly you think I can do for you?"

"We need information," I said. Steve opened his mouth to say something but I waved him off. I figured the more I could keep him out of the conversational loop the more likely Malone might be willing to share his knowledge. "Whatever you can tell us about AT&T," I continued, "so we can figure out why they've targeted our, uh, *associate* here."

Tom brought our coffee. Malone took a moment to arrange his response.

"OK," he said at length. "Every school kid knows the history of the telephone, right?"

I shrugged. "I guess. Alexander Graham Bell…"

"Right. Builds the first working phone in 1876, says to his assistant, 'Mr. Watson, come here, I want to see you,' gets a patent."

"Right," I said. "Bell and Watson. Always thought it was strange that Sherlock Holmes was based on a doctor named Joseph Bell, and his companion was also Watson."

"And Thomas Watson was the head of IBM for decades," Steve volunteered.

"Yeah," Malone said. "And don't forget the Watson who cracked the DNA double helix code with Crick. Coincidences, but curious. History's full of Watsons."

"History, right," I said, attempting to refocus us after the cascade of free association I'd inadvertently set off. "Please go on."

"Well, first off," Malone continued, "AT&T is a large company. A *very* large company. A very, very, *very* large company—actually, it's the world's largest and richest corporation. Assets of more than a hundred billion dollars—*billion*, with a 'b.' Revenues in excess of forty billion. Annual profits exceeding seven billion. More than a million employees, and twenty-seven thousand locations in the United States alone. And I don't think it's an exaggeration to say that their phone system is the largest machine in the world."

"Yeah," I said. "Never thought of it that way. But you're right—it's a single machine that encompasses the entire surface of the earth."

"When the phone was invented," Malone continued, "Western Union, the telegraph company, was the largest company on earth. And they turned down an opportunity to purchase Bell's patents outright. They thought they could save money by building their own system, and even got Edison involved. Bell and Western Union went head-to-head for a few years, building out their phone systems, and at one point it looked as though Western Union might actually win. But Bell had an ace up its sleeve—Alexander Graham Bell's fundamental patent. Bell sued Western Union for patent infringement in 1878, and won. As part of the settlement, Western Union agreed to bow out of the telephone business altogether and transfer all of its phone exchanges and its thousands of customers to Bell."

"So Bell had no competition," I understood.

"Exactly," Malone agreed. "But Bell still had a major problem. Their crown jewels—namely, their patents—were due to expire in 1894, and that would open the field of telephony to competitors. So they formed a new subsidiary: American Telephone and Telegraph. AT&T's mission was to build the first long-distance phone network before its patents expired so they'd have a huge advantage over any upstart, johnny-come-lately competitor. AT&T would be the only company with long-distance telephone service, and they could either charge other companies for access or simply refuse to let them use their network. That became their M.O., and explains how they grew so large over the first half of the century."

"And how they became a monopoly," I deduced.

"Well, AT&T is what's referred to as a 'regulated monopoly,'" Malone said. "Even though it's a monopoly it operates under government supervision. They can't raise rates or make any major changes without the approval of the government—the FCC, for instance, as well as any number of state public utility commissions."

"A leash on the beast."

"Yeah. But that never stopped them from asking for rate hikes so frequently that they became notorious for their requests."

"And those frequent rate hikes do nothing to endear them to their customers," I extrapolated.

"Right," Malone agreed. "Of course, their side of the argument is that they have to build, install, maintain, and replace hundreds of thousands of miles of cable and wire, and millions of residential telephones and business telephone systems, as well as a complicated and sophisticated network of switching stations that directs every call to its intended destination anywhere in the world. Billions of calls. That ain't cheap."

Tom brought my omelet and toast. It looked delicious.

"Continue," I said to Malone as I dug in.

"OK, so the monster is divided into five divisions. AT&T is the parent company, but there are four other branches. One is the aggregation of local telephone companies—the regional companies, like Pacific Bell. Another is what they call 'Long Lines,' which is basically exactly what it sounds like—their long-distance network, national and international, running through cables, or undersea cables, or satellites, or whatthefuckever. Then there's Western Electric, their manufacturing division. All the telephone handsets, all the cables, essentially all the hardware they use is built by Western Electric."

"That's four," I said, wiping a bit of cheese from my beard. He was right: this omelet was good. Damn good. "What's the fifth?"

"Bell Labs," Steve chimed in.

"Right," Malone nodded. "The research and development facility. The *prestigious* research and development facility. At this point, they hold more than nineteen thousand patents and are responsible for such breakthrough technologies as vacuum tube amplifiers, cable television, silicon chips, even lasers. They invented the transistor, for fuck's sake. Three of their scientists got the Nobel Prize for that."

"All right," I said. "But what would prompt a company that large to take such drastic measures against a…a *non-entity* like Apple?" I could see Steve bristle out of the corner of my eye. But he remained silent. Both good things.

"Well," Malone said, "keep in mind that AT&T was founded during the Robber Baron era, early in the century—rapacious, cut-throat businessmen like Cornelius Vanderbilt, John D. Rockefeller, JP Morgan, Andrew Carnegie—"

"Let's leave Carnegie out of it," I said. "He pioneered philanthropy among that class, funding public libraries and the like. He did more for the culture than any of the current tech godzillionaires are doing. Besides, he's Scottish—one of my people, like Alexander Graham Bell, so they're both distant relations."

"Too bad neither of them left you any stock," Malone chuckled. "You'd be rich today."

"Aye, the sleekit sanntach basturts. Anyway, that philanthropy angle is something you oughta look into, in your position. Use your bully pulpit to shame these high-tech captains of industry to stop being such greedy pussies and give something back to the world."

"Not a bad idea," he said. I didn't know him well enough to determine whether he was sincere or simply blowing me off. And I didn't have time to debate the point, either.

"So you think they might still resort to that kind of ruthlessness?"

"They were all spirochetes in those days," Malone continued. "*Spirochetes*. In the early days, in the 1900s, before the FCC was established and assigned to oversee them, AT&T had built its monopoly using shady business practices. Predatory pricing, for instance. Or when a competitor built a new local telephone exchange, AT&T would refuse to connect the exchange with its own network, and would pressure the fledgling company until it sold out to them."

"Just strongarm them out of business," I understood.

"You want to talk about underhanded tricks?" Malone continued. "How about bribing public officials to block the approval of independents building local phone companies? Or using their massive financial influence with banks to force the banks to deny AT&T's competitors the loans they needed to launch a new company? One newspaper of the time described AT&T as a 'ruthless, grinding, oppressive monopoly.'"

"Yeah. Reach out and crush someone," I said. "The government didn't take any action?"

"Well, they tried. The Justice Department launched an antitrust investigation against AT&T in 1913 and recommended stiff regulation...or breaking up the Bell System altogether, or even nationalizing the telephone system as a public utility. AT&T took these mortal threats seriously and engaged in a series of negotiations with Justice to avoid any of those lethal outcomes. By 1914, an AT&T VP—Nathan Kingsbury—gotta love that name, eh? 'I come here to bury the king, not to praise him.' Anyway, this Kingsbury managed to negotiate a compromise with the government, something they've revisited every couple of decades since then. Including now. The thing about Kingsbury was that he was a cutthroat negotiator and the Justice Department was very naïve about dealing with AT&T. The dirty secret of the 'Kingsbury Commitment' was that AT&T agreed to make relatively small concessions that shielded the company from more severe restrictions."

"Yeah, yeah," I said. " 'Please don't throw me in the briar patch!' So Bell is ruthless and arrogant and underhanded. But times have changed, yeah?"

Malone shook his head. "You have to remember it's only been a couple of generations since then—within recent memory, or at least within our grandparents' memory. That kind of manipulation is built into their corporate DNA. You don't change a winning strategy. You find new ways to subvert laws and agreements…or you pay off politicians to change the laws in your favor. It's business as usual, and 'twas ever thus."

"It just seems kind of…old-timey, I guess," I said. "Boss Tweed. Al Capone. Don Corleone. You really think they'd resort to murder? In this day and age?"

Malone chuckled and shook his head. "Yeah, well, 'this day and age' hasn't been particularly kind to old Ma Bell."

"What do you mean?"

"They've had a rough decade," he said. "Scandals, bribery, lawsuits—you name it. Some of the shit they've tried to get away with makes Watergate look like an Amish picnic." He ticked off his points on his fingers. "They had major service failures in big cities in the late sixties and early seventies, for instance. The Equal Employment Opportunity Commission investigated their discriminatory hiring practices in 1970. There was a strike by telephone workers—their own people!—in '71. And they got a lot of bad press about their war against the phone phreaks. Most of their corporate transgressions are hushed up. But a couple of them made headlines."

"Like?"

"Like T. O. Gravitt, a Southwestern Bell exec in Texas who committed suicide in '74. Along with his suicide note, he left a nine-page memo accusing Bell and its officials of an entire catalog of misdeeds. Among other things, he claimed that Southwestern Bell engaged in rate fixing by cooking the data it showed municipal regulators, and that it maintained a slush fund that its executives used to bribe—excuse me, to 'make contributions to'—sympathetic politicians, and that they engaged in illegal wiretapping against their competitors."

"Seems to be a lot of that going around," I mumbled around a bite of omelet.

"Speaking of which," Malone continued, "take Greenstar, the code name for AT&T's toll-fraud surveillance system. The project blew up in their face about five years ago, when the St. Louis *Post-Dispatch* broke the story with a front-page headline that read 'Bell Secretly Monitored Millions of Toll Calls,' which pretty much says it all. The source was a whistleblower inside AT&T, and the exposé was full of details, including specifics of the Greenstar operation and the mind-boggling news that the phone company had monitored something like thirty *million* calls and tape-recorded a million and a half of them. But the story was hushed up and evaporated without any legal follow-up. So, yeah, even today they're well-known for their underhanded business practices…and for avoiding any repercussions or retribution. If you threaten their little kingdom they will put you down like Old Yeller."

I wiped my lips with a napkin. I did this to remove some chili grease. But it couldn't hurt to check for foam.

"But all of these problems," Malone continued, "pale in comparison to the Unholy Trinity they've been charged with repeatedly during the past decade: *competition, antitrust,* and *scandal*. You know that America *does not like* monopolies. That's one reason why everyone hates the phone company." He stopped to chuckle to himself.

"That's funny?" I said.

"Well, what's funny was that just the other day I was down at the local Pac Bell office paying my bill and found myself standing in line behind this little old lady who was arguing with the clerk. When he suggested that perhaps she didn't want to use their service, she says, 'Well then what am I supposed to do…go to the *other* phone company?'"

I laughed. "Like the guy in *The President's Analyst* said, 'I've never been in a country where everybody didn't hate The Phone Company.'"

"Right. Not to mention how much America loved Ernestine the Operator on *Laugh-In* sticking it to Bell."

"'We don't care,'" I recited with a pinched nasal voice. "'We don't have to. We're The Phone Company.' I still don't understand why the government hasn't done its job and reined them in."

"Well, as I said, the Justice Department has been trying to break up their monopoly for decades. Even as we sit here enjoying our gourmet meal all in the golden afternoon, Justice is engaged in a long-term lawsuit against AT&T—a case they opened *six years* ago. It's taking a long time, but scuttlebutt has it that it could be decided as soon as a year or two from now—and all indications are that it don't look good for Ma Bell. The monopoly could be busted up into separate regional phone companies as one part of the outcome, for instance. Once the taffy pull among Bell, the FCC, Congress, and the Justice Department is over, Pacific Bell, for example, could become its own entity rather than a tentacle of the AT&T octopus. They could lose other entire divisions in any settlement or judicial decree as well."

I was intrigued by this detailed information and impressed by this reporter's deep knowledge of the subject—not to mention his erudite summary, delivered in a soft, buttery-smooth voice. This guy would be good on radio, I thought. Or TV, maybe. But Steve was getting antsy. He wouldn't be able to keep his mouth shut much longer.

Sure enough.

"But why would AT&T want me to build a modem into my computers?" he demanded.

Apparently, history was of no interest to a guy whose eyes are always focused on the future. I guess no one had ever introduced him to that famous Santayana quote.

"Why don't they just try to buy Apple?" he argued. "Not that I'd sell. But why would they think they have to coerce us, or threaten me?"

"Your IBM guys?" Malone replied. "The guys tapping AT&T's lines? They didn't overhear them say anything about why?"

"They were baffled," I said.

"Well, why don't you just have them continue their taps?" Malone suggested. "See if they can overhear a reason."

"They won't do it," Steve replied. "It's illegal. They could go to jail."

"They're phone phreaks," Malone shrugged. "They should have no problem with that."

"It's also unauthorized. They could lose their jobs."

"Ah," Malone said with a nod. "A much more pragmatic motivation."

"Well, at least they discovered this conspiracy," I said. "But they couldn't give us a reason, or a timetable, and couldn't point a finger at any responsible individual. But action like this would have to come from the highest level—so who's likely behind it all? The CEO?"

Malone shook his head. "More likely one of the division VPs, jockeying for a better position after the breakup, if and when that happens. Not the CEO. By all accounts, he's a pretty good guy. Charles Brown. Goes by 'Charlie.'"

"That ol' blockhead?" I laughed. "If it is him, then Apple is the football and I'm Lucy."

Malone and I chuckled. Steve did not.

"The hell is so funny?" he demanded.

"Oh, I forgot," I drawled to Malone. "Steve doesn't read the funny pages."

"I read the classics," Jobs announced imperiously.

"Y'ever read *Moby Dick*?" Malone asked him.

"Yeah. It's about a whale."

"It's about obsession," Malone said. "Dangerous, psychopathic obsession. You oughta reread it sometime."

I had to get this conversation back on track and away from their snarky arguing.

"Given this potential breakup of AT&T," I said, "is it possible they're looking to branch out into a new product? Computers, interconnected through their phone lines?"

"More to the point," Steve insisted, "why don't they build their own consumer computer? They have Bell Labs for development and Western Electric to manufacture them. And they already have all the infrastructure they'd need—the phone lines—to connect them. So why don't they just build their own computer?"

Malone shrugged. “Your IBM guys didn’t know?”

“No,” Steve sighed.

“Regardless of that,” I said to Malone, “isn’t there *something* we can do to fight them? Can’t we get the government involved? Can’t President Carter phone somebody in the Justice Department, tell them to order AT&T to back off, leave Apple alone?”

Malone furrowed his brow and looked me square in the eye. “What did you say?”

“I said, can’t President Carter phone somebody—”

He held up a palm to cut me off. He put down his coffee cup and stared off into space for a bit. And at some point he smiled widely.

“Of course!” he exclaimed. I could almost see a light bulb go on over his head. “Makes perfect sense!” he said and began laughing.

“Care to elucidate your epiphany?” I suggested.

He smiled a Cheshire smile and looked Steve directly in the eye.

“They can’t,” he said.

“They can’t *what*?” Steve challenged. “They can’t build their own—”

“They *can’t*,” Malone repeated emphatically. “I mentioned the current anti-trust suit the Justice Department is pursuing against AT&T? And that this is not the first time that Justice has tried to play trustbuster against them?”

He was connecting dots. I wanted to see the picture he’d discovered. I put my fork down and gave him my full attention. Even Steve didn’t interrupt.

“Go on,” I said.

“I mentioned the 1913 Justice investigation, yeah? But Justice also filed suit against AT&T in ’56,” he continued enthusiastically. “It was a crap lawsuit and Justice took it in the ass. One of the concessions they wrenched from AT&T, however, was called the ‘Carterfone agreement.’ Carter was a Texas farmer who built his own long-distance phone device and hooked it into AT&T’s lines. It interconnected mobile radios with phones, if I understand it correctly. He called it the ‘Carterfone,’ and he sold it to people who didn't want to pay Ma Bell's usurious long-distance rates."

"The first phone phreak," Steve said in a whisper that bordered on reverential.

"Yeah," Malone nodded. "And Bell sued him. But since what Carter was doing wasn't illegal at the time, Bell ended up trying to make a case against him using the argument that their system was *so delicate* and *so complex* that any equipment that used their system but wasn't manufactured by them to their tight tolerances could degrade the entire phone network. Well, guess what? The courts disagreed, and that opened the Bell system to all kinds of third-party add-on equipment, like telephone answering machines and off-brand phone units, like those Mickey Mouse and Snoopy phones."

"OK, fine," Steve grumbled, impatient and irritated. "But what does that have to do with my computers? We're actively *not* hooking into their system—"

"Well, let me finish," Malone cut him off. Probably one of the few people who could. "Here's the thing: One of the provisions of the Carterfone agreement is that it blocks Bell from branching out into computers. Now, in 1956, computers were massive and expensive and occupied entire rooms. AT&T had no interest in computers. So it was a small concession for them to make, at the time—the Kingsbury gambit. It was their personal inside joke, and they laughed up their sleeves at the idea that Justice believed they'd won some major concession. But during the past few years, AT&T has seen just how powerful and profitable IBM has become, and they feel like they'd been benched in the Big Game. And now," he addressed Steve directly, "thanks to *you* and your consumer computers, that Carterfone concession is a major obstacle—a billion-dollar punchline to their joke on Justice a quarter of a century ago, except now, the joke's on them. They *can't* build their own computers, they *can't* partner with you, and they *can't* buy you out because it's *against the law*. They *can't*."

I nodded slowly. "Yeah. I get it. 'If you can't beat 'em, join 'em.' But they can't beat him *or* join him, so they have to resort to subterfuge. They have to, uh, *insinuate* a modem into an existing computer in order to get a toehold in the personal computer industry—and to ensure that when computers *are* all interconnected their phone lines are the spiderweb they communicate through. Subversion is their only option. And Steve is the obstacle between their fragmented future and their camouflaged wedge into the computer business. The billion dollar obstacle." We both looked at Steve. "I'd say that was a pretty good motive for murder."

"Only one of many, if we're talking about Steve Jobs," Malone said. But he said it softly, and with a wry smile.

Steve looked at Malone, visibly shaken—as much by the reporter's opinion as by his information was my guess.

"People think I'm an asshole, don't they?" he said plaintively.

Our combined silence served as confirmation.

When Tom came to refill our cups, Steve asked if there was a men's room in the restaurant. He was apparently so shell-shocked that he even forgot to be rude, and actually referred to this greasy spoon as a restaurant. Tom pointed him toward the kitchen and the beleaguered billion-dollar target stumbled off without comment. I counted my blessings that at least he didn't bust out bawling this time.

"All this is a matter of public record," Malone said to me. "You could have found all this out yourself if you were any kind of decent detective."

"I found you, didn't I?" He chuckled. One detail was still bugging me, though. "You said you and Steve go way back? How's that?"

"Jesus, that guy…" Malone sighed quietly, shaking his head. But he quickly pulled himself out of his exasperation. "This valley might be a place where the future is invented, but at heart, it's just a small town. People's lives tend to intersect. Steve and I went to the same elementary school, for instance—Monte Vista, in Mountain View."

"You knew him in grade school?"

"Well, actually, no. I was in sixth grade and he was in fourth. And to a sixth grader, a fourth grader is a baby. Vermin."

I nodded as he polished off his coffee.

"A word to the wise?" he continued, now dead serious. "Look out for that guy. He's charismatic, but like a cult leader. Sometimes he's a silver-tongued devil; other times he's the Devil himself—a bully, abrasive and abusive. If you fall into his orbit there's a chance you could crash and burn. And he would not give two shits. His whole goal in life is to be a paradigm shifter—to, you know, make a dent in the universe—and he just steamrolls over any obstacle or any person who gets in his way. His friends— No, scratch that; he doesn't have any friends, he's alienated them all… His underlings even have a phrase for his manipulative ability: the reality distortion field."

"K," I said.

Steve returned and settled up the bill—the bills; ours and the earlier group's—almost absently. He walked out without thanking Malone, so I did, then followed Steve up the street and back to the car.

"Good news and bad news," I said to silent Steve as I started the car and pulled out onto Fourth Street. "The good news is now we know why they're after you so adamantly. And the bad news is that it's just as serious as you thought it might be."

He said nothing. He just stared straight ahead. But I don't think he was seeing the street. I thought I'd prime the pump—maybe give him something to take his mind off his phone freak fate.

"But no matter how bad the bad news is," I continued, "I think the good news is even better. I think we learned more than we even set out to, and it's given me an idea how we might fight back."

Steve remained closed-mouthed but did turn his head to look at me, so I continued.

"Malone asked why we didn't get your IBM friends to continue to tap AT&T's lines until they found out what we want to know, right?"

"Yeah…"

"Well, I think that's exactly what we need to do. Turn the tables on Ma Bell. Borrow a page from their playbook and eavesdrop on them."

He nodded. Maybe his funk was breaking now that he had a new problem to solve.

“We need an experienced phone phreak to make that happen,” he said. “Someone who knows his way around the Bell system and isn’t intimidated by it. Or reluctant to fuck with it.”

“What about your old phone freak friend, Whiz?”

“Woz. No. No. I don’t want to drag him into this. He’s legit. He’s got a rep to protect. We need someone who seriously doesn’t give a fuck.”

Fourth Street turned into a 280 onramp. I took it.

“I might know a guy,” I said.

Chapter 8.0

"Another one of your 'guys'?" Steve protested as we headed north on 280. "Do you actually know this guy, or is that too much to ask?"

Yeah, he was over his funk and back to ornery normal.

"Known him since college. But I gotta warn you," I warned, "he's an odd cat."

"Odd how?"

"In too many ways to detail right now. James J. Ferrette the Fourth is a font of obscure knowledge, for one thing. And he can get his hands on virtually anything you ask for, but it's best if you don't ask how. It's that ability that earned him the sobriquet 'Jimmy the Ferret'—he can ferret out anything you need. But that only scratches the surface of his talents. You ever see that movie, *The Flim-Flam Man*?"

"No."

"You familiar with George C. Scott?"

"Yeah. *Patton*. Love that movie."

"Right. So in *Flim-Flam Man* he plays a rural con man who claims his degrees are 'MBS, CS, DD —Master of Backstabbing, Cork-Screwing and Dirty Dealing.' That pretty much describes Jimmy the Ferret to a T."

"Do you have any examples of his, uh…craft?"

"References on demand? Sure. Well, for one thing, he insisted we go up to Tommy's Joynt in The City on the Fourth of July, 1976, and order their buffalo stew so for the rest of his life he could say he ate bison on the Bicentennial."

"Amusing," Steve admitted. "But pretty innocuous."

"But total commitment to his gag. Like when he was in high school he took metal shop, but when he thought the teacher was picking on him he welded the guy into his office. He got caught for that one, but he claims it was an invaluable learning experience—don't leave any evidence and don't get caught."

"Still pretty harmless."

"OK, well, how about this: He decided he wanted revenge for getting caught, so he came up with another prank. He went to the same kind of California high school you and I went to. Same kind of architecture—you know, a series of long, one-story buildings with covered outdoor walkways. His school was built around a central quad—a big open grassy space that sloped gently to a drain in the middle. So one night he covered the drain, turned on the fire hoses, and flooded the quad. Turned the grassy space into a little lake."

"Clever, but once again, pretty benign."

"Not so much after he dropped a dozen baby alligators in the pond."

"Alligators? Seriously?"

"Well, caimans actually. Babies. About a foot long, but half of that is tail. I think he got them from Orchard Supply Hardware or maybe Andy's Pet Shop in San Jose. They were selling them as pets for a while. Cute little buggers, actually. Cops never were able to identify the buyer. And Jimmy got away scot-free. But that's nothing compared to the prank he pulled just a few months ago. You remember last December seventh—'a day that will live in infamy'—when all of San Francisco woke up to see a giant rising sun flag unfurled on the Golden Gate Bridge?"

"That was this Ferrette guy?"

"It would be a betrayal of confidence to say…yes."

This actually made Steve smile. "Woz and I pulled off a stunt like that at Homestead. During the graduation ceremony we unfurled a huge banner congratulating the students with a drawing of a hand flipping the bird. Woz's mom painted it. We told her it was a Brazilian good luck gesture. But what this Ferrette did is, like, what we did times a thousand."

"Yeah, whatever Jimmy does he does a hundred and crazy percent. He's the most, uh, *individual* individual I've ever known. The most liberated, free from the agendas of others. Most people have laws, morals, ethics, peer pressure, public opinion, religion, and that kind of shit to keep them on the straight and narrow. You know—got to keep the loonies on the path. To Jimmy, all those things are just suggestions. Quaint beliefs and primitive superstitions."

"Sounds like this guy Ferrette and I will get along just fine," Steve chuckled.

Chapter 8.1

I pulled off 280 onto Lawrence Expressway, heading toward Sunnyvale. When traffic allowed, I took a left on Lochinvar and pulled into the parking lot of the Lemontree Square Apartments. I parked in the guest lot and we walked along a series of sidewalks toward one of the outlying units. It was a big complex; many buildings but none over two stories. The whole complex was painted in shades of gray and white and was nicely maintained. Quiet, with numerous flowerbeds and trees, although—as if to evidence my Valley Replacement Theory—any actual lemon trees which might have once populated this area had long since vanished.

"The one thing you need to know about Jim right now," I said as we approached his apartment, "is that he always pretends he's not home. I phone, I phone, I phone, but he never answers. So here's how we're gonna play this: You go to the door, bang on it really hard and yell, 'Police! Open up!'" He looked at me askance. "I know what I'm doing," I said and headed around the corner to the little veranda outside his sliding glass doors.

Steve sighed but went to the door of apartment 108 and beat on it.

"Police!" He yelled. "Open up!"

Less than thirty seconds later the glass doors slid open silently and Jimmy appeared, carrying his go bag. As he started to climb over the porch railing to make his escape, I confronted him.

"Busted," I said cheerily.

"Ah shit," he spat. "What do *you* want?"

"I want you to go back in and open the front door," I said.

He did. He cast a suspicious eye on the two of us. "Wait here for a sec," he said, then closed the door.

Steve turned to me and cocked his head.

"Not to worry," I said. "He's just a little bit ultraparanoid is all."

The door opened once again and Jim gestured us into his tiny foyer. I'm six feet and Steve is a couple inches taller, but we towered head and shoulders over Jimmy. Ironically, he had the deepest voice of all three of us. Steve's was high-pitched, mine was average, but Jim's came from six feet below his cowboy boots.

He was sloppily dressed in blue jeans and a blue work shirt covered with floral embroidery, and looked like he had maybe once, long ago, read that there was a personal grooming device known as a "comb," but had never believed it. He stepped ahead of us and closed the bedroom door on his right. From the quick glimpse I caught, it looked like a bookstore had exploded. There was a galley kitchen to our left and a bathroom on the right. But the living room was spacious. Or would have been if there weren't boxes everywhere and discarded Sunday newspaper sections strewn all over the carpet.

"I just moved in," he explained. "Haven't unpacked yet."

"You moved in a year ago," I reminded him.

The living room had a trio of bowed old couches arranged in an open rectangle. The fourth wall was all bookcases, all stuffed. Steve and I each took a seat on one of the facing sofas. Jim dropped onto the middle one, next to a bulge covered by a sheet.

"Can I offer you guys something," he said, "to leave?"

"Not until we talk to you."

"So what's the 411?"

"We need your help," I said. I cocked my head toward Steve. "He needs your help."

"You must be in some deep shit," he said to Steve, "if you're hanging out with a Luddite like this guy."

"Hey," I objected. I don't know what a Luddite is, but from the sound of it, I didn't want to be one.

"He doesn't need my help," Jim informed me, aiming a thumb at Steve. "He's a fucking millionaire."

"You know who I am?" Steve said.

"Of course I know who you are. Steve Jobs. I saw you hawking your Applesauce a couple of years ago at the West Coast Computer Faire."

"How'd you get an invitation to that?"

"Who said anything about an invitation?" Jimmy laughed.

"Do you have a phone?" Steve asked him.

"Oh, hell no," Jim replied. "There's a payphone in the shopping center across the street if you need a phone."

"How do you order pizza?" I asked.

"Dude, I live across the street from Pizza & Pipes. A quick walk and I can get pizza *and* a concert featuring the fabulous Wurlitzer organ. And I've heard rumors they're gonna build a Bullwinkle's over there, too."

"We don't need a phone," I said. "We need a … a *no* phone. A *lack* of a phone. Tell Steve your phone story."

"Oh, you're gonna love this," he said, launching into his anecdote. "Before I moved here, I called the phone company to ask them about installing some additional outlets. And the girl looks up the address and says, 'Oh, there's a jack in the kitchen on the counter next to the stove, and one in the bedroom on the baseboard under the window, and another one in the little hallway that leads to the bathroom. Won't that be enough?' And I thought, 'Fuck! Some random chick sitting at a console in a Bell building taps a few buttons and calls up the floorplan of my house? What the fuck else might they know about me?' So from that moment on I opted out of plugging a phone into *any* of the jacks just, y'know, *just in case.* I never trusted the phone company in the first place—a conclusion which was totally validated once I started looking into their nefarious business practices."

James J. Ferrette IV was a magician in some ways—he could tell a compelling story, for one, and always had something brilliant or outrageous to say. But he was no stage magician. He didn't know much about misdirection, for instance, proving this as he kept glancing over and inching closer to the sheet-covered lump on the couch as he talked.

"What's in the bag, Goose?" I said in an exaggerated bandito accent, pointing to the bump. "Money, eh?"

He laid a protective hand on the sheet covering the bulge. I was no magician either, but I did know the value of a good reveal. I stood up, grabbed the sheet, and whipped it off whatever he was trying to hide…which turned out to be an open box full of electronics. A small plaque on the front displayed a rainbow-striped apple and the word "apple" followed by what looked like three bold slashes: ///

I had no idea what it was, but Steve clearly did. He waved a long finger at the box.

"Where did you get that!" he demanded.

"It fell off a truck," Jim replied.

"It's not shipping yet!" Steve yelled, his face turning red.

"I found it," Jim suggested, nonchalantly. "Some guy left it on a bar stool in a taproom in Redwood City. The Gourmet Haus Staudt. Hey, why don't we all head up there and have a few beers?"

"It's closed Sundays," I said calmly…but to little effect.

Steve was on his feet, nearly apoplectic.

"That's a *prototype*!" he screeched, his voice rising two or three octaves. "That's an Apple III *prototype*!"

"Yeah, well, it's a piece of shit," Jim shot back. "It over-heats, the real-time clocks don't work, it craps out and crashes every few minutes because the connections are so loose, and the chips pop out of the sockets. To name just a few of its problems."

"I'm taking it," Steve threatened.

Jim barked a laugh. "Hard to believe that a person of your stature would stoop to busting into a private home and confiscating someone's personal property. That's a dick move. An asshole move. Bush league. So fuck off. Say hello to your brother Hand and your sister Blow for me."

Steve ignored the taunts. "I'm taking it," he repeated, moving toward the coverless computer.

Jim just sat back slowly. He spread his arms out along the back of the couch and crossed his legs. "Not if you want my help, you're not," he said calmly.

Steve stopped and stood seething. I could feel him over-heating. I hoped one of his chips didn't pop out of its socket.

"Then I'm calling the cops," he announced.

Jim reached under his couch. He pulled out a red touchtone phone and held it out to Steve. "Be my guest."

"I thought you said you didn't have a phone," Steve accused.

"Of course I have a phone," Jim laughed. "How else would I order pizza?" He waggled the loose jack clip at the end of the wire at Steve. "I just never plug it in. They can't spy on you if you're unplugged."

“But you said—”

“Welcome to the wonderful world of James J. Ferrette the Fourth,” I said to Steve, “where reality is whatever you can make people believe. Hey, Jimmy, why don’t you get us all something to drink, will ya, so we can all simmer the fuck down.”

“Orange juice,” Steve said, still simmering.

Jim went to the kitchen and returned with a couple of cans of Pepsi-Cola. He handed one to Steve. “This is all I have.”

He handed me a can but I waved it away. “No Pepsi. Coke,” I said in a comic Greek accent.

Steve popped the top of his can, took a swig, and choked. “That’s the worst fucking thing I’ve ever tasted,” he said, coughing.

“It’s a billion-dollar business,” Jim said.

“Oh yeah? Well, whoever makes that shitty sugar water oughta be fucking shot.” He put the can down on the floor, resting it on top of the comics section of the Sunday paper.

“Careful there,” Jim admonished. “I haven’t read ‘Peanuts’ yet.”

“What the hell is ‘Peanuts,’” Steve grumbled.

“You know,” Jim replied. “That ol’ blockhead Charlie Brown?”

“The only Charlie Brown I know is trying to kill me,” Steve said sharply.

“Steve doesn’t read the funny papers,” I stage whispered to Jim.

“No, I don’t,” Steve spat. “I read the classics. Shakespeare.”

Jim cocked his head and addressed Steve. “Thou art a boil, a plague sore. I do desire that we be better strangers.”

Steve glared at Ferrette with his unblinking gaze. I braced myself for another tantrum, ready to kiss goodbye any assistance we might get from my recalcitrant friend.

At length, Steve addressed him. “O gull, o dolt, ignorant as dirt. I’ll beat thee, but I would infect my hands.”

“Thou hast no more brain than I have in mine elbows,” Jim replied immediately. “More of your conversation would infect my brain, thou beetle-headed flap-eared knave.”

Steve was not long to retort. "Quintessence of dust," he spat. "Canker-blowworm. Poisonous bunch-backed toad."

"*Thou* art like the toad," Jim responded. "Loathsome as a toad; loathsome and venomous."

I had no idea what was going on in this game of dueling a-holes. All I knew was that this whole meeting was going south, pear-shaped and to hell in a handbasket.

"Thou cream-faced loon," Steve parried. "Thou art unfit for any place but hell."

"Foot-licker!" Jim cried, leaping to his feet.

"Lump of foul deformity!" Steve retorted.

Jim let him have it with both barrels: "You starvelling, you eel-skin, you dried neat's-tongue, you bull's-pizzle, you stock fish…*you vile standing tuck!"*

But Steve was not about to be bested, and held his own: "You scullion!" he yelled. "You rampallian! You, you… *fustilarian*!"

The parrying pair broke out in raucous laughter and fell back onto their respective couches. And when the laughter subsided, Steve looked at me and said, "I think I can work with this guy."

"Right back atcha," Jimmy chuckled. And to me, he said, "So what kind of fine mess have you gotten us into this time, Ollie?"

I summarized our current dilemma. I told him about the tail, about the IBM guys, revealing their taps and their revelation about AT&T's conspiracy against Apple. I filled him in on the highlights of what the tech reporter Malone had revealed about AT&T's legal restrictions preventing them from engaging in the computer industry in any way but subversively, and on AT&T's current legal and image problems.

Steve listened carefully and wisely kept his mouth shut as I gave Ferrette my data dump. But I could tell he was getting fidgety, squirming around in his chair with nothing to say and nothing to do. He clearly wasn't used to being the least important guy in the room, or the third wheel on a bicycle of the mind.

"Did Malone mention that some of their image problem is because of the way they deal with phone phreaks?" Jim asked.

"He did mention that, among their many other PR problems. Didn't go into any details. So," I sighed, "I guess I can assume that you will, if only to flaunt your deep knowledge of the subject."

"That's OK," Steve assured me. "I'd like to hear what he knows. But guys, I'm feeling a little claustrophobic here. Is there somewhere we can take a walk? Nature? Walk and talk?"

"Yeah," Jim said, rising from the couch. "Good idea. C'mon."

Chapter 8.2

Jim led us out the front door and into the ivy growing between his building and the cyclone fence surrounding the complex.

"This isn't exactly the kind of nature walk I had in mind," Steve grumbled.

"Oh, don't have a kitten, man," Jim replied. Steve did not respond. I could only assume Jim's eccentric earlier performance had somehow earned him the right to backtalk the boss.

We followed him to the cyclone fence, where he pulled back a loose section near a pole and motioned us through. We found ourselves standing on a sidewalk on the corner of Lawrence Expressway and Homestead Road.

"My personal shortcut," Jim explained. "Otherwise we'd have to walk completely around the building inside the complex to get to an exit, then completely around the other side of the building to get to this corner. This hack cuts my travel time down by ninety percent."

He pointed toward the strip mall directly across Lawrence. "Over there, other side of the street, that's Santa Clara," he said, then pointed across Homestead. "Over there it's Cupertino. My apartment is in Sunnyvale—tucked away in the very uppermost corner of Sunnyvale at the confluence of three towns."

We crossed Homestead then headed away from Lawrence. The area was a vast expanse of open space, bordered by a double line of mature trees set a few yards apart from one another. We ambled along the grass through the leafy tunnel created by the tall trees, three abreast.

"So," Jim began, "AT&T versus the phone phreaks—"

"Hey, listen, before you get any deeper into this," I said. "Everybody keeps talking about these 'phone freaks,' but I'm still not sure exactly what they are. Who are they, and what do they do?"

"You want me to field this one?" Steve asked.

"Nah, I'll take the bullet," Jim replied.

"You were a phone phreak?" Steve said.

"You ever hear of Captain Crunch?"

"I know Captain Crunch," Steve said. "John Draper is Captain Crunch. You're not Captain Crunch."

"No sir I am not," Jim replied with a straight face, meaning a punchline was coming. "I'm his superior officer, Rear Admiral Crunch."

"Jesus," Steve said, shaking his head. "Easy to see why you two assholes are friends."

"We prefer 'butthole buddies,'" I corrected.

"Just FYI," Jim said to me, "the 'freak' in 'phone phreaks' is spelled with a P-H. It's not an 'f' word."

"I got an F word for you," I grumbled under my breath. Jesus… Jobs corrects my grammar and pronunciation; the Ferret corrects my spelling. Like I knee'd those either things.

"So, yeah," Jim continued, returning to his own train of thought, which was already leaving the station. I just can't seem to get away from engineers. "I got turned on to phreaking by Abbie Hoffman's book, *Steal This Book.*"

"You still have a copy?" Steve said.

Jim smiled a Cheshire smile. "I have seventeen copies."

"He's very literal-minded," I deadpanned to Steve.

"Let's define phone phreaks as an informal network of telephone enthusiasts," Jim suggested. "Curious, tech-minded guys—mostly guys—who have a deep interest in how the Bell system works. The first recognized phone phreak, a guy who called himself 'David Condon,' discovered he could use a toy—a little Davy Crockett bird-call whistle—to duplicate the tones that accessed long-distance lines. So he started making free long-distance calls."

"And became king of the wild phone phreak phrontier?" I suggested. "I'll bet that made Walt proud."

"Other people got their hands on phone company manuals from libraries," Jim continued, "and figured out a way to cobble together a little electronic gizmo that made the tones needed to control the network."

"A blue box," Steve said. "That's what we did, me and Woz. He built the first one. The first digital one, anyway. We built them and sold them until Bell started cracking down, even though it wasn't illegal. Then."

"Yeah," Jim agreed. "Not even malicious mischief, since it was all just fun and games. No maliciousness involved or intended. Nobody ever got their eye poked out."

"And the Valley was the epicenter," Steve said with a touch of pride.

"Yep," Jim nodded. "The capital of phreakdom."

"But you're right," Steve said. "It wasn't malicious at all. It was the magic of the fact that two teenagers could build this box for a hundred bucks and use it to control hundreds of billions of dollars worth of infrastructure throughout the entire global telephone network—and they could do it from a podunk place like Los Altos or Cupertino. That was just magical! Those blue boxes were our first foray into electronics, Woz and me," Steve claimed. "Not to mention our first experience with manufacturing and sales. Apple would never have existed without the blue box."

"Turns out there were no laws restricting what the phreaks were doing," Jim continued his lecture, or monolog, for my benefit. "So it wasn't illegal. But Bell could never differentiate between the curious and the criminal, so they came down hard on anyone they found screwing with their system."

"Right," Steve agreed. "It wasn't illegal. But Bell engaged in all kinds of illegal ploys to stop the phreaks."

"Such as?" I asked, if only to prove I was listening.

"Once they caught on to the existence of blue boxes," Jim continued, "they'd send security agents to photograph attendees at phone phreak conventions, for instance. They placed private residences under surveillance, illegally tapped the lines of the, uh, the *scofflaws* they suspected were taking advantage of phone system loopholes."

" 'Scofflaws,'" Steve chuckled ironically. "Captain Crunch was a fucking folk hero in those circles."

"Yeah," Jim agreed. "There were a lot of young radicals back in the day who thought they were fighting a kind of holy war against The System by liberating money from, uh, The System. The Bell System. They pointed out that the ten percent excise tax added to everybody's phone bill went directly to the government. Uncle Sam collected more than a billion and a half dollars from that tax in 1971 alone—enough to pay for about ten percent of the Vietnam War that year. So the radicals figured that if you can make free long-distance calls, you deprive the Bell System of their long-distance revenue and therefore deprive the war machine of the tax revenue it needed to send young men off to fight and die in Southeast Asia. Make free phone calls and fund the anti-war effort, they reasoned. A win-win."

"You know about *Ramparts*, right?" Steve asked Jim.

"Oh, yeah," Jim nodded, then addressed me. "*Ramparts* was a radical left-wing magazine that had the brilliant idea of publishing everything any tech-savvy reader needed to know to build their own blue box. But AT&T got a court injunction to stop them from distributing the issue to newsstands—something like ninety thousand copies. The editors of the magazine estimated that the recall cost them about sixty thousand bucks. They wrote an editorial to the effect that within a week, AT&T had achieved what the CIA, the Pentagon, the FBI, and other targets of *Ramparts'* journalism over the last decade hadn't been able to accomplish: the nationwide suppression of the magazine. *Ramparts* didn't do anything illegal, yet they were pounded into the ground like a circus tent stake in a clear violation of their First Amendment rights."

"OK," I said, "so the only thing these guys were doing was cutting into Bell's profits. Illegally or not, they were costing The Phone Company money. I guess we know how that worked out for the phreaks." I said it with a "ph."

"Yeah," Jim said. "By '72, Bell was losing more than twenty million dollars a year in long-distance revenue, and they decided these ripoffs had reached epidemic proportions. By the end of the year, they'd come up with a new strategy to squelch the phreaks—invoking a little-known law about 'electronic toll fraud,' which was in fact illegal—and they used that strategy to make fifty-seven arrests of phone phreaks."

We'd been walking quite a while—long enough to reach Wolf Road. No wolves greeted us. As Steve had noted earlier, occasionally Valley Replacement Theory worked in our favor.

Across the street was a shopping center, not nature, so we reversed direction to walk back along the perimeter of the tree-lined field. Before we did, Steve took a look around at the vast tract of meadowland.

"You don't see many open spaces this big in suburbia anymore," he said. Given our previous conversations, I found it difficult to believe he was succumbing to nostalgia. "Damned waste of good real estate," he concluded. Yep, not nostalgia. "Somebody oughta build a big business park here."

"That's never gonna happen," I said.

"Why not?"

"Tell him what you told me when you moved here, Jim."

"This whole area," The Ferret explained, waving his hand at the field, "is a toxic superfund site. Used to be a couple of semiconductor manufacturing plants here—Intersil and Siemens. They leaked a lot of trichloroethene into the ground."

"The only thing that will ever occupy this space," I added, "is if a flying saucer lands here."

Chapter 8.3

We headed back towards Jim's apartment complex.

"How do you know AT&T knows you can add a modem to your computers?" Jim asked Steve as we strolled down the grassy path through the tunnel of trees.

"We hired Draper—Captain Crunch—to work on the Apple II," Steve replied. "He and Woz built a pirate modem into the prototypes. They called it a Charley board and it integrated everything the phone phreaks know how to do. I know Draper had a prototype with him when the Phone Company cops had him arrested in Pennsylvania. The way I figure it is they confiscated his Apple II with the Charley board installed and reverse engineered it."

"Yeah," Jim said. "Probably sent the Charley board to Ken Hopper or Charlie Schulz at Bell's Telephone Crime Lab."

"Hold on," I said. "They sent a Charley board to a guy named Charlie Schulz who works for Charlie Brown, the CEO of AT&T? That's some weird coincidence."

"Keep in mind they have a million employees," Jim said. "They probably have at least one Lucy and a Linus somewhere on their payroll as well."

"But no Snoopy or Woodstock," I said. "And if they're in hot water for EEOC violations, probably not many Franklin Armstrongs."

"Probably not."

"All right," I said, to get us back on track, "now we know what AT&T is up to, we need to come up with a defense, or even better, a counter-offensive. But I still don't think we know enough about what they're planning to counteract their subterfuge against Steve and Apple. We really need more information. Hard data. Facts."

"Well," Jim suggested, "I read that ninety-five percent of phone company business is conducted—prepare yourself for a real surprise—over the phone. Can't you get those IBM guys to keep tapping their lines?"

"No," I said. "They're out of the loop altogether. They've recused themselves to avoid further jeopardy to themselves or IBM. We're on our own here."

"What do you mean 'we,' Kimosabe?"

"Well, you know," I shrugged. "You're either on the bus or thrown under the bus."

"I'd rather be omnibus," Jim said. "So it sounds like *we're* gonna need to tap their corporate phone lines."

"That's why we came to you—because you were a phone phreak. Do you still have a blue box?"

"Oh my, no," Jim gasped. "Those things are illegal!"

"I'll take that as a yes."

"Well, that's not the tool you need anyway."

"So we're wasting our time with you?" Steve grumbled.

"Mmm… Not necessarily. Lemme think about this for a sec."

We continued our pleasant stroll in silence while Jimmy ferreted around in his brain for some straightforward revelation or convoluted, conspiratorial inspiration. It took longer than the second he'd requested. But not much.

"Did you guys ever pull that telephone magic trick?" he said at length.

"That game we used to play in grade school?" I said. "Where one kid whispers a message to another kid, and that kid whispers it to the next kid, and by the time you get to the last kid the message is total gibberish and unrecognizable? That one?"

"No, not that game. The idea of that game was to teach kids to listen carefully and communicate clearly. I'm talking about the magic trick, which is entirely different."

"Well, enlighten us, then."

"OK. So you're sitting around with a group of friends, right? And the phone rings, and you answer it, and you hang up and just shrug and say 'wrong number' to your buddies, or 'telemarketer,' or whatever, and you go back to your card game or ballgame or whatever. And the call is ignored. Forgotten. Then a few minutes later you say to your buds, 'Hey, did I ever tell you about this guy I know who's got ESP?' And they tell you you're full of shit, and you say, 'No, really, this guy is incredible. He can tell you anything you're thinking of—a number, a color, an animal, whatever. He does it over the phone. Here, I have his number—you guys tell me some things we can get him to divine with his psychic abilities.'"

"Is this like Karnak the Magnificent?" I said.

"Something like that, yeah. But you're getting ahead of me. Which, given that it's you, is almost comically ironic. Anyway, you get your friends to tell you out loud what number or color or animal they've chosen. Then you go to the phone, dial the number, and the voice from the other end repeats all the choices your friends just made."

"So what's the gimmick?"

"The gimmick is a little-known bug in the phone system."

"And you turn the bug into a feature," Steve intuited.

"Exactly. The whole trick is built around the fact that when you get a call and hang up, it doesn't disconnect the call. Your hanging up doesn't shut down the line. The call isn't ended until the guy who called you, the guy who *placed* the call, hangs up as well—pushes the hook switch on his phone. If he never hangs up, he just stays on the open line. This turns your telephone into a microphone, and the caller can listen in to everything you say, like when you decide what number, color, animal, and so on you want the 'psychic' to psych out. It's like tapping a line, but legal. In phone tech talk, it's called 'holding the line.' Any telephone can be turned into a microphone if the line is held open. You can listen to anything said in the room."

"Bell knows about this?" I said.

"Yeah. Bell knows about this. They used held lines to catch some of the phone phreaks."

"And the phreaks turned the tables on them," Steve added.

"Of course. One guy who suspected his line was being tapped hooked up a circuit to 'hold the line' so he could monitor his own phone while it was still on the hook. That way he could leave his phone hung up and still hear what the telephone company was up to as they monitored his line."

"Tapping the tappers," I marveled. "Well, turnabout is fair play. And that's not illegal?"

"All depends on your point of view," Jim shrugged. "Is it illegal wiretapping to leave a call incomplete? Or are you merely taking advantage of a flaw in the phone system that Bell never assumed anyone would ever discover, much less find a way to use? The bigger question—especially in your case—is not the legality, but the lethality. If the way Bell deals with phone phreaks proves anything, it's that if they don't want you to do something, it doesn't matter to them whether it's legal or not."

"Right," I said. "They'll still try to stop you."

"So the real question here," Jim said to me, "is, Do you want to save your client's life?"

After a few moments of silence, Steve exclaimed, "Well?"

"I'm thinking," I said. "I'm thinking."

Jim had a good laugh, but it took a minute or two of walking before Steve unpeeved.

"So how would you go about this?" he asked Jim at length. "Tapping the tappers."

The Ferret thought it over for a few seconds…then a manic grin spread over his face. I knew that look. It was trouble.

"OK, what?" I asked reluctantly.

"Well, there might be another solution," he giggled maniacally. "You brought up IBM, AT&T, the FCC, the FBI… If the problem is a three-letter acronym, maybe so is the solution: EMP. We could fire a warning shot over Bell's head using an electromagnetic pulse to knock out the entire phone network in some city. If they're threatening Steve, we blackmail them into a stalemate and make them back off. You know, 'If you take out Jobs, we take out Chicago.'"

"Hmm…" I said, pretending I was considering this insanity. "That might be a little…overkilly, y'know? I think we need something a *liiiittle* more, uh…*subtle*. Besides, to create an EM pulse big enough, you'd need to set off an atomic bomb. Even you might have trouble getting ahold of one of those."

Jim just smiled and giggled to himself. "Oh, yes," he said in what I could only hope was actual, not mock, seriousness.

"Jimmy, that's a road I do not want to stumble down," I said, "even if it is paved with good intentions."

"How many roads must a man walk down," Steve added, "before we can call without qualms?"

"Well, we're not taking that one," I said. "We'll leave that road less traveled. So let's think a little more practically. Jimmy, how would you go about eavesdropping on AT&T?"

It didn't take him long to come up with a plan.

"They've got, what, a million employees?" he said. "So we couldn't even begin to monitor them all."

"I don't think we'd need to," I said. "A scheme like this, it would have to originate at the highest echelon."

The Ferret nodded. "Probably all we need is a few key lines…the CEO's office, his top execs, a couple of executive conference rooms at their headquarters in New York. A dozen taps would probably be enough to catch at least one of them discussing this openly, even if they never discuss it on a call. We just listen in on everything anyone says in those offices. The advantage we've got is that they're too arrogant to think their own lines would ever be tapped."

"And you don't think they'd notice these open lines, these lines you're holding?" I said.

"Well, eventually, yeah. But keep in mind there are a hundred and seventy million telephones in this country alone, and half a billion calls made daily. As long as we limit the number of held lines, it'd take weeks for them to notice—particularly if they have no reason to suspect anything or to start looking. Months maybe. Far longer than we need. It's the needle-haystack dilemma, and the trick is to never let on that there even is a needle. Fly under their radar."

"But how exactly would you do this?" Steve insisted. "Technically, I mean. Could you do it from your apartment with a blue box?"

"Absolutely," Jim said, "not. No way. That's monkey business. We're into guerilla warfare, way beyond what a blue box is capable of." He thought for a bit while we continued strolling down the tree-lined tunnel. We didn't interrupt him. "I'd need physical access to one of their switching centers," he finally decided.

"Where?" Steve asked. "San Francisco?"

"No, there's one in San Jose that'd do. The problem is access. I'd have a hell of a time getting in there for long enough to do what I need to do in there. Could take hours."

"So what you're saying is we're SOL," Steve said.

"It's like I always say," I said, "Where there's a will, there's a won't. Looks like you're up Stevens Creek without a paddle."

"Hmph," Jim grunted. Then he smiled a crooked, cocky smile and addressed our guest. "This might just be your lucky day," he announced.

"You know a way to get in?" Steve said.

"I think I might. Let's go back to my place."

Chapter 8.4

We crossed Homestead, entered the apartment complex, and took the internal sidewalk back to Jim's unit. He unlocked three locks and led us back in.

"Have a seat," he said and began picking up discarded sections of the Sunday paper from his living room floor. "I know it's around here somewhere," he mumbled, checking out the various pages. He pulled a sheet off a light table in the corner, checking underneath it for stray pages.

Steve went to the light table and ran his hands along the frosted glass surface. "You do design?"

"Yeah, I guess you could call it that," Jim answered absently. "I've been working on fonts for various, uh, documents."

"I audited a calligraphy class at Reed," Steve said. "Fonts are a lot more important than most people realize."

"Oh, yeah," Jim enthused.

"Nice to see not all of your interests are criminal," Steve said.

"Oh, wait for it," I counseled.

"Yeah," Jim said. "Fonts are vital. You get 'em wrong on a government document and you've blown the whole scam."

"And there it is," I said to Steve.

"You like calligraphy?" Jimmy chuckled "You're gonna love this, then. You been to a Post Office lately?"

"Uhh… No," Steve admitted.

"They've been putting up these signs. 'Thank You for Not Smoking.' Very ornate script with so many flourishes you can barely read the goddamn thing. Hardly make out the words. Very poor design—more like a Rorschach test. I found myself standing in line one day staring at the sign, almost hypnotized by the ambiguity of the calligraphy. Then I saw a hidden message, so I drew up my own version.

He dug in a pile of papers on the light table, pulled out two, and placed them side by side.

"This is the original," he continued, tapping one. He was right; the script was so florid and flamboyant that it was in fact difficult to make out that it read *Thank You for Not Smoking.*

Then he showed us his version. It was virtually identical, but, like an optical illusion, when our eyes adjusted to Ferrette's literal handiwork, a new message became clear: *Thank You for Not Fucking*.

Steve and I started laughing. Jim joined in, proud of his own subversive joke. "I've been switching them out in Post Offices anytime I go to one."

"You pranked 'em!" Steve enthused. "I love it!"

We all returned to our couches. Jim picked up another section of the paper.

"Ah! Here it is," he announced. He folded the newspaper into quarters and used a red marker from his art table to circle a spot midpage, then handed it to me.

What he'd located was the Want Ads section, and the one he'd circled read:

OPERATORS WANTED
Full-Time/Temporary Position

> PACIFIC BELL is hiring 50 full-time telephone operators for a month-long assignment in our San Jose call center. This position is temporary and does not include any employee benefits. Candidates must speak English. No heavy lifting. Minimum wage. Apply in person at 95 S. Almaden Ave., Monday, April 14, 8 AM

"Yeah, so?" I said.

He looked at me agog. "You fucking kidding me?" he whined. "Are you really that thick?"

I may be thick, but his intention sank in quickly.

"Are you really suggesting I get a job at Pac Bell?"

"Yes!"

"What're you, my father ten years ago? 'Get a job!'?"

"This is our ticket in!"

"So why don't *you* do it?" I challenged.

"I'll be busy. I'll rig the gig. I'll do the data analysis afterward. But I don't take…*jobs*. I don't…*work*."

"Damn it, Maynard, why do *I* get stuck with the grunt work?"

"Look," he said. "I have to get all the equipment together to make this happen. That'll take a couple of days. I can't be sitting around at Pac Bell answering phones all day. I could never smuggle all my tools in anyway. And Steve has his little company to run—"

"Hey!" he protested. Jimmy ignored him and continued.

"Bottom line? I have shit to do. He has shit to do. And you don't. You get hired, we've got access to the building. You let me in one night and I'll handle the hack—the tech details."

"And just how am I supposed to get hired?" I protested. "I haven't worked for anyone for years. I have no job record, no résumé…"

"Do you speak English?"

"*Si.*"

"Can you look presentable?"

"I can look it, sure."

"Then you're in. All they're looking for is warm bodies and clear voices. If you can sit in a chair eight hours a day and repeat a couple of phrases, you're hired."

"Just be yourself," Steve suggested.

"Oh, Christ, no," Jim protested. "Don't be yourself. You'll never get in. Be someone normal."

"What about the background check?"

"You fucking kidding me? For a temp job like this? Ain't happenin'. You don't even need a résumé—just a Social Security number."

"I don't want to give them my real name and Social Security number," I argued, "just in case they *do* check and it sends up a red flag."

Jim went to his light table and rooted around in a drawer. "You don't wanna be yourself?" he said. "Then be this guy." He pulled out a small card and handed it to me. A Social Security card.

"Forged?"

"Trust me, they won't know and they don't care."

"So now I'm… Who is this guy? Glenn Bullish? Bullshitz?"

"I think it's pronounced Bull-itch. Doesn't matter."

"How'd you come up with a screwy name like that, anyway?"

"Threw some Scrabble tiles in the air and just used whatever they spelled out when they landed."

"Shoulda used more vowels," I grumbled, pocketing my new identity and resigning myself to going to work for the phone company. As Glenn Balls-itch, or whoever. But I wasn't going to let him off the hook that easily. "So if I'm using a fake Social Security card, how'm I supposed to get paid?"

"Well, you're not," Jim growled.

Clearly, I was getting on his nerves. Payback's a bitch.

"They aren't gonna pay you much anyway," he continued crossly, then pointed at Steve. "And you're already on *his* payroll, right? He's paying you a lot more than you're ever gonna make working for Ma Bell, is my guess. Besides, it's not for long. A couple of days, tops. When I'm all set up, I'll call you."

"Not if AT&T is onto me," I said. "The guys behind this little conspiracy. They might have found out who I am and be tapping my lines. So you can't call my office. Or my house. And you will *not* call Laurel's house. We keep her entirely out of the loop. Goddamn it, we can't use the phone *at all* and be safe. Besides, how the fuck are you gonna call me while I'm at my fucking desk at my fucking job in the Pacific fucking Bell call center?"

One of us had to calm the fuck down, and it was his turn, apparently. He took a few deep breaths before he answered.

"I'll find a way to contact you," he said evenly. "When I do, that's your cue that we're a go for the following night. You hide yourself away somewhere in the building before closing time—in the john, or a janitor's closet or something—then let me in later in the evening. We'll have the entire night for me to set up the taps."

"There are no guards at this place? No night watchman?"

"The place is a fortress, man. Besides, who'd want to break in there in the first place? Nothing worth stealing. They're too arrogant about their security to waste money on night watchmen. Not to mention too cheap."

"Jesus," Steve said, shaking his head. "You guys really are pirates, aren't you?"

"Yes, we *yarrr*," I sighed morosely.

"It's better to be a pirate than join the Navy," Jim said, barely able to contain his glee at his own half-witticism.

"And what if I don't get hired?" I said.

Jim sighed. The devil is in the details, and there were a lot of details.

"I'll tell you what," he said patiently. "If you aren't hired, just come on over tomorrow and we can regroup and revise the plan. But if you *don't* show up here by noon, say, I'll know you got the job. Cool?"

"Yeah," I grumped. "OK."

"And what'm I supposed to be doing while you guys are setting all this up and monitoring their calls?" Steve asked.

I was still a little irritated at Jimmy, not only for forcing employment on me but for coming up with these plans at all. That was my job. Jobs was my job. I was Dortmunder in this outfit. I was the White Knight in this looking-glass world. So I fielded his question.

"You just go about your normal routine," I said. "Go to work, go to meetings, verbally abuse people—"

"Hey!"

"Make calls," I continued. "Work-related, but innocuous. Don't discuss any secrets on the phone. Try to keep yourself surrounded by sycophants at all times so you can't be abducted. Again."

"What about the tail?"

Oh shit.

"Um… Yeah. That's a detail we overlooked," I said to Jim. "If I'm shackled to a desk all day, who's gonna play guardian angel to Steve?"

"I don't think they're gonna hurt him," Jim determined. "He's the goose that lays the golden egg."

"Wait a minute," Steve said. "Didn't they gut that goose in the end?"

"Oh yeah…"

We all sat thinking for another minute or two until I beat them both to a plan.

"We need somebody to take my place and watch over Steve," I said to Jim. "You must know somebody. How about that mystery writer friend of yours? The guy who helped me do research a couple of years ago. Bragg. He's an odd duck."

"He's not odd," Jim said evenly.

"What's he up to these days?"

"Working as a process server. And he hates it. Probably would jump at a cushy job like surveillance."

"Does he have a gun?"

"Of course he has a gun. He's an American, isn't he?"

"Better warn him guns make Steve a little nervous."

"They should," Jim insisted. "I don't trust anyone who isn't a little nervous around guns. Nervous enough to be cautious, anyway." He looked over at Steve. "I wouldn't worry about this guy with a gun," he said, cocking his head toward me. "The only thing he ever shoots is the shit."

"Will you contact Bragg and fill him in?" I asked Jim. "Give him the make and license plate of the AT&T guys following Steve. What did the IBM guys call them? Mad Hatter and White Rabbit? And give him a description of Steve's car. And his license plate number."

"My car doesn't have any plates," Steve said. I'd forgotten that detail. I said there were a lot of them.

"New car?" Jim inquired. "New lease every six months?"

Steve nodded warily.

"The grace period scam," Jim identified. "I'll bet you park in handicapped spots as well."

"No I don't!"

I caught Jim's eye and nodded.

"OK," I said to Steve. "You're covered."

"What about the tail? What do I do about them?"

"Nothing," I said. "Ignore them. Bragg will keep tabs on them and step in if they try to approach you. He'll take over doing what your IBM guys were doing—watching the watchmen. Just think of it as a shift change. Don't try to lose the tail—it might tip them off that you're onto them. I'll get in touch when we know something definite."

"How are you gonna do that, without phoning me and them eavesdropping?"

"I'll call from a pay phone," I said. "I'll call your secretary—"

"We don't call them secretaries," Steve interrupted. "After Women's Lib, we call them 'area associates.'"

"You know how many secretaries it takes to change a light bulb?" Jimmy asked. Steve and I just looked at him askance. "It's moot," he continued. "There are no 'secretaries' anymore." He chuckled at his own joke, but we just shook our heads.

"You can go ahead and use that one," Jim said to Steve.

"Anyway," I continued, trying to get us back on track, "When we're ready to regroup, I'll call your office that morning with a Wong number."

"A wrong number?"

"No, a *Wong* number. It's an old phone prank, y'know, like 'Is your refrigerator running?' or 'Do you have Prince Albert in a can?' Don't worry, you'll know it when you hear it. So even if they're listening, they'll just take it for a prank call. That'll be the signal that I'll pick you up at noon and bring you here, so we can see what Jim has discovered."

"Same ruse? I park in back and sneak out the front door?"

I thought that one over for a beat. "No, they might have figured out that trick by now. We have to stay a step ahead of them…and without tipping our hand."

"So… What then?"

Again, I took a moment to let a plan coagulate in my brain. When I thought of it, I had every reason to believe that Steve would hate it, which was an unexpected bonus.

"Your offices are in that building on Stevens Creek, yeah? Next door to the Good Earth restaurant? Where I picked you up yesterday?"

"Well, no," he said guardedly. "That was our first building, but most of us are in a building on Bandley now, a couple blocks from the Stevens Creek building. Big place. Surrounded by orchards, like in the old days. I forgot to tell you about that Friday, so I let you pick me up at the Stevens Creek building yesterday—the address on the old business card I gave you years ago."

"So who's in the Stevens Creek building?" I asked.

"Oh, we still lease it. But we turned most of it into a test bed for the Apple III."

I looked over at Jim.

"A place for testing something under development," he explained. He knew what I didn't know and he knew I didn't know it. The bastard. "In this case, I'd bet money it's a model factory. Manufacturing and assembly for the new product line," he said, patting the prototype of the Apple III next to him on the couch.

Steve nodded. "A pilot factory, right. For Apple III assembly. The facility is fully operational, but small scale."

"OK, so that's the Stevens Creek building. But your new offices are close, right? Walking distance to the Good Earth, right?" I asked.

"Oh yeah. Less than half a mile. We walk there for lunch a lot."

"OK," I said. "Here's how I think we should work this. Give us a week to get the taps set up and for Jim to start monitoring them. Then a week from tomorrow, you start taking a few of your people to lunch at the Good Earth every day. Five, ten, twelve—a group. Tell 'em it's your way of showing your appreciation for their effort and dedication or something."

I was right. He gave me a lemon-sucking look.

"Hear me out," I said before he could be a twat and protest. "You do this every day until Jimmy uncovers some hard details and we're ready to meet again. That morning I'll call your office with the Wong number. You take a group to lunch just like you'd been doing every day. The tail will take it for granted that you'll all be going there at noon and coming back as a group at one, one-thirty, since you've established that as your routine."

"But the day you call," he intuited, "when I get to the restaurant, I give it ten minutes or so then announce I forgot something back at the office and beg off."

I nodded. "Be sure to pay in advance so your people don't think you're just jumping the check." Again with the scowl. "Then go out the back of the restaurant and I'll pick you up there. Doesn't matter if they're watching the front door or back door of Apple or the front door of The Good Earth because you won't be ducking out of Apple or leaving through the front door of the diner."

"So the tail will be expecting a group to leave after lunch," he said. "They might not even notice I'm not with them."

"Right. And even if they do, it doesn't matter—we've already bought an hour to elude them. We'll be back here before they even know you're gone."

Steve nodded. Jim nodded. So I nodded, too. What the hell.

We sat in silence for a minute or so. I don't know about them, but I was doing a mental idiot check, trying to make sure we hadn't overlooked anything important. So many friggin' details…

"One more thing…" Jim said at length. "Perhaps the most important thing of all."

We both looked at him and awaited his revelation. What could we have forgotten that could possibly qualify as "the most important thing of all"?

"What's in this for me?" he said.

I relaxed. "Jesus. Is that all? Steve, can you put him on the payroll? Same terms as me?"

"Bragg, too," Jim added. He might be a loose cannon, but he has balls.

Steve just gave Jim his silent glare. It was a pleasant change of pace not to be on the ass end of his attempt to intimidate using stares and silences. It might take him a while to realize that his antisocial strategies would never intimidate James J. Ferrette IV, the poster boy for antisocial behavior. But he'd learn very soon how futile it was to attempt to negotiate with Jimmy the Ferret.

"I'll pay you half what I'm paying him," Steve said at length, pointing at me. "And this bozo Bragg, half what I'm paying you."

I could sense the tension rising between these two stubborn egos. I couldn't let them blow the whole scheme over a few dollars, so I attempted to defuse the situation with some humor before Steve threw another hissy fit.

"C'mon, man," I said to Steve. "You told me you're not in this for the money. What kind of nickname do you want, The Great Humanitarian Jobs or Minimum Wage Jobs?"

Jim, however, didn't need anyone to fight his battles. He just sat back on the couch, relaxed, and smirked. Just a little.

"So let me get this straight," The Ferret stated. "You require my skills. You need all this done immediately. And you're gonna be penurious? My best offer is this…" He ticked off his points on his fingers. "Expertise. Timeliness. Cost. Choose any two."

Steven Jobs was not at that moment the happiest millionaire. "This is all getting to be very expensive," he sulked.

"Steve," I counseled, "it costs a lot to win. And even more to lose. So you and me better spend some time wonderin' what to choose."

"You and *I*," he snarled. "Grammar."

He sat stewing for a while. But to his credit, he eventually recognized an ironclad argument and the inevitability of the conclusion, and reluctantly relented to Jim's Chinese finger puzzle style of negotiating by nodding curtly.

"So everyone is clear on their assignments?" I asked. They nodded. I put my hand out in front of me, palm down. Jim placed his on top of mine.

"C'mon, Steve," I said, cocking my head toward our hands. "The Three Muscatels."

"I don't drink," he deadpanned.

I sighed. "If you did, you might understand why that's funny."

"I'd have to be pretty drunk to find that funny."

Steve and I rose to leave. Jim aimed a thumb at the bootleg Apple III resting next to him on the couch. "You wanna take that with you?"

Steve sighed. His shoulders drooped. He shook his head slowly. "You're gonna need that to screen the calls you intercept. I'll send one of my guys out here tomorrow to install a plug-in card that'll let you connect to the phone system, and a word filter program like the IBM guys had so you don't have to listen to every call."

“Thank you, Steve,” I said.

“…for the free shit,” Jim added.

Steve looked at the naked prototype like it was a child he was giving up for adoption.

“Congratulations,” he drawled to Jim. “You’ve just become a beta tester.”

Chapter 9.0

Monday, April 14

And that's how I found myself far too early the next morning wearing a dress shirt, stiff slacks, and hard shoes, my hair and goatee neatly combed, battling commuter traffic from Los Gatos to downtown San Jose, prepared to join the ranks of the gainfully underemployed. The irony is that for all this discomfort and irritation, it was still more pleasant than spending another day with Mr. Steven P. Jobs.

The Pacific Telegraph & Telephone building was located at 95 Almaden Boulevard just outside downtown San Jose. The place looked like a beige fortress: a solid cube of walls. It was tough to estimate how many stories the windowless edifice contained, but I guessed at least five, maybe six.

I parked and walked into the lobby a few minutes before the 8 AM interview time listed in the ad. A few dozen people were sitting, standing, or milling around in the spacious but spartan space. A quick headcount topped out at 48. The ad said they were looking for 50, so I was confident they'd have to take us all, unless one of the candidates started waving a gun around. I was smart. I'd left mine at home.

Against all odds, I recognized one of the other jobseekers—a guy I hadn't seen in years. Last time I'd dealt with him he'd provided me introductions to several writers who provided data vital to solving the case I was on. In those days, he was a clerk at a used bookstore in downtown San Jose—not far from the Quality Café, in fact. I noticed he was still wearing a Mickey Mouse t-shirt as he had in those days. I hoped it wasn't the same shirt, or at least that he'd washed it since then.

The clerk was my height and build with sandy brown hair and a goatee. About the only thing that dismissed us as mirror images were his glasses. I wear very simple gold wireframes with round lenses—timeless, classy, elegant—but his, with their teardrop-shaped lenses surrounded by huge black frames made him look like a raccoon. Or the Hamburgler.

I tried to stay out of his line of sight but he spotted me and headed my way.

"Hey," he said, "the fuck're you doing here? Give up the P.I. biz?"

I held a finger to my lips. "Ixnay on the etective… ectec… dectective… Shut up."

"Ah," he said nodding and squinting. "Undercover. On a case. Got it. My lips are sealed."

That'll be the day, I thought, recalling his proclivity for verbosity.

I thought correctly.

"So who you working for?" he whispered.

"You know I can't tell you that. Client confidentiality."

"Apples," he mumbled.

"I beg your pardon?"

"Short for *road apples*," he said. "In other words, horse shit. Who's your client?"

"His name wouldn't mean anything to you. You've never heard of him."

"Oh, but he's heard of famous you, huh? You're so beloved as Mr. TV that being a celebrity can get you jobs, right?"

I knew the only way to get him off the topic was to get him talking about his favorite subject: himself.

"So what're you doing here?"

He puffed out a deep breath then launched into a hyperverbal overexplanation. "I spent the last six months bumming around South America," he thought he'd explained. "I got back a few weeks ago, broke and homeless. I needed work. I was over at my friend Jim Ferrette's last night and he showed me an ad for this"—he gestured to the Pac Bell lobby—"and the rest, as they say, is history. Or current events."

"Did he mention me?"

"Why the fuck would he mention you?"

Good. At least Jim didn't blow my cover.

Precisely at 8 AM, a door behind the receptionist's desk opened and a trio of woman entered the lobby. They were all in their mid-40s and all dressed in pants suits filled with double-wide asses—no doubt the result of spending 20 years of sedentary service as phone operators. One took the lead. The others stood flanking her, a step behind. In deference to her Authority, I assumed.

"Good morning," declared the dominant boss. It was the last pleasant thing we would ever hear from her. All fidgeting ceased; all conversations cut off short. "Thank you for responding to our ad. If you follow us, we'll get the employment agreements signed and get you your badges and workstations."

She turned and started down the narrow hallway. Her entourage followed, single file. The rest of her new recruits followed them two by two, like Noah's zoo queue. I glanced above the doorway but did not see an inscription reading, "Abandon all hope ye who enter here." Probably covered that in the Employee Handbook.

The Supes led us down the hallway waddling like Donald Duck and his kin.

"I love a parade," I mumbled to the bookstore clerk, walking beside me.

"I guess that makes us the clowns," he whispered back.

I pointed covertly to our lumbering leaders. "And that's the March of the Elephants."

He snorted a laugh. "That's because we're making peanuts. Like Charles Schulz."

"All that's missing is the Calypegian Calliope," I added.

The Supes led us into a large room with long folding tables and small folding chairs. Bookstore boy insisted on sitting next to me.

The Boss Ladies distributed job applications. We filled them out. Or filled them in. Even though the two phrases sound like opposites, they mean exactly the same thing. Like flammable and inflammable. Is all language that ambiguous? I suppose the only answer is maybe yes, maybe no.

A few minutes later, the women collected our applications and began reviewing them. And while they were busy with the paperwork, the Dominatrix addressed her new submissives.

"The reason you are here," she explained, "is that an entire quadrant of the Santa Clara Valley with the area code 408 is being broken out into a new area code. All calls to this new area code are being routed through our call center. Your job is to inform the caller that this number now has a new area code, and they should make a note of it." One of the second-in-commands handed out three-by-five cards with this printed on them:

That area code has changed.
The new area code is 510.
Please make a note of it.

"This is your script," the Uberboss continued. "You will repeat it exactly, with no alterations or embellishments, or you will be fired. Your shift begins precisely at eight o'clock AM and ends at five PM. If you are late, you will be fired. By law, you are allowed two fifteen-minute breaks and a one-hour lunch break. Times will be assigned. If you return late, you will be fired. We will be listening in at random to your calls from our booth. If you are not answering calls, or are deviating from the script in any way, you will be fired." It was like a high school language lab. In 1943 Germany.

That's when it hit me—why she was treating us with such disdain, if not open contempt. We were not fellow employees. We were not even people. We were *temp workers*—the human version of the automation that they really wanted...the automation that would soon replace us, and, if there was any justice in the world, them.

Ilsa the She Wolf of the Telefongesellschaft looked over at her two henchbiddies. They tapped the pile of applications. One nodded and the other gave her a "thumbs up." Apparently, we'd all passed the rigorous interview process and were all hired.

And thus, for the first time in years, I became a minimum-wage slave.

The Axis Trio passed out our temp badges then led us down another hall. My bookstore buddy walked alongside me, both of us watching the wiggle-waddle-wiggle from behind.

"My dad would say, Looks like two pigs wrestling in a gunny sack," I said.

"My dad would say, The bigger the cushion, the better the pushin'," he replied.

"Your dad is a wise man."

"My dad is a milkman who drinks his coffee black," he said. I had no idea what that meant.

They led us into another large room. This one was dimly lit and contained several rows of workstations…not desks, exactly, but long tables with dividers every three or four feet to separate us and our voices from one another. I silently congratulated myself for pegging the place as a high school language lab earlier.

"Please check your badge for your assigned workstation," Adolpha ordered. Mine was #40. The clerk's was #6.

He held up his badge for me to see. "I am not a number," he growled in a severe British accent. "I am a free man!"

"Good luck with that at the DMV," I said. "Or the IRS. Or the SSA."

I took my seat at Slaughterhouse-5, aka Workstation 40. I was not a free man. I was a number.

My cubicle contained what I assumed every other cubicle contained: a headset with an earpiece and a microphone connected to a small box with a few square, raised buttons in a line. Posted on the wall in front of me was the Holy Scripture, from The Book of The Phone:

That area code has changed.
The new area code is 510.
Please make a note of it.

One end of the room was raised, walled off, and had windows that overlooked the rest of the workspace. I could see the trio of Aryan Supers in the little room. From their vantage point, they could see the sea of repeaters.

Der Boss's voice came over a PA: "Please put on your headpieces." We did. "This is a mic check," she said through the headsets. "If you can hear me, please raise your hand." We did. "Excellent," she continued. "If you encounter any problems, just raise your hand and we'll contact you through your headphones. We are live in five…"

Great, I thought. Five minutes to relax.

"…four…three…two…one…"

In the dim of the gloomy room I could see the glow of phone lines lighting up the buttons on the boxes in front of us—including mine.

I pushed the flashing button. "That area code has changed," I said. "The new area code is five-one-zero. Please make a note of it." The caller hung up.

OK! First call, big success! Woo-hoo! I'd followed the complicated, convoluted instructions precisely and was ready to claim my first victory. Until the next button lit up and I had to do it again.

And again.

And again and again and again…

And that is exactly what I found myself doing every few seconds, for eight solid hours.

The only appreciable break during our shift was a lunch hour. Fortunately, our staggered breaks were based on our badge numbers, which prevented my bookstore barnacle and fellow inmate from insisting we eat together. But when my platoon was dismissed for lunch, I followed several co-workers to the cafeteria, where I received a shock: there was no cafeteria. There was only a break room. I realized the ad for this job should have included the instructions "Pack a lunch," because there was nothing substantial to eat in the stark, sterile break room. Sure, there were vending machines for soft drinks and snacks, but no sandwiches, no sustenance of any substance. And despite our downtown-adjacent location, there was nowhere close enough nearby to get lunch and return before the sands in the Wicked Witch's hourglass ran out. *Return late and you're fired.* That was enough to make anyone lose their lunch. I mourned my lost lunch but had a Coke and some chips and resigned myself to spending the afternoon listening not only to my repeated phrase but to the repeated growling of my stomach.

Chapter 9.1

At five o'clock I was able to rouse myself from my hypnotic robotic slumber and stumble to my car. But rather than enjoy the bumper-to-bumper commute home—no wonder so many people love their jobs—I decided I needed dinner, and I needed a treat. I knew where I could get both. I maneuvered my way over to San Carlos and headed west. Once past Highway 17, San Carlos became Stevens Creek, and about 15 minutes later I drove past the Apple building and The Good Earth. Neither was my destination. I needed something more substantial than sprouts and tofu tonight. And I'd had chips for lunch.

I took the next left on DeAnza and headed due north into Sunnyvale. It only took about ten minutes to reach my destination: the Dairy Belle Freeze on Mathilda, just before the entrance to the Lockheed compound beyond Highways 101 and 237.

The Dairy Belle Freeze was Mr. Peabody's WAYBAC machine, and it was set for the '50s—the era of real food, not fast food or junk food. Or sprouts. I parked, strolled past the outdoor picnic tables and opened the squeaky screen door. The order counter was directly ahead, under a plastic menu that offered pretty much anything that can be cooked on a flattop. A row of vinyl diner swivel stools stood like stainless steel mushrooms along the front windows. A few tiny, bare-boned booths lined the side wall. The hiss and fragrance of frying food filled the cramped little building. Dairy Belle Freeze served both kinds of food: fried and deep fried.

Henry Choe was manning the counter. He smiled when he saw me. I greeted him and his wife Bong ("our best cooker," Henry had once confided), who was not so busy scraping the griddle that she couldn't give me a wave and a smile. It might be unnecessary to point out that I was clearly a regular, but one thing that is definitely worth pointing out is this: Who'd believe it would take a Korean family to keep the American hamburger stand, the cheap and delicious fast-food dive, alive?

Henry knew what I wanted without even ordering: a jumbo deluxe cheeseburger, large fries, and a chocolate malt. There was no question about how the burger got its name: it came with a jumbo patty, a jumbo slice of tomato and one of onion, and a jumbo handful of dill pickles. The fries were always fresh potatoes, cooked to order and delivered too hot to eat. They made McDonald's fries taste like the cardboard container McDonald's fries come in. And a malt? Seriously? Who even made malted milks anymore?

While I masticated my cowburger I ruminated randomly on my case. Jobs' choice of the name Apple for his company might indicate that the little martinet might actually be kind of brilliant. The name didn't sound cold and sterile and technological, but as round and inviting and sweet as Mickey Mouse and as American as some kind of pie.

The humble apple certainly had its place in history, metaphor, and folklore as well, and was laden with associations. The fruit of the Tree of Knowledge, for starters. Steve probably meant that his computers were the gateway to knowledge—but with the bonus meaning that they were also the "forbidden fruit," which surely appealed to his anti-authoritarian attitude. Hell, half the time he went out of his way to look Satanic.

Apples were all over our lives. A is for Apple in the earliest readers. An apple for the teacher (if you were an apple polisher). An apple a day and the ditto of my eye. Then there was Johnny Appleseed, spilling his seed across America. So to speak. This is not to overlook William Tell—although in this case it wasn't Swiss William Tell but American Tel & Tel trying to shoot the fruit off Steve's head. Or shoot his head off and grab the Apple.

And Steve. Jesus, Steve. Both a genius and Jesus…in his own mind. Certainly a legend in his own mind. Was he a difficult genius or was he just difficult? Was there more to him than chutzpah and hubris? Was he Lucifer or Prometheus? Was he a snake oil salesman, a bad apple, a phony, or was he genuinely precocious and misunderstood? Was he Snow White holding a poison apple, or Snow Jobs, selling harmless snake oil? Was he a perfectionist, as he claimed, or was that just a polite way of saying "anal retentive control freak"? A selfish, sarcastic scofflaw, or…

Screw Steve. My fries were getting cold and my malt was getting warm, so I finished them both then drove home fat and happy. Screw the cholesterol. Screw the salt. Some things are worth the risk. Dairy Belle Freeze was definitely one of them. But Jobs? Not so sure…

Chapter 9.2

Tuesday, April 15

Tuesday I packed a lunch. (Despite massive evidence to the contrary, I am in fact capable of learning.) I also packed a pocket notepad and pen which I placed on my cubicle desktop to tick off the number of times I repeated our 510 Mantra during the eight-hour shift. The final count: 700.

By 5 PM I was so bored and desperate for stimulation that I drove a few blocks to the main branch of the San Jose Public Library to do some research on Steven Paul Jobs. It should be a measure of how bored I was that I went to the library for stimulation.

I spent most of the evening doing research, or trying to. But I ended up with exactly nothing. Squat. Zero. Goose egg. Bupkis. A complete strikeout.

There was no mention of Steve Jobs in the microfiche archives of either San Francisco paper, the *Examiner* or the *Chronicle.* This was to be expected, perhaps, since The City considered The Valley beneath its notice and often failed to even acknowledge our existence. To them, we were the embarrassing red-headed stepchild of the Bay Area.

That was strike one. But even the local rag, the San Jose *Mercury News*, had no mention of either Steve Jobs or Apple. Strike two. And the all-inclusive *Readers' Guide to Periodical Literature* listed no magazine articles about the unknown entrepreneur, either. The tourist on East Brother said he recognized Steve from an article in a computer magazine. Apparently, any magazine devoted to computers was too new, or its circulation too small, for it to surface in the *Readers' Guide*. Strike three.

It was late. I was hungry. And I was tired…but not so tired that I didn't drive a few miles up The Alameda to the Stuft Pizza in Santa Clara, near Santa Clara University. The thought of Italian sausage, red onions, and that thick, buttery crust was immensely motivating. I drove home, "stuft" my face, washed the pie down with a couple of beers and promptly fell asleep. I couldn't even stay awake for Carson. I had to get a good night's sleep to be capable of being a perky Pac Bell parrot.

That area code has changed.
The new area code is 510.
Please make a note of it.

By Wednesday afternoon, the third day on the job, even the monotony was getting monotonous. Where the hell was Jimmy? How long until he reached down into this hell world and rescued me? And took me somewhere different, somewhere better? Somewhere in area code 510, maybe.

Chapter 10.0

Wednesday, April 16

What can you say about a 28-year-old girl I loved? That she was beautiful. And brilliant. That she loved Beethoven and Bach. And the Beatles. And me. I'm pretty sure.

No, I can't say that. Erich Segal already said that, mostly. And if it sucked when he said it (and it most assuredly did), it would suck balls if I plagiarized it. Besides, if we learned one thing from the '70s, it's that the word should be "woman," not "girl." And that disco sucks. OK, two things. But I digress. (And it does.)

Speaking of digressions, let's turn back the clock to…

Chapter 10.1

September 1965

Despite the fact that my parents insisted I go to Sunday School through most of my childhood, I'd never been a religious kid. But when Laurel entered my universe on our first day of high school I suddenly realized there was a God, or at least Angels, and that I was in the presence of one of His favorites.

Hundreds of adolescents were roaming randomly around the schoolyard blacktop that morning, waiting for the bell to order us, Eloi-like, or Pavlov-like, to our first class. I saw her from across a crowded quad and had to know her. Her flame-red hair stood out like a heart waiting to be embraced. Her pale, lightly-freckled face was serene even in the roiling, hormonal crowd. Purple tights under a flowered skirt accentuated her chiseled legs. Is it wrong for a guy pushing 30 to still get a twinge when recalling that first vision of a 13-year-old? If it is, I don't want to be right.

She arrested my attention, but not my adolescence. If anything, I wanted to grow up as fast as possible so I'd know how to approach this waking dreamgirl.

I immediately determined to pursue her, as uncomfortable as it made me, as risk-averse as I was to rejection by any member of the fair sex. I made a point of sitting in front of her in our science class, for instance, and always asked her to partner with me for our experiments, even though talking was discouraged. (The clever teacher had posted a sign that read "This is a LABORatory, not a labORATORY." Yet another reason to hate high school.) We learned a little about the physics of audio vibration and olfactory sensitivity, but we didn't learn too much about one another. What's a 13-year-old boy supposed to ask a 13-year-old girl, anyway? What do you want to be when you grow up? Are your parents married—I mean *still* married? Do you believe in love at first sight? Who's your favorite Beatle? (But what if she didn't say John?) Do you watch *The Man From U.N.C.L.E.*?

Sometime during our freshman year, my parents announced they were taking the family to see Bill Cosby perform at the

Circle Star Theater in Redwood City. Even then I knew he was the funniest man alive, and probably always would be, and I asked Laurel if she'd like to join us. She demurred. I was crushed. More than a decade later, when we began seeing each other regularly, I mentioned this abortive attempt to secure a first date. Her eyes grew wide and her mouth made a big red O. "I wasn't *ready* for dating!" she explained. That relieved some of the trauma that I'd carried for over a decade. Some.

As Seniors, I sat in front of her in our AP English class, another venue in which we were (ironically, since it was English) discouraged from talking. But we managed to talk. By then she'd matured into a brilliant, strong-willed woman with what was clearly a perfect body. Is it creepy for a guy pushing 30 to lust after his current adult girlfriend when she was 17? It seems like nature…so if it is cringey, I blame Mother Nature. Or society.

After high school, we went our separate ways and took our separate paths—her to maturity; me to arrested adolescence. But she was always on my mind, and once I graduated and obtained my P.I. license, I looked her up. During my absence, she'd become a nurse. She spent her days saving lives, which made me feel a bit guilty wondering if I was wasting mine doing little more than living out my private detective fantasies.

Laurel was currently working in a Pediatric ICU at nearby Good Samaritan Hospital. I'd visited the unit once and it broke my heart. Later I asked her how she dealt with a room full of doomed, dying infants.

"They're no different than you and me," she explained with a beatific smile. "They live. They suffer. They die. They just do it quicker." Couldn't argue with Buddhist logic like that. My only hope to obtain that level of compassion and detachment would be if I became the understudy to the Living Incarnation of the Buddha of Compassion, His Holiness the 14th Dalai Lama. Even then it would be a crap shoot.

Chapter 10.2

Returning to Wednesday, April 16, 1980

And now here we were, sitting in the little kitchen of her cozy cottage in Los Gatos—mere blocks away from my downtown office—with its carefully tended garden and her radiant serenity.

"You staying for dinner?" she asked.

"Sure. What're we having?"

"All I have is leftovers," she said. "Sorry."

"No, that's great. Your leftovers are better than most restaurant meals. Right this moment, however, what I really need is a drink."

She went to the cupboard for a wine glass then went to the fridge and poured herself a glass of white wine. I don't drink white wine, so I have no idea what kind it was, other than it came from Mirassou, which showed her good taste. Then she went back to the cupboard for a tall glass and got some ice from the freezer. She grabbed a can of ginger ale from the fridge and returned to the cupboard for the bottle of Wild Turkey she kept on hand, just for me. And she made me a perfect highball, just like my Scottish Grandpa's, *och aye*.

She removed some covered casserole dishes from the fridge and stuck them in the oven, then returned to the kitchen table to talk over our cocktails.

"I tried calling you a couple of times over the weekend," she said. It wasn't an accusation, just a comment. "I had Saturday and Sunday off, which is unusual, and I thought you might like to do something."

I could hardly expect her to understand that I'd had a romantic weekend getaway planned for us but spent it shacked up with another guy. Out of context, it could easily be taken the wrong way. And providing context could take all evening.

"Yeah, sorry," I said. "I'm on a case." That, she would understand. We were used to one anothers' eccentric schedules. Neither of us worked a standard Monday-to-Friday 9-to-5, or wanted to, as my recent days as a smooth operator had reminded me. Speaking of which… "And I got a job," I said with mock pride. "At the phone company." I took a deep drink of my highball. Even the effervescence of the ginger ale and the astringence of the Wild Turkey wasn't enough to remove the bad taste those two sentences left in my mouth.

"You?" she said, wide-eyed. "A job?"

"Don't sound so surprised," I said. "I'm employable. And anyway, I'm working undercover."

She started to say something, but the phone rang.

"Sorry," she said. "I should get this. Might be the hospital."

"Mrs. Peel, you're needed."

She answered, listened, then said "No thank you" curtly and hung up.

"Telemarketer," she spat as she sat back down and took a sip of wine. "So you were saying…?"

"Uhh… Yeah. I've got this new client. Guy named Steve Jobs. Works in electronics. Apple computers?"

"His name sounds vaguely familiar," she said quietly, looking off into the distance as though she was trying to place where she'd heard it before. Could take a while, since "Steve Jobs" was not exactly a household name. "So, wait…" she said. "Aren't you violating some sort of client confidentiality telling me about this?"

"No, no, I cleared this with him. I told him I tell you everything. He had no problem with that, except he didn't seem to understand the concept of sharing."

"Sounds like he's—" she started to say when the phone rang again. She sighed and shrugged. "I should really get this…"

"Yeah. Might be the hospital."

She answered, listened, said "No thank you" curtly, then hung up and returned to the table. "Telemarketer. Again."

"How do they always know when we're having dinner?"

"OK, so since you *can* tell me what you're up to, tell me what you're up to. Nothing illegal, I trust?"

"Well…" I said with a chagrined shrug, "not so far…"

She pursed her lips and shook her head slowly. "You know I—" she began when the phone rang. Again. She rose to answer. Again. Might be the hospital. But of course it wasn't. Again.

"Damned telemarketers," she grumbled.

"OK," I declared. "That's it. Get your shoes on. I'm taking you to Chart House."

"Ooo! Swanky. We celebrating something?"

"Yeah. Celebrating no more interruptions during dinner."

"But Chart House? Can you afford that?"

"I'm making the big telecommunications bucks now, baby. So, no."

Chapter 10.3

Laurel decided she needed to upgrade her outfit to be presentable outside the house—ah, the infinite mysteries of women—and I finished my drink while she changed. It was worth the wait, however, since she reappeared a few minutes later in a chic skirt and blouse and in full makeup. Maybe I was the one who was underdressed. Wouldn't be the first time. Or the last, I'm sure.

The leftovers in the oven had barely even had time to warm the chill off, so she removed them and returned them to the fridge. We left her little villa and walked a couple of blocks up Broadway to Montebello Park, then took a left on Santa Cruz Ave. As we crossed Main, I glanced up at my corner office on the second floor. I'd left a light on even though I wasn't there, which would reinforce what I'd overheard my alleged friends say occasionally, that the lights are on but nobody's home.

As we strolled past the chichi shops, I asked her about her day—days, actually, since I hadn't seen her for a few. I may be self-centered and self-indulgent, but I'm not stupid. As far as I know. I was in fact the very model of the modern Major Gentleman—the Attentive Boyfriend who always asked about her day. The sad fact that I rarely remembered what she told me, however, was a clear indication that there was still work to be done.

We strolled down the long block, crossed Bean Street, and arrived at the Chart House. The restaurant occupied a classic two-story Queen Anne mansion, gray with white trim and recessed from the street. For 60 years before it was converted into a surf 'n turf joint it had been a funeral home. The staff considered it in bad taste to ask how long the meat had been in the freezer.

The restaurant billed itself as "California Casual," which seemed redundant. I suppose it meant that even though it was decorated like a fine dining establishment with plush carpets, cloth napkins, and crystal stemware, the wait staff all sported aloha shirts—those flashy Hawaiian blouses decorated with surfboards or sailboats or tiki heads or hula girls or other images designed to invoke a South Seas ambiance. It would be a cold day in paradise before I'd be caught dead in one of those garish garments.

It was Wednesday evening, so the place wasn't busy. It was empty enough, in fact, that I asked the hostess if we could be seated in the Turret Room–a private alcove on the second floor just big enough for two. She led us there and our waiter appeared almost as soon as we were seated. He was wearing a green aloha shirt, untucked (as is the fashion) with an orange Birds of Paradise print. An abomination. I could barely look at him. I'm not colorblind, but a shirt that loud could make me color deaf. We ordered drinks—another white wine for Laurel, Drambuie rocks for me (it was a classy joint, after all, not a highball dive) and he left us with menus printed on a pair of paddles. Thick, wooden paddles, a foot square, with handles—the kind of utensil that would come in handy during a pledge hazing, I thought. Or a very special Saturday night…

By the time our drinks arrived, along with a basket of warm bread, we were ready to order. The waiter insisted on reciting the Specials, which included Blackened Catfish. I love Cajun food. But I knew it would never catch on as a trend. I ordered the filet mignon, medium rare; Laurel, the lobster. "Well done," I added. The waiter chuckled. Oh, he was getting a tip.

We'd hardly had time to sip our drinks and butter some bread—home-baked white for her; delicious, dark pumpernickel for me—before the waiter returned with our salad. This was always one of the high points of a meal here, not so much for the pedestrian chilled romaine but for the house blue cheese dressing, the best I'd ever had. He served. He peppered. He left. Perfect service so far.

"So tell me about your client," Laurel encouraged.

"Nah, I want to enjoy our dinner," I said, sprinkling croutons and bacon on my lettuce. "He's frustrating and exasperating. Dealing with him is like wearing fiberglass underwear."

"Please…" she protested. "I'm trying to eat here."

"OK. Like wearing Velcro underwear? Better?"

"Only marginally."

Once I had a chance to think it over, however, I realized that she was, as usual, right. It might in fact help to talk about Steve.

"You took some Psych classes to get your RN, right?" I said.

"Yeah. Didn't you, to get your Police Science degree?"

"Yeah, but only aberrant psych."

"I bet you got an A."

I chose not to interpret what she meant by that.

"I've been reading this series of mysteries," I began.

"I'm shocked."

"Writer named Robert B. Parker. He's got a series character, a private eye named Spencer. And Spencer has a, a paramour who's a therapist."

"A 'paramour'? I guess that Word of the Day calendar I got you for Christmas was worth the money."

"Indubitroubley. Every one of his books has at least one chapter where the couple share a gourmet meal and discuss the psychology of his latest client. Maybe we could do that?" It's not plagiarism if he never knows.

"Sure. Tell me about him."

"OK. Well, he's whip-smart and whippet-thin. Profile like a hawk. Taller than me, but slouches. Long black hair and thick eyebrows. Kind of Satanic, actually. Long, delicate fingers."

"Artist fingers."

"Brown eyes. Thin, angular nose. Pale."

"Oh my," she sighed. "The police science training. Always so literal."

"Yeah, but only figuratively. You want character traits, not a description, right? Personality traits."

"Well, I'm not looking to pick him out of a police lineup, so… yeah."

"OK," I said. "Well, he's a Pisces."

"Like you. Interesting."

"And he's a prickly, arrogant control freak, convinced he's something special, better than everyone else. Smarter."

"Sounds a bit familiar."

"He's obnoxious. Stubborn. Petulant. Everything has to be his way."

"Oh, my!" she exclaimed. "You've found your long-lost twin!"

There weren't many ways I could respond to that and still have a girlfriend. I thought of one. Maybe.

"You remember that tape I showed you of Dick Cavett interviewing Federico Fellini and Marcello Mastroianni?" I said.

Her fork hovered above her salad plate. No salad fell off. That's how classy she is. But she cocked her head and narrowed her eyes. "Yeahhhh," she said. "And?"

"And Marcello was pulling some goofy faces because he couldn't speak-a de English very good, and Fellini watches him for a minute then says to him," I imitated Fellini's high, heavily accented voice perfectly, " 'Marcello? Are you-a *feenish* with your gag?' "

She almost dropped her fork laughing but didn't. That's how classy she is.

"OK, OK," she said, laughing around her lettuce. "I'll try to be good. Let's start off easy. Can you describe your client in, say, three words?"

"Oh, hell, I can describe him in three words for every letter of the alphabet," I said. "A: Arrogant. Abrasive. Asshole. But also articulate. And abrupt. B: Bastard. Bully. Butthole. But also brilliant. C: Capricious. Contrarian. Conceited. But also kind of charismatic. I: Intense. Irritating. Impatient. Oh, also intelligent. And irascible. And so on."

"I think you skipped a few letters there," she pointed out.

"I'm exhausting the alphabet."

"You're exhausting, that's for sure," she said brightly.

"If I'd been an ancient Greek, my name would have been Thesaurus," I declared. "And if I'd been an ancient Roman, my name would have been Smarticus."

"I'm Dubious," she said. I let that slide because I didn't understand it.

"He's got a lot of issues," I continued. "Issues with authority. Anger issues. Family issues. He's got more issues than *TV Guide*. He certainly has issues with socialization and emotions. My sense is that he wants to be Mr. Spock—cold, calculating, emotionless. He thinks like a computer. Binary. Everything is either great or it's shit—everyone, too. Either it's cool or it sucks. The guy is such a butthead."

"Details?" she prompted.

"Well, his whole history is a study in contrasts. He's adopted, but his adoptive parents went out of their way to make him feel special. So he has both abandonment and entitlement issues. Sometimes simultaneously. He's got an illegitimate daughter—but despite his own abandonment issues, he refuses to acknowledge paternity."

"Why?"

"Because it's inconvenient, maybe?" I guessed. "Or because it might affect his stock price, or because she might get kidnapped and held for ransom? Or something. I suspect these are all rationalizations and he's making them up as they occur to him."

"Contradictory?"

"Yeah. Everything's a clash of opposites with him. I think he was bullied as a kid and grew up to be a bully, for example. He claims to be a vegetarian but he loves sushi. His Buddhist beliefs tell him we shouldn't be attached to material possessions, but he wants everyone to own one of his computers. He's a walking contradiction. An oxymoron."

"Your friends call you that, too," Laurel said. "Except for the oxy part."

"Hey! I thought you said you were gonna be good!"

She waved her hand and laughed into her napkin. "I said I'd try. I can't help it if you're contagious."

I ate some salad. I wasn't pouting or sulking. At all.

"Eccentric behavior?" Laurel asked at length.

"Well, he has these bizarre beliefs about food. Like for instance, he thinks an all-apple diet reduces mucus and keeps him odor-free so he doesn't need to bathe. And let me tell you, he could not be more wrong about anything. And he's mercurial. One minute he's berating someone, the next, he's crying."

"Moodswings?"

"Yeah, I think so. Maybe manic depressive?"

"The American Psychiatric Association just released a new edition of the DSM—the DSM-III—and they're calling that 'bipolar disorder' now."

"DSM?"

"*Diagnostic and Statistical Manual of Mental Disorders.* The ultimate authority for psychological diagnoses."

"A little light reading, huh?" I said. "How'd you get ahold of that?"

She groaned a little under her breath. "The Chief of Psychiatry at the hospital got an advance copy and asked me to read it and give him a summary. Makes me want to go to med school just so I could become the only doctor on the planet who is not arrogant and dismissive of nurses. But that's beside the point. We're talking about your favorite subject now."

"Me?"

"Of course. So go on. Your client, this Jobs, is…?"

"Overbearing. Confrontational. Guy's got balls so big he'd need the blimp hanger at Moffet Field to store them. And he's a control freak—but when I suggest a plan he likes, he's fine going along with it. Maybe because he later claims he thought it up in the first place. I have to out-bully him to get any control at all. He does seem to concede to people who stand up to him and know what they're talking about, however."

A busboy whisked our empty salad plates away.

"Great salad," I said. "All that lettuce. Steve would love it."

"He'd object to the blue cheese dressing," she said. "Causes mucus." She catches on quick. Quickly.

"Here's my new joke," I said. "What's the difference between Steve Jobs' Mercedes and a porcupine? Porcupines have their pricks on the outside." She chuckled a little at that one.

"So how'd you find all this out?"

"Well, y'know, mostly from observation. From doing— I mean, *spending* time with him. I also did some research at the San Jose Public Library."

"Did you bring your pencil to connect the dots in the books?"

If anyone else had said that, I might have been insulted. But Laurel saying it was the opposite of insulting: it meant she remembered my joke.

Our waiter appeared and served our entrées. We took a minute away from conversation to savor the presentation and the heady aromas before we dug into our meal. I gave Laurel my sautéed zucchini and carrots. I loaded butter and bacon on my baked potato and sprinkled salt on the potato and the steak. She cast a brow-furrowed glance at my plate.

"Better watch that cholesterol, buddy," she admonished. "And the salt." She reached over and took the shaker from me. "I'm just gonna keep this over here so you aren't tempted."

I shrugged. "I don't eat like this every day."

"No," she said. "Worse."

Chapter 10.4

And all that could be heard for the next few minutes was the sound of silverware, punctuated by the occasional, inevitable *"Mmmm..."*

At length, Laurel broke the silence.

"I suppose if we're imitating the conversations you read in your mystery novels," she said, "I'd better hold up my end of the psychological analysis."

I nodded. I couldn't reply verbally as I had a mouthful of meat. That would be rude. Not to mention the meat might fall out.

"You've heard of Carl Jung, right? The Swiss psychologist?"

I swallowed, so I could speak once again. "Of course I've heard of Carl Jung," I said. "I'm not a perfect idiot."

"Oh, sweetheart, nobody's perfect," she said sweetly, and continued before that could sink in. "He observed that people perceive and interact with the world in four major ways, OK? Everyone has all four of these psychological tools in their tool chest, but one always dominates a person's way of understanding the world. They fall on two spectrums, like this..." She crossed her fork and knife at right angles, like I was a vampire she was banishing. "And they stack up, one two three four, in terms of how developed they are, how *conscious* they are, and how much one relies on the function."

"And just what are these fantastic four?" I asked around a mouthful of meat.

"One is the Thinking function," she said. "That's probably the easiest to understand. People who have that as their primary method of engaging with the world use an intellectual approach—analytical, objective, reductive. Scientists. Mathematicians. The other end of that spectrum is the Feeling function—emotions, basically, and gut instincts about right and wrong, good and evil, justice, that kind of thing. Holistic rather than compartmentalized. In a Thinking type, this Feeling function, this valuation function, is usually underdeveloped. Thinking types might be brilliant people, but can also be awkward socially and childish emotionally. Like a lot of these computer nerds. Especially the software guys. Or the guys who developed the H-bomb just because they could, not because it was of any benefit to humanity or society. The *idea* is the important thing to them. What it means, how it affects people, well, that's irrelevant."

"Yeah, I'm thinking I got it. What's the other spectrum?"

"At one end is Sensation—physicality. These are hands-on people, who understand life at its most tangible, tactile level. Jocks. Athletes."

"Guys who ride motorcycles, just for the vibration on their butts and the wind in their hair and the bugs in their teeth," I said. I catch on quick. Quickly. "Risk takers. Mountain climbers, surfers, sex fiends."

"By George, I think he's got it!" Laurel said in an English accent for some reason. "And at the opposite end of that spectrum are the Intuitives. They're the most difficult to understand. They read unconscious clues and are very easily detached from reality. Poets. Artists. Mystics."

"Druggies," I added. "Head in the clouds."

"Right," she said. "And the farther away they are from the opposite pole, Sensation, the looser their grip on reality. You know how shrinks often tell patients they need to be 'grounded'? That's precisely what the Intuitives need—to tie the string on their helium balloon to something solid to keep them from floating away to Cloud Cuckoo Land."

"I used to be grounded all the time when I was a teenager," I said. "But probably not the way you mean."

"These functions are inextricably intertwined," she said, once again proving her vast intelligence—not by her erudite use of language, but by ignoring me, "and they all influence one another. Like I said, everyone has all four but is inclined to use each to a greater or lesser degree. One function is dominant, then there's a backup function from the other spectrum, and both of them are relatively conscious. After that, things get a little dicey. The other functions are less developed and more unconscious. The goal is to bring those undeveloped functions to consciousness and integrate them...get them all working in unison. In harmony. Balanced."

"I'm not entirely certain I understand the ramifications of all this," I said, thus proving my own vast ignorance...unless the smartest response to confronting the unknown is to admit that one is clueless. If that was the case, I was a stone genius.

She dug back into her lobster and I into my steak.

"OK," she said at length. "Let's talk about this in terms you understand."

"Words of one syllable or less?" I suggested.

"You're into the whole detective genre," she said. "Which private eye would you peg as an example of the Thinking type?"

"Oh. Sherlock Holmes. Clearly. High intelligence, logical and analytical, but cold, calculating, emotionally stunted. A social outcast."

"There ya go! How about the Sensation type?"

"Mike Hammer," I stated confidently. "Ain't no problem that can't be solved with a punch in the face or a bullet in the gut, or vice versa. Baby."

"And the Feeling type?"

That took a second. "Kojak. Not the brightest bulb, but his moral compass was always working overtime. And the Intuitive type can only be Colombo. He always knows right from the get-go who the killer is and doggedly pursues clues to create a chain of evidence that proves his intuition correct. And as an Intuitive type, his weakest function would be the opposite pole, Sensation, which explains the rumpled suits and overcoat, his fondness for cheap cigars, and his ancient automobile. Always love the way he acts like a scatterbrain, and ends every interrogation with his signature phrase, 'Just one more thing, sir.'"

"Well, congratulations," Laurel said with a smile. "You passed the pop quiz."

I was feeling very proud of myself.

"Every one of them an exemplary practitioner of the detectionary arts," I said. "And where would you rank me in this pantheon of detective luminaries?"

She offered a forkful of lobster. "Want a Scooby snack?"

"Zoinks," I mumbled to myself. But I took the lobster.

"I'll go ya one better," I said, swallowing the morsel. But not my pride. "Show you I know what you're talking about. Mr. Spock: Thinking type. Dr. McCoy: Feeling type, damn it, Jim. Mr. Scott, the engineer in charge of the Enterprise: Sensation.

He can tell the state of the ship just by feeling its vibrations. Mighty fond o' his dram. And Captain Kirk: Intuitive. Always with a brilliant, unexpected solution that logic, grumbling, or drinking could never devise."

"Going for extra credit. Proving you're worth your salt."

"Then can you please pass the shaker?"

"You've gotten to know this client of yours a bit, I trust?" she said as she handed over the salt shaker. "How would you analyze him in terms of Jungian functions?"

I took a bite of salty steak and gave it some thought while ruminating. Or I ruminated while chewing my steak. Either way.

"I'd say he was a Thinking type. He's clearly brilliant, intellectual, well-read. It seems to be a point of pride to him to always be the smartest guy in the room, which would indicate the high value he places on thinking…and the poor judgment of his Feeling function, if he thinks a person's worth is based on how smart they are. And if he's a Thinking type, that would explain why he's so inconsistent and scattered emotionally—the Feeling function would be his least developed trait, so he has trouble relating to people. He's cruel, he berates them, he breaks down crying… He has little control over his own emotions. He can't help himself—he's as much a victim of his anger and moods as his targets are."

"And his backup function?"

"Intuition," I said. "He has a great appreciation for art and design, and he often seems to know what people want before they know themselves. Reading unconscious clues intuitively, isn't that what you said? That would make his Sensation function relatively unconscious, which might account for his weird attitudes toward food and dress and hygiene. But even his intuition is often out of his control, ambushed by that undeveloped Feeling function and wielded as a weapon. He seems to have an uncanny insight into what a person's biggest fear or most egregious weakness is, for example, and he exploits that ability ruthlessly in order to control them."

"Congratulations," Laurel announced. "You pass the final exam."

"Does that earn me another Scooby snack?"

Chapter 10.5

We returned to eating as I mulled over her tutorial. I wanted to feel smart and smug—my favorite internal states—but something was gnawing at the back of my alleged mind. It took a minute to put my finger on it.

"This is all well and good," I said, "but a quarter of Humanity falls into one of those four categories. An eighth, if we figure in the backup functions. Less accurate than astrology. It's like I always say, there are two types of people—those who divide people into categories."

This time it took her a second to catch on. I win that round.

"What I'm trying to say," I tried to say, "is that when we're talking about an *individual*—and an outlier in this system of psychological categorization at that—details can get lost. Overlooked. We need a finer-grained view of this guy. There's something just a little...*off* about him. I mean, there are plenty of Thinking-Intuitive types, but his personal psychology goes off the charts in places unaddressed by a simple, general analysis like that. Why is he so cruel, for instance? Why the unconscionable rudeness and active insulting? How can he be sensitive to art and design in objects but aggressively, unrepentantly insensitive to people? Why does he seem incapable of displaying empathy or remorse? And so on."

She sipped some more wine and pushed some lobster shell around her plate. I kept quiet, waiting for her to activate her monumental Thinking function and formulate a response.

"OK," she said at length. "Let's dig a little deeper. What do we know about him—specifically him—rather than some theoretical person or textbook example? Can we, for instance, safely say these things about him: He has unusual eating habits and strange work habits."

"Yes."

"He's contradictory but either doesn't recognize it or doesn't care."

"Yes."

"He's arrogant, entitled, competitive, and hypersensitive to criticism; he feels he's destined to do great things in the world."

"Definitely."

"He's emotionally unstable occasionally, cruel sporadically, and has a seductive power to manipulate people and get them to do what he wants."

"Oh my, yes."

"He sees other people as pawns on his chessboard rather than human beings with their own thoughts, feelings, hopes, dreams, and desires. They are objects to be exploited to get him what he wants."

"Yep."

"Well, from what I recall of my recent reading in the DSM, that's the very definition of Narcissistic Personality Disorder. And beneath all the other traits—maybe even the core pathology—is a demonstrable lack of empathy. No conscience, no remorse for his actions. Expecting him to be more considerate and less self-centered is like asking a deaf man to critique a Beethoven symphony. He simply lacks the capacity."

"Wow," I said. "Wish I'd taken that class."

"No," she demurred. "The last thing you need is a mirror."

"Not true," I objected. "I never met a mirror I didn't like."

"I rest my case," she said sweetly. Sometimes she can be enigmatic, I reflected.

"That's a pretty spot-on analysis," I said. "But there are details that don't fit. He's got a pretty good sense of humor, for one."

"Does he laugh at your jokes?"

"No."

"Well, then, maybe you're right."

"I thought you were gonna be good." She gave an exaggerated shrug. "Besides, from what I understand, narcissists don't typically believe in religion, and Steve claims to be a Buddhist. Made a journey of self-discovery to India, spent a lot of time in Buddhist monasteries and retreats. Although the way he tries to mind-control people, I think he thinks he's a Jedi." I adopted a nasal British accent. " 'The Force can have a strong influence on the weak-minded.' "

She shrugged again, this time as acknowledgment. "Not every sociopath exhibits every one of those traits."

"So you're saying he's a sociopath? If he's a sociopath, how'd he become so successful?"

"Well, there is the concept of the high-functioning sociopath," she said. "People who actually get big things done even if they have to steamroll over people in their way. Thomas Edison, for instance. Think entrepreneurs, business magnates, political aspirants."

"Not to mention many sociopaths."

"The danger for that type is that the worse they act the more success they achieve."

I nodded. "Makes sense. If their controlling and manipulative behavior is rewarded, they have no reason to change it and every reason to double down. But that's a long-term risk. That's an assessment that can only be made over the long haul. Steve is young. We can't know if he qualifies."

"Only time will tell," she agreed. "And don't overlook the possibility that he's not an actual sociopath at all, but just a pretender."

"Like Chrissi Hynde?"

"Not that kind of Pretender. A performer playing a part. He might have known some sociopaths in his life and observed their behavior and their ability to bend others to their will, and has just adopted their strategies. He'll use unexpected bad behavior as a tool to manipulate others, to catch them off guard or knock them off balance, for instance. And if he doesn't try to hide it, like you say, it could be because he's a victim of it himself and can't help himself, or it might be because he's mastered those antisocial techniques and uses them as tools, purposefully.

"Yeah. He's got brass balls. Or brass in pocket."

"Or maybe he's decided that the end justifies the means."

"Maybe," I said. "Or could be we're just overthinking it."

"I'm sure that's an accusation you deal with almost constantly," she said.

"I mean maybe he's just a prima donna—a spoiled brat who throws tantrums when he doesn't get what he wants."

She nodded. "An *enfant terrible*."

Three years of high school French and I could still only guess I understood what she was saying. I might as well have taken three years of French from Marcel Marceau.

"Well, he's young," she continued. "What did you say? Twenty-four? Maybe he'll outgrow his terrible two-ohs."

"You say that like we're old."

"We're pushing thirty, buddy," she said quietly, as though revealing a secret. "We *are* old."

"Eh?" I said, cupping a hand to one ear. "Speak up, dagnab it. I left my ear trumpet in the Model T."

"There's one other explanation I can think of," she said, dipping a last bit of lobster into the melted butter and gracefully tasting it. "It might be us."

"You mean, *we* might be sociopaths? That would explain a lot..."

"No, no. What I mean is our ability to interpret extreme behavior might be limited. We might be analyzing his unusual personality through the lens of our own expectations as late twentieth-century, white, middle-class Baby Boomer Americans. Our own programming that defines us but also imprisons us."

"Not sure I follow you."

"What I'm saying is he might be so eccentric—so many standard deviations from the average personality—that we simply *can't* understand his complexity. I mentioned Edison? He was a total asshole to his employees, but he changed the world. Tesla was fixated on the number three, he was in love with a pigeon, and he had any number of additional quirks. But he changed the world, even though a modern shrink would probably label him obsessive-compulsive."

"Never heard that one before."

"Another new diagnostic term from DSM-III. Always finding new and improved ways to label us crazy. But anyway, Tesla's research virtually created the modern world: alternating current electricity, radio, and on and on. Disney was a tyrant to his employees, despite his public image as genial old 'Uncle Walt.' Henry Ford was an antisemite. Picasso was by all accounts a sex addict. Gandhi used to sleep with a pair of thirteen-year-old girls because he thought it kept him young—and he changed the world for the better despite his, uh, unorthodox behavior. We'd probably label him a pervert today. A pedophile. And if we're listing world-class eccentrics, do I even need to mention Howard Hughes?"

"Oh. OK. Yeah. I get it. I think. It's like the guy from the Mothers of Invention said in their movie *200 Motels:* 'Jeff's imagination has gone beyond the fringe of audience comprehension!'"

"There you go," she agreed. "And we're the audience."

"Interesting theory. But it still doesn't help me determine whether he's a visionary or a sociopath."

"It does, however, indicate that the two are not mutually exclusive, even though there's no question that the behavior of all those visionaries is clearly..."

"Aberrant," I finished for her.

"Unconventional," she suggested.

"Bizarre," I redefined.

"Idiosyncratic," she re-redefined.

"Abnormal," I insisted.

"Offbeat," she proposed.

"Outlandish," I determined.

"Quirky," she euphemized.

"Oddball."

"Kooky."

"Fucked up," I decided. "Fucking nuts."

"OK, have it your way, King Burger. But every one of them made significant contributions to modern society. My point is it's possible that their...*unusual* behaviors are as difficult for us to understand as their accomplishments. Could you think up the light bulb or AC power or a personal computer?"

"I can barely think up what to get you for Christmas."

"It's almost impossible for people like you and me to get into the heads of people like that," she continued, "especially without interpreting their behavior in terms of what *we* consider normal. All I'm saying is that maybe we *can't* understand someone who's that eccentric because our own interpretive tools are too limited. Our own view is blindered."

"Well, if it's a choice between my blindered interpretation and his reality distortion field," I said, polishing off the last of my baked potato, "I choose me. Even if he is maybe a sociopath."

"Well, be careful," she cautioned. "You're very suggestible."

"If you say so," I shrugged.

"And you already hang out with one flagrant sociopath."

"Oh, Jimmy's harmless," I protested. "He walks a yellow brick road, not a socio path. Not to mention he's very useful. I can talk him into doing a lot of things for me."

"Mm-hm. Like Steve talks you into doing things for him? Birds of a feather?"

I couldn't argue with her. Or, apparently, manipulate her. But if I was a sociopath, maybe later I could seduce her. And make her believe it was her idea, heh heh. I was beginning to see the advantages of sociopathy.

By now we'd finished our banquet. Ordinarily, I would have suggested dessert and we'd dawdle over coffee, but it was getting late and I had to be up early to go to f'in work. When you work for Pacific Bell, you can't just phone it in.

Fine dining etiquette informs us that when done eating, one places one's knife and fork (tines down) angled across the plate at 10 o'clock and 4 o'clock. I was a classy guy, so I did this. I'd read recently that fine dining etiquette also insists that one leave one's final bite on the plate. Apparently, this was a signal to the waiter that you were done, which seems contradictory. How can one be done if there is still food left on the plate? In addition, it seemed to me to be an egregious waste of food, of money, and of one last taste of a gourmet meal. So this I did not do. Since I am a class act, however, I refrained from either belching or licking the plate. Such are the sacrifices we make to local social mores. Once again, I found myself considering the advantages of sociopathy…

"So was any of this helpful?" Laurel asked.

"Yes and no," I shrugged. "Maybe he's a sociopath; maybe not. Doesn't matter. I'm still gonna try to save his life."

"We could expect no less," she said. She might be undecided about Steve's personality, but not about mine—for better *and* for worse, damn her anyway.

Our waiter approached us. But instead of clearing, he asked me, "Are you Mr. Wong?"

I knew where this was going. "Close enough," I replied.

"There's a call for you. You can use the phone at the bar downstairs."

I excused myself (since I am both polite and aware of etiquette) and went downstairs. The phone was sitting on the bar. I picked it up and said hello. As I suspected, it was Jim with his Wong number.

"I'm calling from a pay phone at the airport," he said without preamble. "No way they can eavesdrop on us this way. We're a go for tomorrow night."

"How'd you know I'd be here?"

"Where else would you take Laurel when you had a few extra bucks?"

"Am I that predictable?"

"Only about food."

"Speaking of which, if we're gonna be there all night you better bring me a sandwich. I don't think I can smuggle one in. But not Blimpies."

"'The World's Second-Best Taste Treat'?" he said. "Of course not. You want a veal parm from All American on Moorpark—the place across the street from Arthur Treacher's Fish & Chips."

"Yes," I said. Predictably. "And fuck you." Bet he didn't predict that.

He hung up without saying goodbye. If anyone else did that I'd think they were terribly rude, or in a movie, where no one ever says goodbye before they hang up.

"What was that all about?" Laurel asked, one eyebrow raised, when I returned to our table.

I put on my best poker face.

"Telemarketer," I said.

Chapter 11

Thursday, April 17

The following morning I reported to work a few minutes early. Not dedication…I didn't want to risk blowing the whole caper by being late and being fired. And, as I'd done yesterday and the days before, I sat in my cubicle wearing my headset and repeated the PhoneCo mantra 700 times, although by late afternoon it was less Om and more Omigodwillitneverend?

At 4:51, I raised my hand.

"Yes?" said a voice in my earphones.

"Bathroom break please."

"Your shift is over in less than ten minutes," the voice informed me. "Can't you, uh, hold it until then?"

"Afraid not," I apologized.

"OK, go ahead."

I went. But I did not go to the Men's Room, and I did not return to my station. Instead, I turned my bathroom break into a prison break. I ducked into a supply closet and locked the door. Always worked for Superman. With fifty bodies to shepherd, I knew my corporate mistresses would never miss one that wasn't escorted out. I further assumed that no one would be looking for office equipment after hours. And if anyone did, I could always just jump out and yell, "Supplies!"

I took a seat on a stack of boxes and waited over an hour, until I couldn't hear any human activity. At 6:00 I left the closet and scouted the first-floor offices cautiously. As Ferrette had predicted, the building was a ghost town—no workers, no janitors, no security guards.

I rolled an office chair down a hallway to the back door we'd agreed would be his point of entry. Now all I had to do was wait for him to show up. I wouldn't have any dinner until he arrived, but I did have a paperback in my pocket to keep me distracted, and I settled in to read.

The book was a comic crime caper entitled *Sand Dollars* by one Dmitri S. Abbott, and concerned a Jersey wiseguy wannabe who witnesses a mob hit and goes into the Witness Protection program. WITSEC relocates him to Silicon Valley, and once he assesses the territory ("cases the joint"), he hits on a scam in which he pitches some impossible product (known locally as "vaporware") to groups of venture capitalists with the intention of collecting the millions of dollars they invest and then absconding with the dough. ("He put the 'con' in Silicon Valley" read the blurb on the back cover.)

The book had caught my eye precisely because it was set in Silicon Valley—a location unused in fiction to date, mystery or otherwise, but so ripe for mockery it was a wonder no one had thought of it before. I was not disappointed when I read the opening lines:

I thought there'd be more people at my funeral. The fucks.

I'd just reached the point where, after settling in and scouting the lay of the land, the protagonist, Tony Jehovah ("no relation"), has given up on "tryna find a decent hoagie in this jerkwater berg," when I heard a tiny tapping at the door.

I opened it. And there was Jim, dressed all in black and wearing a black watch cap.

"Going commando," I observed.

"How'd you know that?" he said, tugging at the crotch of his jeans.

He stepped inside. He had a duffel bag nearly as big as he was slung over one shoulder.

We headed off down the corridor toward the lobby.

"What have you been doing for the past four days?" I said, trying to keep the irritation out of my voice. Unsuccessfully.

He shook his duffel bag. "Following phone company trucks around. To get the equipment I need. The lineman goes to lunch, I go shopping."

"With a five-finger phone phreak discount. No wonder you don't mind a bit of B&E."

"It's not Breaking and Entering if you let me in."

We'd reached a bullpen full of desks but empty of employees. Jim dropped his duffel bag on one, unzipped it, and pulled out a foot-long, paper-wrapped tube. "Speaking of lunch, here ya go." He handed me the sandwich. "Veal parm from All American, as requested. Couldn't carry a drink, though."

"I can get a Coke from the vending machine. Thanks, man."

"Don't thank me. Thank Steve—I'm adding the cost of that sandwich to my itemized expense invoice. Where're the stairs?"

"Right around the corner. I'll take you."

"Nah. Have your dinner. I need to do some recon."

I shrugged. "Your call."

Jim disappeared into the building. I sat at a desk, unwrapped my sandwich, and opened my paperback.

Maybe half an hour later, he returned. He'd left empty-handed but now he was carrying a console of some sort, about the size of a large typewriter. He stowed it in his bag.

"What're you, uh…liberating there?" I asked reluctantly.

"It's a PBX. A multiline phone console. Kind of a mini-switchboard businesses use to route calls internally. I'll need it to consolidate the lines we'll be piggybacking on. Ready to go?"

I tossed my sandwich wrapper in a trash can.

"Rookie error, grasshopper," Jim admonished, retrieving my wrapper and stuffing it in his bag. "Leave no trace."

"Yeah, OK," I agreed. "No paper trail. Literally."

We headed off down the hall. I slipped my book into my pocket

"What're you reading?" he asked.

"Comic crime caper." I pulled out the book and showed him the cover.

"What, no Chandler? No Parker? No John D. MacDonald?"

"This one is more like Donald E. Westlake. I love his stuff. I wish I could write like him."

"I've read his comic crime capers," Jim said sarcastically. "Shit like that never happens in real life."

"I know," I sighed and slipped the book back into my pocket. "So what do you want me to do?"

He hitched the duffel bag up on his shoulder as we walked. "Can you find a cart or something so we can move around without having to carry all this stuff?"

"Wait right here." I went back to the supply closet I'd hidden in and returned pushing a wheeled cart.

"Perfect," Jim said. He transferred the bag to the cart and off we went into the bowels of the beast.

He stopped at a freight elevator and pushed the button.

"Your reconnaissance pay off?" I asked.

"Found an elevator, anyway," he shrugged.

When the car arrived, we entered and rolled the cart in.

"I gotta tell ya, man," Jimmy said, pressing the button for 3, "that client of yours is some piece of work."

"He thinks he's some piece of fruit. An apple."

"Crabby Appleton, maybe. Remember him?"

"From the Tom Terrific cartoons?" I recalled. " 'Crabby Appleton…he's rotten to the core.'"

"But I think he's more like a pear. A prickly pear."

"Yeah, before they made him they broke the mold."

"Well, he's got a wild hair up his ass, that's for sure."

"He's a Pisces, so it's probably a March hare," I said as the elevator rose slowly. "Laurel thinks he might be a sociopath, or at least that he, uh, exhibits numerous sociopathic tendencies."

He nodded. "High-functioning sociopath. Probably Narcissistic Personality Disorder."

"How do you know that?

He grinned widely. "Takes one to know one."

" 'Behold the lowly sociopath'," I recited from memory. "'He does not give a damn. I wish I was a sociopath. My God, perhaps I am!'"

We exited on the third floor. Jim set off into the building and I rolled the cart along behind him.

"We're gonna have to move fast," he said.

"OK. Move fast but don't break anything," I counseled.

The corridor we were walking through stretched from one wall to a virtual vanishing point at the other end of the building. The entire passageway was lined with metal racks stuffed full of mechanical and electrical equipment. It looked like the Quement Electronics store had exploded, but symmetrically somehow. I peered around the corner and saw another identical corridor. Same on the other side. I had no doubt this entire floor consisted of these equipment corridors—possibly every floor of the building except the ground floor. Bell had come a long way from banks of women in long dresses and puffy blouses sitting on stools in front of switchboards and plugging cords into jacks all day long.

Jim stopped in front of one panel and began unloading his tools, which included a set of screwdrivers rolled up in a leather pouch along with wire cutters, wire strippers, and pliers, both regular and needle nose. He removed several binders, which I could only assume were technical manuals, as well as little boxes full of wires and wire wrap caps, jacks and plugs, alligator clips, tiny light bulbs, and other arcane bits and pieces. And, of course, since he was a guy, a roll of duct tape. The most unusual tool he had was a telephone handset with a dial built into it—probably a piece of equipment liberated from some lineman who'd have to explain where he'd lost it. The handset had alligator clips attached to the end of a pair of loose wires.

Jim consulted his binder, scanned a panel, and set to work with a screwdriver. He was absorbed, so I took the opportunity to wander up and down the numerous corridors. Each one consisted of a lattice of gray metal frames filled with rack after rack and bank after bank of components, both mechanical and electrical: crossbar switches, junction boxes and wiring frames; markers, meters, and modules; senders and relays; vertical cylinders the size of my sandwich jam-packed with wipers, ratchets, pawls, blades, armatures, miscellaneous widgets, and numerous other oddly-shaped mechanical clockwork pieces I could not identify and had no words to describe. Bundles of black cables and miles of wires in a rainbow of colors stretched through every cabinet like nerves running through a skeletal frame.

Every corridor also had a console with a keyboard, a computer monitor, and dozens of lighted buttons on its panel, as well as switches and digital displays flashing various numerals. And each mechanical panel had line after line of tiny lights—mostly green or white; some flashing yellow or occasionally, red. The entire corridor was lit up like a festive Christmas tree or like your insane neighbor's overambitious Christmas display. Each panel, each tiny component, each rack and frame and piece of equipment was labeled with a number or an alphanumeric code. I'd expected the place to be an ear-irritating concatenation of clicks, clacks, and clunks, but was impressed by how quiet it was, what with all these hundreds and hundreds of devices whirring ceaselessly in peripatetic movement. The whole building hummed, but only as background noise.

Eventually, I circled back to Jim, who was standing in front of another rack. He'd removed its front panel and had his handset hooked up to it. When he saw me approaching, he held up an index finger to caution me to be quiet while he was on the phone.

"San Jose node," he said. "Number one test board." He listened for a moment then disconnected his handset. "Shit."

"I feel like I've been swallowed by Robby the Robot," I said as he replaced the panel. He looked something up in a binder, then moved the cart down to another rack, where he removed the front panel with the screwdriver and scanned the contents. He attached his handset and dialed a number.

"San Jose node," he said. "Number one test board." He listened for a second then detached the clips and muttered "Shit."

And this is how we spent the next several hours, in an infinite loop of removing panels, testing a line and pronouncing it shit, then replacing panels, checking manuals, and rolling the cart to the next rack or box or mechanical tower Jim thought might serve our needs.

We exhausted the third floor and moved to the fourth which, as far as I could discern, was identical to the third, and proceeded with our seemingly unproductive task.

While he stayed busy checking boards, I was just getting bored.

"What exactly are you trying to do?" I asked at one point, in an attempt to stay awake and stave off the monotony.

"The Bell System," he said distractedly, poking around inside the panel, "is the single biggest integrated machine in the world. All the parts—and there are millions of them—interconnect and work in harmony. I'm trying to exploit a loophole in the technology to get the machine to do something it was never designed to do. And I'm trying to get it to do that without leaving a footprint, or any trace of what we're doing."

"Yeah, but, y'know, what exactly?"

He sighed and tapped his screwdriver on the massive machine in front of him.

"I'm trying to capture a unicorn," he said. "I'm attempting to access various electromechanical stepping switches—tandem switches that route trunk lines—using a line finder. It might have been easier if they still used the mechanical Strowger switches, where the selection shafts and wipers are right out in the open in bank assemblies and easy to access, but it looks like most of the Bell system has been upgraded to Four-A computer units, which are now the brains of the long-distance network. The Four-A's are electronic switching machines that automatically figure out how to route a long-distance call. I'm attempting to circumvent them. To trick them into ignoring our held lines once I complete the circuits. I'm trying to create a stable artificial pathway for the lines we want to hold."

"OK, I'm with you so far."

"This requires juggling three balls," he continued. "I want the most direct route, for one, so we don't have to pass through multiple switching stations, because the more complicated these connections get, the higher the risk that something could go wrong. I also want to route our lines across minimally-traveled circuits and through fully automated nodes in various obscure switching stations. Minimally-traveled because we don't want the calls to be rerouted if the line experiences heavy activity, in which case it might drop our call and we'd lose our connection, and fully automated because we don't want some random operator noticing our unusual activity and reporting it. So I'm searching for idle trunks to establish a path. The unicorn part is that the least used nodes are the last to be automated, so I keep getting live operators on the line, which disqualifies it as a line we can use. OK?"

"Well, what are the steps you're taking?"

He grimaced and snorted.

"Even if I could spell out the technical steps, do you really think you could understand what I'm trying to do?"

We both knew the answer was no.

"Yes," I said.

"Yeah, when pigs fly," he scoffed. "C'mon, man. What was it Elvis said? 'A little less conversation, a little more action, please?' What I need right now is a little less conversation, a lot more concentration. We don't have all night, y'know."

"Actually, we do, but..." I had to choose my words carefully. There was more than one way to make what I wanted to say sound insulting. *"If you were really as smart as you claim to be..."* would be one. *"If you were really as smart as you think you are..."* would be another. But I think I landed on a winner:

"...but if you're really as smart as I think you are," I continued, "you'd be able to explain this to me in a way I can understand."

He considered this for a few seconds.

"This building is the string. I'm attaching our tin can to theirs."

"All right then."

"So could you please do me a favor and just back the fuck off?" he said irritably. "Read your book. Take a nap. Do some fucking thing. But leave me alone and let me work."

"I don't have to be told twice," I said, hoping I didn't sound petulant.

"Yeah," he grumbled. "More like three times."

I took the hint and shut up. He returned to work.

Around 4:30 AM I saw him smile. "Bingo," he announced. "Yahtzee." He wiggled his fingers like a cartoon safecracker and aimed a crazed, wide-eyed smile at me. "We're in."

"Cool," I said, suppressing a yawn. Didn't want to rain on his parade.

And he got to work, attaching alligator clips and switching out plug-in jacks. "Hand me that small needle-nose, would you?" he said, motioning toward the cart where his tools were laid out. "And one of those little white lights."

I found the pliers and the tiny bulb and handed them to him. He pried a bulb out of the back of the panel he'd removed and replaced it with the bulb he'd brought.

"Do I dare interrupt you to ask what you're doing, or is it something so clever that you can't resist interrupting yourself," I said, knowing full well the answer.

"If the bulb never blinks red, no one will ever know there's a problem," he chuckled, replacing the panel.

I'd spotted something sticking out of an unzipped pocket on his bag and out of sheer boredom returned to snoop. It was a pair of airline boarding passes. One was for San Jose to JFK on a red-eye last Tuesday night—two days ago. The other was for a return red-eye Wednesday night. Yesterday. What the flying fuck?

"Hey, Jimmy?" I said, risking his wrath at being interrupted once again. "How were you able to follow phone company trucks around while you were in New York?"

He stopped dead in his tracks and looked at me, head cocked. "How did you…?"

"You forget I'm a detective."

"Who wouldn't? What makes you think I was in New York?"

I waved the boarding passes.

He grimaced and clenched his fists. "God*damn*it! I forgot to toss those."

"Yeah," I chided. "Paper trail. Rookie error, grasshopper. So why were you in New York?"

He sighed deeply.

"OK, so here's the deal," he admitted. "Once I had a chance to think through the details of this little caper, I realized I couldn't tap into AT&T's phone lines remotely. The corporate offices."

"You said the FBI and NSA can do it."

"Yeah. But I'm not the FBI or the NS fucking A. Not to mention that they work *with* the phone company to establish those legal taps. I just don't have the resources or the equipment they have. I realized that the only way I could make this work was if I had physical access to the switchboard in their main offices, where the phone lines we want to tap are located. 195 Broadway. In Manhattan."

"So you take a red-eye to New York…"

"I bring a tech uniform with me, and before I leave I forge a company ID badge and a work order, and I stroll right in. They're too insulated to think anyone would want to infiltrate their HQ and too presumptuous to believe anyone could. Bunch of arrogant narcissists. If Jobs had any introspection, he'd probably understand them perfectly. And I spent a couple hours locating the lines and installing my, uh, upgrades."

"Which were...?"

"Well, essentially what we discussed. I split each of the lines so all calls go to their destination and also to our destination. Irony is, I hacked a couple of their own services, call forwarding and third-party calling, to do this. And on our lines, I'll make them 'held calls,' so they're always connected to my recording device. The microphones on their phones will always be on...as soon as I make the connections, anyway, and hold the lines. Even when the handset is in the cradle, the microphone and the line to us will still be live. Each desk phone becomes a full-time, never-ending phone call. To us."

"So what are we doing here?"

"Connecting the other end of those lines. Switching them from their HQ through this switching station to our little local switchboard—my numbers, the one with the computer and tape recorder attached. Connecting their tin can to our tin can."

"Now wait a minute," I said. "Hold the phone. You've been working 'round the clock for the past, what, three days?" No wonder he was grouchy. "Did you get any sleep on the flights?"

"No, I was busy reviewing the technical manuals I picked up at AT&T. Another bonus of going there in person."

" 'I'll sleep when I'm dead,' huh?"

He took a deep breath.

"For the billions of years since the universe big banged into being," he said, "and until about thirty years ago, there was no James J. Ferrette the Fourth to enjoy this earthly paradise. Fifty or sixty years from now—despite what the cryogenics and life extension evangelists say—the universe will once again be devoid and deprived of the presence of James J. Ferrette the Fourth for the rest of its billions of years of existence. During that brief slice of eternity, I intend to take full advantage of what this crap planet has to offer. So as long as there are gourmet meals uneaten, exceptional liquor undrunk, and nubile young women willing to explore the depths of their sensuality and sexuality, I will remain steadfast in my hedonistic mission."

I nodded. "Eat, drink, and make merry."

He nodded soberly. “As long as it’s spelled M-A-R-Y.”

“Well, I’m impressed by your involvement.”

“*Commitment*,” he insisted. “It’s like ham and eggs—the chicken is involved, but the pig is *committed.* And it was only because of that commitment that I was able to wander around AT&T’s library and score those binders full of technical specs that I needed for our little mission…not to mention *this*.” He dug around in his duffel bag and pulled out what looked like a large paperback book with the AT&T logo on the cover.

“And that would be…?

“The Holy Grail, man! The internal phone book for AT&T headquarters…including the private phone numbers and extensions for every executive and every conference room in the building, informing me about exactly which lines I need to tap. They’ve got a million employees but I only needed a dozen phone numbers, and I could never have known which ones without this internal phone book. This is pure gold! Totally worth the time and the cost of the trip. Especially since I’m adding the plane tickets to my itemized expense invoice to Jobs.” He laughed his deep, crazy laugh.

I laughed too. Maybe I was just giddy from being up all night, but I also realized that my four days of boredom, sitting in a chair and repeating the same phrase over and over, paled in comparison to the effort Jimmy the Ferret had put in.

“I think we’re done here,” he announced once we’d stopped laughing. We packed up his bag and headed for the elevator.

“Here, yeah,” I said. “But you still have to, what, hook up the held lines?”

“Yeah. Well, establish them. First I have to run a dozen lines to my apartment and into that multiline console they’ve so graciously loaned us.” He patted his duffel bag.

“That’s not a problem?”

“Nah. My apartment complex is huge. You’ve been there. They have their own switchboard. Fully automated, and with dozens of unused lines reserved for future growth, future tenants.”

“And they’ll just let you monkey around with the switchboard?”

"Man, give me some credit, will ya? I fix things for the management all the time. I go out of the way to ingratiate myself to them. Because I'm a swell guy."

"Of course," I agreed vehemently. "Certainly not so they can return the favor in circumstances like this."

"Duh. It's called 'quid pro quo,' Smarticus. All I need to do is make a couple of garbled calls to the rental office, then show up, and they'll beg me to check out the switchboard and fix it instead of waiting days for Ma Bell to send out a tech minion. I hook up the lines to my apartment, feed 'em into this mini console, then into the computer Mr. Jobs so graciously loaned us, then to the tape recorder. The tricky part is establishing the held lines. I have to call each one and make sure they answer, so I can hold the line."

"What're you gonna use to make the connection, the Wong number?"

"Nah. These guys are top-level execs. They have admins whose job is to shield them from calls like the Wong number prank. Or irate customers calling to complain. I'll probably use the one that never fails."

"Oh. 'This is Doctor Steinberg's office calling with his test results.'"

He chuckled. "Yep. They always take those calls. If the admin gives me any resistance, I just insist that the exec specifically requested to be contacted the minute the results of his syphilis test were returned. They put me through immediately then. They might have a stake in the answer themselves. And once I get the connection I hold their line. I'll do all this early tomorrow."

"You mean later today."

"Yeah, whatever. It's Friday, so most of the AT&T execs will probably be in their offices. I'll place the calls and hold the lines, test the recording and Jobs' word filter. Then Monday I'll start monitoring seriously."

"What?!" I exclaimed. "Nothing over the weekend?"

He shrugged. "A nap, maybe."

"You're sure nobody's gonna notice your hack?"

"Maybe someday," he said. "Not in the next week or two, which is probably all we need. First they'd have to suspect something. They're too arrogant for that."

"They're not gonna notice any odd tones or clicks from your taps?"

He scoffed. "You think those guys dial their own phones? That's what their secretaries are for. That, and getting coffee. And, you know, the ol' slap and tickle."

"Jesus, Jim, it's like the Women's Movement never happened in your world."

"The only woman's movement I like is—"

"No, no, don't drag me down that rabbit hole."

He giggled a deep, dirty giggle. "Speaking of rabbit holes, remind me to tell you sometime about a book I read, *Oedipus in Disneyland*, that claims *Alice in Wonderland* is actually Queen Victoria's coded sexual memoirs. That's some mind-bending shit there, man."

We reached the back door and walked out.

"Ladies and gentlemen, Elvis has left the building," Jimmy said expressly.

"Back through the looking-glass," I sighed. "Still not sure which side is which, though."

"What's the problem?"

"Well, it's just kind of…anti-climactic, is all. In those Westlake comic caper novels, they usually manage to evade all laws except Murphy's Law, which is strictly enforced. At some point, everything they plan goes kablooey and they have to improvise. But everything we've been planning has gone off without a hitch. Except maybe your detour to the Big Apple."

"I told you that stuff never happens in real life," he said.

"Still," I sighed. "No car chases, no shootouts. Just nerd stuff and a lot of blah blah blah."

"Speaking of nerd stuff," he said, "it's nearly eight AM. You gonna stay for your shift?"

We both had a good laugh over that. Then we went down the street to the Quality Café and had a hearty breakfast. On Steve's dollar.

Chapter 12.0

Friday, April 18

I took Friday off to sleep. Jim still had work to do and Bragg was covering Steve, so there was really nothing for me to do but wait. I hate waiting. I beat my brains up for something I could do to move this case forward. I could relieve Bragg on watching-the-watchmen duty, maybe. I even considered returning to my temp job at Bell. Sometimes I make myself laugh. Too bad it's far more often than I make other people laugh.

Eventually, I decided to take the day off, just to take a breather—to decompress a bit from the events of the previous week. Choosing to do nothing qualifies as doing something, I reasoned. As Tweedle-Dee and Tweedle-Dum put it, "That's logic!"

I was so proud of my reasoning abilities that I decided to take the weekend off as well.

See you Monday!

Chapter 12.1

Monday, April 21

Monday I was back in the office, doing little more than waiting. Again. I hate waiting.

Sometime in the afternoon I got tired of waiting and headed over to Ferrette's place. He didn't try to escape this time, but let me right in.

He'd turned his living room into a kind of makeshift call center. He'd set up a long folding table in front of one of the couches and organized his tools on the table: the multiplex phone switchboard console he'd spirited away from the phone company building, the Apple III computer Steve had, um, *loaned* him, and a cassette tape recorder. Which I assume he had, or found. Or stole. I did not assume he'd purchased it, unless it, too, was going on his invoice to Steve.

We settled onto opposite couches. "So how's it goin'?" I asked, shooting a chin toward the table of tools.

"Technically, perfect," he said. "Screw Donald E. Westlake." He pointed to each piece of equipment as he explained his setup. "I managed to connect with all twelve lines we wanted, and held them. I channel them through my makeshift switchboard, that PBX unit. Steve's guy came by last week and plugged a Charley board and a voice analyzer board into the computer—the thing that alerts to keywords I programmed into it. And I rigged a switch that activates the tape recorder whenever the computer hears a keyword."

"Anything interesting?"

"Nah. Not yet, anyway. Only a couple of those guys were in their offices over the weekend. I didn't wait for a keyword to be detected—I just listened in at random, to check that the system works. It does. I hear them and everything that goes on in their offices, whether they're using the phone or not. And they don't hear me, or seem to notice me, uh, hovering over their shoulder."

"Like an angel," I deadpanned.

"If you insist," he shrugged. "So now I just sit and listen."

"It's a stakeout."

"I wish I had a steak. I can't even call for pizza—all my lines are held."

I congratulated him on his technical expertise and left. But I went to the Round Table in Santa Clara, near Santa Clara University, and to the Safeway next door, and returned an hour later with a large sausage and onion, a large pepperoni, and two six-packs of beer.

"Nothing for yourself?" Jim said when I showed up on his doorstep again unexpectedly. I didn't expect him to thank me. But I did expect a slice of pizza. Five, actually. And two beers.

And once we were gorged, I belched and left. Without even saying goodbye. Etiquette would be wasted on a Philistine like the Ferret.

Chapter 12.2

Tuesday, April 22

I was back in the office, doing little more than waiting.
And waiting.
And waiting…

Chapter 12.3

Wednesday, April 23

Waiting…

Chapter 12.4

Thursday, April 24

I was sitting in my office waiting and thinking. When I got tired of waiting, I dusted my Snoopy phone, cleaned my Beretta, and thought about Chekov. And when I got tired of thinking I picked up my paperback of *Sand Dollars* and continued reading about the exploits of a con man in the world of high tech. I noticed something about the book that most people might overlook, namely the author's accurate portrayal of Silicon Valley geography and his spot-on descriptions of our local landmarks, like restaurants. He must have actually spent some time around here, I determined, if he didn't actually live here to begin with.

I'd just reached the point where our anti-hero hits a major snag: some of his investors want to tour his imaginary manufacturing facility and he scrambles to cobble together a fake factory in order to keep the scam alive.

And in a brilliant epiphany, I came up with a plan that—as they say in the movies—was *so crazy it just might work.*

As I was reaching around to pat myself on the back, the door to my office opened and who should walk in but my old buddy the bookstore clerk—the same guy I'd run into when applying for the temp gig at Pac Bell a couple of weeks earlier. What the hell? Was he following me, like some kind of stalker?

He plopped down in my client chair without being invited. A lot of that going around these days.

"Nice place you got here, not," he said by way of greeting.

"And what're you doing here?"

"Groucho sent me," he said. "Actually, The Ferret."

"You mentioned you knew Jim," I said. "But one thing I never got to ask you is how."

"Oh, Jimmy and Casey Bragg and I go way back. You *know* I know Bragg—I introduced you to him when you were trying to figure out why everything Harshlaw wrote came true. I met Jim through Bragg. They were roommates in college or something. So there ya go, and here we are."

"Yeah," I said, "which returns us by a commodius vicus of recirculation to my original question: What're you doing here?"

"Well, The Ferret has Bragg playing watchdog over your current client—but he noticed there were now *two* teams of bad guys tailing your guy around the clock, in twelve-hour shifts, and he couldn't keep up. So Jimmy conscripted me to be another guard dog. Or seeing eye dog. Whatever."

"You left the cushy operator job at Pac Bell for that?"

He laughed. "The phone company was only temp work, and the pay was piss poor. Jimmy says your client is picking up the tab for this stakeout—and that he's a millionaire. I need some of that dough, or I want a slice of that pizza, or whatever you kids are saying these days. And this job is even cushier. I just sit in a car all night and watch the bad guys."

I nodded. "You don't even need to repeat the same phrase seven hundred times a day," I said.

"Right. Bragg and I take twelve-hour shifts and bring each other food when we make the switch. Let the other guy go use the, uh, the facilities. You know, to take a dump. We keep a bottle in the car to—"

"Can you get to the point?"

"Yeah. Sure. Anyway, we each stop by Jimmy's place after our shift and report any activity. In person, so we don't have to use the phone, which is apparently some vital aspect of this surveillance—either that or you guys have all gone completely off your nut with paranoia, but as long as you're paying me, I'll pretend you're sane and doing God's work or whatever."

"And?"

"And nothing. No activity. But when I saw Jimmy a few minutes ago, he sent me here to tell you he's finally hit paydirt and has proof of whatever it is you turkeys are trying to prove. He also said to bring your client around tomorrow, about noon, like you planned. He'll do the big reveal then, whatever the fuck that means."

"Thanks," I said. I reached for my book but picked up my Beretta instead. "Got it. Beat it."

"Hey, don't kill the messenger, man," he whined, waving his hands. "Take a chill pill. And take a fucking cue from Charlie Schulz, not Charlie Manson. Or John Lennon. Happiness is a warm *puppy*, not a warm *gun*!"

Chapter 12.5

Friday, April 25, 11:30 AM

I arrived at The Good Earth in Cupertino, next door to the (old) Apple HQ, about 11:30. I parked behind the restaurant, near the back door, then went in and found a pay phone. Must be an upscale place, I decided, since the phone worked.

I dialed Steve's number—his private, direct number from his business card, and one assuredly tapped by AT&T, so I needed to make the call in code as we'd arranged. He answered promptly. Maybe he was as impatient as I was.

"Dis Mistah Jobs?" I said. After a second or two of silence, he replied yes. "Dis Mistah Wah Wen Wong, your vendor, cawring from China."

"Is this a Wong number?" Steve asked. He'd gotten the coded message. "What can I do for you, Mr. Wong?"

"You overcharge me, you plick!" I said. "Yuan not same as dollar today!"

"Fluctuations," Steve explained.

"Yeah, well, fluc you 'Mericans, too!" I said and hung up.

I went back to my car and waited. About 12:30, Steve ambled out the back door. I pulled up to him and he climbed in.

"You're running late," I said.

"Picked the wrong crowd to take to lunch," he grumbled. "Too many questions. Gotta kick ass every once in a while to keep the bozos motivated. This is wearing me out."

"There's a nap for that," I suggested.

"Y'know, I've been thinking," he said as I pulled out onto Stevens Creek.

"Yeah, first time's always the hardest, innit?"

"That asshole Malone," he continued, ignoring me. "He mentioned the Carterfone agreement between the Justice Department and AT&T?"

"Yeah, what about it?"

"AT&T used what he called the 'Kingsbury Commitment' to trick the Feds. Bell agreed to make what they thought were small concessions to prevent more severe restrictions and to put the lawsuit to rest, right? Isn't that what he said?"

"Yeah. So?"

"So I'm wondering if I couldn't adopt that same strategy against Apple. They're suing us."

"Apple is suing Apple?" I said. "How does that—"

"The other Apple," he explained. "The Beatles' Apple Corps. They're suing us over the use of the name Apple as a corporate name since they had it first. Their lawyers claim it might cause confusion among consumers, which is total bullshit. But that suit's been dragging on for two fucking years now. I'm wondering if we can't offer them a deal: they don't manufacture computers and we don't get into the music business."

"Sounds reasonable," I said. "As long as you never get into the music business."

"Well, I'll burn that bridge when I come to it," he chuckled.

"I guess you should be thanking Malone, then," I said. "For the inspiration as well as the information."

He chuckled a dark, throaty chuckle. "Yeah, right. I know his type—lean and hungry. Writers never make any money. They're always scrambling. I have half a mind to hire him for some impossible, meaningless task, like writing our annual report, and making his life a living hell."

Thus spake The Great Humanitarian…

It was only a ten-minute drive to Jim's apartment. I spent the remaining time filling Jobs in on our exploits in the Bell building the previous week.

"By the time we were done, we were so deep inside the beast I was afraid we'd never find an exit," I wrapped up my saga.

Steve chuckled.

"That's funny?"

" 'There must be some kind of way out of here,'" he replied, " 'said the Joker to the Thief.'"

Before I could ask what that was supposed to mean, he continued—in good humor for once. Will wonders never cease?

"Man, that plan we came up with was pure gold," he enthused. "Brilliant."

I felt certain that if "our" plan had failed he would have disavowed any involvement and branded both Jim and me as dumb shits. But at least he gave us some credit.

"We gotta give The Ferret some strokes, since he did most of the heavy lifting," I said.

"I have to admit," he said, "I gotta wonder what makes a guy like Ferrette tick."

I remembered a favorite line from humorist Jack Douglas. Steve couldn't have given me a more perfect setup.

"That's easy," I said. "Years ago he swallowed a small boy wearing a watch."

Steve did not laugh. Instead, he furrowed his brow and responded, "The kid should have gotten a digital watch. They're silent."

Hoo boy.

Speaking of silence, we drove in it until Steve asked point blank:

"Ferrette. You trust him?"

"As far as I can throw him."

"Typically that's not a good thing."

"You've met him," I said. "He's a little guy. I can throw him pretty far."

Chapter 12.6

A few minutes later we showed up on Jim's doorstep. This time he let us in with no shenanigans and we all took seats in his living room.

"I hear you have some news," Steve said, foregoing any amenities. I wasn't sure whether the tone in his voice was anticipation or trepidation.

"Yup," Jim said with a radiant smile. "Do I ever." He took a minute to fill Steve in on his call center setup and the dozen lines he'd tapped.

I pointed to a green card in the Apple III.

"Is that the word filter?" I asked.

"That's a computer bus," Steve answered, beating Jim to the punch. If you insist on being the smartest guy in the room you occasionally have to prove it. "It's a communication system that transfers data between components, or between computers. It's binary—the data is either on the bus or off the bus."

"I've been on the bus," I reminded him.

"If you're on it, it must be a short bus," Jim said.

"It'll still get me there, as long as the wheels on the bus go round and round."

"Jesus, you guys are bozos," Jobs sighed in exasperation.

"Buddy," I said, "I think we're all bozos on this bus."

"So Jim," Steve said, ignoring me. "What did you find out?"

"First, let me tell you," he said, "it's snooze city to listen to these suits talk business. Finding what we want is like panning for gold. The computer keyword filter swooshes maybe ninety-nine percent of the dreck away, but I have to remove the rest myself. And interpret it."

"The filter works for you, then?" Steve asked.

"Yes and no," Jim replied. "It works almost too well. It picks up on the word 'Jobs,' for instance, but it's ridiculous how many times that word shows up in these calls. Jobs reports, jobs forecast, job security. It picks up 'apple,' but it also alerts if one of them puts in a lunch order for a Waldorf salad 'with apple.' Like it would be a fucking Waldorf salad without apple, for

Christ's sake. And then there's the exec I caught calling an escort service and asking the price of blow—"

"Moving right along..." I encouraged him.

"So it works, but the problem I encountered was that the keywords triggered the tape recorder, but not until the keyword was detected—*after* the word was spoken. So I ended up with a lot of half-sentences out of context."

"Can you get to the point?" Steve snarled.

"Patience, grasshopper. I did find a few flakes of gold and one big nugget. I lucked out when a couple of calls and conference room discussions mentioned both Jobs and Apple—so either keyword started the recording, and we caught the second one on tape so we know they're talking about you."

"And what were they saying about me?"

The Ferret dug around on the table and held up a cassette tape. "I put together a mix tape."

" 'Bell's Greatest Hits'?" I said.

"Yeah. Number One with a bullet."

"I suppose that's appropriate since they sent out hit men."

"Yeah," Jim chuckled, loading the tape into the player. "To fire at Jobs."

"I'm so glad that my impending murder can serve as such great fodder for amusement for you two assholes," Steve growled. "Will you just play the goddamn tape?"

Jim hit PLAY and we listened quietly. Between recordings he stopped the tape and filled us in on each call's origin.

There's nothing to be gained by including a transcript of the conversations. It's probably enough to mention that there were three total—two personal calls and one conference room conversation. The gold flakes and the nugget, in Jimmy's terms.

One of the two individual calls was from the office of a specific VP of Western Electric—probably, as Malone had intuited, attempting to position himself for a promotion if the Bell System was broken up as a monopoly. He took a call from the guys assigned to tail Steve, who made the bush league error of mentioning Jobs by name. The VP was none too pleased with their performance, we discovered, when he drawled sarcastically,

"You haven't lost him again, I trust?" and went on to order a second team to follow Steve round the clock.

"We know that happened," Jim said. "So we know we're getting good data from the right guys."

"Great," I said. "Go on."

"The second call was a happy accident," Jim continued. "Someone in a conference room happened to mention a couple of our keywords in an innocuous conversation—the recording starts '…spoils the bunch,' so I think he must have said something like 'one bad apple,' and it tripped the recorder. And what we got was this top-level discussion about the Justice Department's antitrust lawsuit."

He played the recording of a presentation admitting that the lawsuit was not going well. The AT&T execs expressed their concern that they would probably lose the suit and be forced to dismember the corporation.

"The dialogue goes on for another twenty minutes," Jim said, turning off the recorder, "but that was the gist of it. They're preparing for the worst-case scenario."

"And how does that affect—" Steve tried edgewise.

"At one point," Jim continued, cutting him off, "they specifically mention the Carterfone prohibitions…and they are not optimistic about getting those restrictions repealed. If that's the case, they're still stuck without an entry point into the computer industry."

"Which is what inspired this whole subterfuge against Apple in the first place," I said.

"Yeah," Jim agreed. "*Et voila*, the *pièce de résistence*… Just listen to this call from that same Western Electric VP to his Bell Security agents who've been shadowing you for the last few weeks."

He played the call. It was in fact the gold we'd been panning for. And it was chilling. The VP laid it all out to his minions, no holds barred. No secret code, no pseudonyms, no euphemisms. He told them that he was "moving up the timetable." He told them that it was "time to take action and confront this asshole Jobs once and for all, as soon as you can catch up with him and corner him." He delivered his ultimatum: "If you can't bring him in, take him out." And just in case there was any ambiguity in his direction, he paraphrased the line from *Apocalypse Now* that the IBM Wonder Twins had heard him quote: "Terminate with extreme prejudice."

Jim clicked off the recorder.

"Dylan called it," Steve whispered faintly. "The world is ruled by violence."

"OK, Jimmy," I said. "One question: Is there any chance we're misinterpreting these conversations? Are they in any way ambiguous enough to include some alternate, less sinister explanation?"

"I know why you're asking," Jim said. "Your whole association with that dancer was based on misinterpreted conversations. But these? No way. These guys are saying exactly what they mean, and they mean exactly what they say. Off with his head."

"Yeah," I sighed. "Sentence first, verdict afterward. First we find out their sentence is death, then we discover they're guilty."

All three of us sat ruminating over this revelation. It was our worst-case scenario, and it was true. It was happening. Jim's taps verified everything, with no possibility of ambiguity.

Jim sat quietly, smiling, pleased with himself and the success of his plan.

Steve sat quietly, hunched over, hands clasped between his knees. I was afraid he was going to break down crying again. This was no time for crying. This was time for something entirely different. This was the time to tip over the first domino in my plan.

"Only one thing to do now," I said brightly. "Let's get lunch!"

Chapter 13.0

"There are guys coming to *kill me* and *you* want to go to *lunch*?" Steve protested, rousing slightly from his stupor. "How can you even think of eating at a time like this?"

"A time like what?" I said. "It's lunchtime. I think better on a full stomach."

I got up to leave and Jim followed. Steve's only options were to sit there alone or tag along. He chose wisely and followed us out of the apartment. Reluctantly, maybe, but he did come along.

We piled into my car, Steve sitting silently in the back seat, head bowed, while we drove.

"That Vietnamese soup place you took me to?" I said to Jim. "That's right around here somewhere, yeah?"

He directed me down Lawrence Expressway to a shopping mall just before 280.

"There," he said. " 'Real Pho.' Best soup in town."

I pulled into the parking lot. "I love fur," I said.

"It's pronounced *fuh*," Jim protested.

"Then I guess it's a good thing they didn't call the place Pho Q, innit?"

"Or Pho Q'duc," Jim replied. "Why do you call it *fur*?"

"Guy who introduced me to it," I said. "G. Kelly Sides. He's a Texan, and apparently that's how they pronounce it in Tex-ass." I was just making conversation, trying to amuse Steve out of his fatal funk.

"Well, now you know better," Jim admonished. "And you're not from Tex-ass, so you don't have any excuse to be culturally insensitive. Although a lot of people here pronounce it *foe*."

"Hey, you think it's some kind of multilingual pun that they call the place 'Real Pho'? Because if you pronounce it *foe*, it's the French *faux,* for 'fake'…and we know the French were mired in Vietnam long before we were and traded culinary tips with the locals. So 'Real Faux' would be a pun. Or an oxymoron. Right, Steve?"

I gave him a perfect straight line but he was still in shock and didn't reply. What an oxy.

"C'mon, Steve, snap out of it," I said, hoping a little humor would get through to him. "You read Ram Dass. Be here now. Which reminds me: What did the guru say to the hot dog vendor?"

Jimmy knew this one: " 'Make me one with everything!' "

Even this bit of sophisticated jocularity failed to get a rise out of the morose millionaire.

We led the sleepwalking Steve into the restaurant, which was nearly as big as a supermarket. Every foot of floor space was filled with tables. It was a no-frills joint, though: linoleum floor, second-hand kitchen tables and mismatched wooden chairs, no decorations aside from some Vietnamese flags hanging limply on the walls. Even the walls were innocuous—the kind of generic pale green that was the worst possible color for a restaurant, since it looked like nausea. Plastic soup bowls, wooden chopsticks, paper napkins. Made the Quality Café look like the Chart House.

We sat at a table that was being bussed and wiped. I asked the teenage busboy to leave half a glass of water behind, which he did. When the boy spotted Jim, he smiled and nodded.

"Guys," I said, "I want to show you a test my girlfriend taught me." I put the glass between them. "Is this glass half empty or half full?"

"Both!" Jim replied.

Steve took a few seconds to shake off his torpor and mumble an answer. "It's a sixteen-ounce tumbler containing eight ounces of water," he said.

OK, so much for that…

"You want a test?" Jimmy challenged. "I got a test for you. Ever hear of the Turing test?"

I said I hadn't. Steve remained silent, still lost in a world of his own and still seeing the end of it.

"Alan Turing," Jim continued. "Father of theoretical computer science, and an early pioneer in artificial intelligence."

"As opposed to real stupidity?" I inquired.

"A concept with which I'm sure you're familiar," he replied.

"What's that supposed to mean?" I said.

"Turing," he continued, "said that if you want to discover whether or not a computer is conscious, you sit in one room and you put a terminal or another person in another room, and you have a text conversation with him. Or her. Or it. If you can't tell the difference—if you can't determine whether you're talking to a person or to a computer—then for all practical purposes, the computer is sentient."

"What's that got to do with anything?" I said.

"We'll get to that," he replied. "Just play along for a minute. What one question do you think you could ask that would reveal whether the reply is coming from a person or a computer?"

I had to give that some thought. Who wouldn't? What separates human self-consciousness from a machine, I asked myself? A sense of humor? Something that could not be understood using logic? Maybe a good question would be: *Is this a rhetorical question?* But I think I had a better question as an answer.

"The question I'd ask," I said, "is: *What are people for?*"

Jim nodded. "Yeah. Good. No machine could answer that."

"Yeah. But then again, neither can most people."

"So what's *your* answer?" he asked.

Again, this required some thought. Damn it. "To help each other out," I said at length. "To show some empathy."

Jimmy aimed a thumb at Steve, who was still just staring at the tabletop, or into the bleak blackness of his future. "In his state, this guy wouldn't pass."

"If kindness is the criterion," I said, "he might *never* pass."

"Guys," Steve mumbled irritably, "I'm sitting right here."

"Yeah," I said. "But are you listening?"

"If you are," Jim added, "listen to this: Did you know Turing committed suicide by biting into a poisoned apple?"

"Like in *Snow White*?" I said.

"Yeah. Apparently one of his favorite flicks."

We were approached by a waiter, a skinny young Vietnamese man, maybe college age. He handed us menus then looked startled.

"Mistah Jimmy!" he exclaimed. Ferrette smiled back at him. "I terr evyone you here!" And he headed off towards the back of the place.

I didn't ask what that was about. I already knew. Maybe Steve would be curious, though.

"Thank whoever for immigrants," Jimmy chuckled. "This place couldn't have existed ten years ago."

"Yeah," I said, still searching for leverage to crowbar the boy genius out of his coma. "Steve and I were talking earlier about all the changes in the Valley in the last decade or so. Used to be the Wild West, now it's fucking Futuropolis."

"Yeah," Jim agreed. "Like that Godard movie...careening toward *Alphaville*, a dystopian vision of what Silicon Valley could become when science meets sociopathy."

"That idea of Cowtown versus Futurama," I mused, "...you could probably come up with some image for that...a cowboy fighting an astronaut or something. Might be a story there."

"Tough to get those characters together in one story," Jim said. "Maybe a movie?"

"Yeah. Maybe a cartoon."

"I love cartoons," Jim said animatedly.

"Anyway, it's just a story I'm toying with. You guys know what you want?"

Jim didn't need to look at the menu to know what he wanted. I worked by a process of elimination but finally winnowed the menu down to a single choice. Steve sat stock still, staring at the menu or at his own mortality.

"There's not much I can eat here," he mumbled robotically. "I'm a vegan."

"And I'm a Martian," Jim replied. "So what?"

"You eat sushi," I reminded Steve. Jim snorted. That got Steve's attention.

"Yeah, I eat sushi," he said defensively. "And I know what you're gonna say—I'm a hypocrite to call myself a vegan and still eat sushi."

"Naw," Jim replied. "I wasn't gonna say that. I was gonna say, you're a Pisces and you eat fish? Isn't that cannibalism?"

I thought that was funny. And Jim, like me, thinks all his jokes are funny. Steve's scowl indicated he clearly disagreed with both of us, but we had a quorum and he was outvoted. Verdict: funny.

The waiter returned and took our orders. Before he could walk away, however, Jim addressed him.

"Tôi có the nhan du'o'c môt cái gì dó dac biêt cho ban cua tôi?" he said. I think.

The waiter glanced over at sullen Steve and chuckled.

"Bat cú dieu gio cho ban," he said. I think.

"Súp rau," Jim said. I understood "soup."

"You got it," the waiter replied. I got that. I think.

"Cam on nhieu," Jim said, and the waiter hurried away.

"You speak Vietnamese?" Steve asked. Clearly, Jim's little performance had broken his robotic hypnotic trance. And then Steve made his big mistake—a novice error, but one I counted on him to make, not knowing Jimmy the Ferret as well as I did. "What's the story on that?" he asked.

Bingo. Second domino pushed over, to mix game metaphors.

Jim shrugged. "Started in college. You go to college?"

"No. I started a million-dollar company in high school. But I audited a few courses at Reed, in Oregon. Small liberal arts college."

"Nobody ever matriculates to a conservative arts college," I opined. They ignored me.

"I never saw the point, really," Steve continued. "I mean, what'd you learn in college? What did you actually learn?"

Jim thought about this for a minute before he gave Steve his answer: "How to get what I want without paying."

There was clearly no response to that, so Jim continued his story.

"So I was in ROTC in college in 1970," he said, "and I expected to be shipped off to Vietnam, so I studied the language. Figured it couldn't hurt to be able to communicate with the locals."

"Did you have to go?"

"No. I lucked out. By the time my Two-S student deferment expired they'd gone to a draft lottery, and my birthday number came up way low."

"Wai Lao is not Vietnamese," I said, just to hold up my end of the conversation. "It's Chinese. Like Hung Lo."

They said nothing but both looked at me blankly. I decided it wasn't that they objected to the joke because it was racist. They objected to it because it was bad.

"Then I discovered pot and LSD," Jim continued, "and I decided I didn't want to kill anyone. And later I discovered that my language skills came in handy when San Jose became one of the two main destinations for Vietnamese refugees in the mid-seventies. A hundred and twenty thousand refugees came to America in 1975 alone. Eighteen percent relocated to Los Angeles, but eight percent settled in San Jose. The Vietnamese were occupying us so fast you'd think we'd lost the war."

"We did," I reminded him.

"And they had a tough time," Jim continued. "They were widely discriminated against. Locals called them 'boat people,' for instance. They had little education, spoke little English, and had no marketable job skills in a high-tech area like this was becoming. They had no local community until they built one here. But they were industrious. They started businesses and clustered concentrations of Vietnamese-owned businesses. There was a time when they owned every store on entire blocks of downtown San Jose, for example. But the same discrimination that encouraged them to stick together also encouraged them to exclude outsiders, I think."

"Caucasians," I said.

"Right," he continued. "I'd go shopping in their stores—or try to, at least—but as soon as whitey entered their store they'd all stop talking and just give me the stink eye, trying to make me uncomfortable enough to leave. Suspicious of The Man. That's not integration—that's separation. One time a young guy made a racist comment about me in his native tongue, and I said to him in his own language, 'You better be careful. I've heard that some roundeyes speak Vietnamese.' They were shocked, then amused. And that started a conversation. Eventually, I offered to help them, and they began to trust me. Nice people. Good people. Been through a lot. I felt sorry for them and decided to help them."

"That's very altruistic," Steve remarked.

"Wait for it," I said.

"You remember," Jim continued, "when we were growing up, we were taught that America was a 'melting pot'? Immigrants and refugees came to America to become *Americans*. And it seemed to work. My best friend in high school, for instance—his parents were both from the Philipines, so he was one hundred percent Filipino. But he was as American as I am—he was into baseball, comic books, sci-fi, TV, cars. It wasn't until I heard some asshole call him a 'gook' that I realized my friend wasn't a WASP. That really opened my eyes…and numbed my butt. Much later I figured out that if I caught enough new immigrants early enough, I could turn them into Americans rather than allowing their culture to infect ours, like a virus. I wanted to be an antibody."

"Aaaaaand there it is," I said.

"So I set out to make myself into a melting-pot factory—a factory that manufactures Americans," Jimmy the American Altruist continued. "I help them integrate. I sponsor families. I act as their interpreter and Caucasian liaison with local merchants, neighbors, schools, government agencies. I teach them to drive so the jokes will stop. I even started a little league team so they could learn baseball."

"Not to mention that the government is very generous with grants and aid for this kind of work, I imagine," I said. I didn't have to imagine. I already knew.

"Absolutely! They want the refugees to be economically self-sufficient as quickly as possible. That's what I want, too," he chuckled. "So we're on the same page. The bonus is that I've become well-known and, if I might be so bold, well-loved among the Vietnamese community."

As if to prove this point of pride, when the waiter arrived with our soup he was followed by a wizened old guy wiping his hands on a soiled chef's apron.

"Mistah Jimmy," the old cook effused while the waiter served our bowls. "We are honored to eat you here," he said. Jim did not correct him.

"Best pho in town," Jim said. "Say hi to your wife for me."

"She busy make broth. I say hi. I say hi to grandkids, too. Their team in prayoffs. You good coach!"

" 'Prayoffs'?" Steve whispered to me.

"Basebawr," I whispered back.

The staff bowed politely and left, and we attacked the garnish plate. We split the fresh basil three ways and granted Steve all the sprouts. There were enough lime wedges for six people, so we didn't have to compete for those. And I was the only one who wanted a slice of jalapeño. Just one slice, for the teeny tiny tingle.

Steve peered deeply into his bowl.

"It's all vegetables," he said.

"And noodles," Jim reminded him. "I asked for something special for my, uh, *special* friend."

And we ate. Chopsticks in one hand, soup spoon in the other. And yea, it was good—too good to continue any conversation. At one point our waiter brought us Vietnamese coffee, the thick French roast sweetened with evaporated milk. A gift, apparently, since none of us had ordered it. If Jim had to prove his relationship with the Vietnamese community to Steve, this gift would be just the thing to do it.

I could only echo James J. Altruistic Ferrette IV's earlier sentiments: Thank whoever for immigrants. Like the cook who made this pho. And maybe even some Syrian guy named Jandali.

Chapter 13.1

The moment was as pleasant as the pho. But we'd have to return to the reality of our situation soon. Once we'd paid—once Steve paid—and we returned to my car, I decided it was time to spring my idea on the morose millionaire.

"So Steve," I said. "You had three goals when you hired me. We discovered you were in fact being followed. We discovered by who, and why. The third item on your request agenda was to get rid of them. Is that still what you want?"

"Yeah," he said. "I just want to get AT&T to leave me the fuck alone so I can run Apple without these distractions."

"You willing to do something to get rid of them that will win you no friends?"

"Absolutely. Friends are orthogonal to my interests."

"You really don't care what people think about you, do you?" Jim said.

"No," he replied. "But I care about what people *think*. I care about fresh ideas they have. Unfortunately, ninety percent of people are bozos, and ninety percent of what they think is shit."

"Ah, Sturgeon's Law," Jim said.

Steve furrowed his brow.

"Steve doesn't read science fiction," I said to Jim.

"Theodore Sturgeon," Jim explained. "Science fiction writer. Damn good science fiction writer. Also wrote a couple of classic *Star Trek* episodes, and came up with the Vulcan salute, 'Live long and prosper.' When someone complained to him that ninety percent of science fiction is shit, his response was that ninety percent of *everything* is shit. And that became known as Sturgeon's Law."

"I think he was generous in his assessment," Steve opined.

"He's also famous for his saying, 'Ask the next question.'" I said.

"OK, so what *is* the next question?" Steve asked.

"I think the question," I said, "is what's next?"

"You mean, like what's the next big thing?"

"Are you planning another big thing?" I said. "Next?"

"What makes you think my big thing will be next?"

"I'm getting confused," Jim announced, cutting this Gordian knot and allowing us to escape this infinite loop. "You of all people really never read science fiction?" he continued, addressing Steve.

"You must have at least watched some sci-fi," I said. "*Star Trek*, maybe? With those cool handheld communication devices? And weren't we talking about those old Hanna-Barbera cartoons like *The Jetsons* and *Jonny Quest*?"

Steve cocked his head.

"*Jonny Quest*," I repeated. "The genius kid adventurer who always wore the same outfit—black turtleneck sweater, blue jeans, and sneakers?"

Steve just shrugged.

"I bet your pal Wozniak was into sci-fi," Jim said.

Steve nodded. "Yeah. I always thought sci-fi was for awkward adolescents, and he was always a kid at heart."

"Reminds me of an old joke," Jim said. "When was the Golden Age of science fiction? Whenever you were fourteen."

"OK," I said. "So you never read any sci-fi. But you must have read *Profiles of the Future*, Arthur C. Clarke's book about predicting future technologies, yeah?"

"Uhh… No. But I know who Arthur C. Clarke is. Guy who wrote *Space Odyssey* with Kubrick."

"Well, he was a lot more than that," I said. "He was the first person to suggest that satellites in geosynchronous orbit would make great platforms for telecommunications, for one thing."

"Probably more appropriate that he read that Clarke short story, 'Dial F for Frankenstein,'" Jim advised. "The one where the global telephone system gets so large and complex with so many potential interconnections that the wiring acts like neurons in a giant brain and the system develops consciousness. Self-awareness. Which leads to global chaos. Like consciousness always does."

"You should definitely read *Profiles of the Future*," I continued. "Book's nearly twenty years old and still seems fresh. It's part prediction, part speculation, part long-term imagination. That's your playground, isn't it? Imagining future technologies?"

Steve shook his head. "I don't think anyone can predict the future. I'm with Stewart Brand on this—if you want a future, build it. We probably can't even imagine what technological products will be manufactured twenty years from now."

"Or how they'll fuck us up," I amended.

"You mean to tell me you never read the Tom Swift books?" Jim said.

"I read Jonathan Swift," Steve replied.

"Well then I got a modest proposal for you," Jim said. "I'll bet you money your buddy Woz was totally into Tom Swift."

"And Tom Swifties," I said to Jim. "According to Steve, Wozniak has a reputation as a joker." And that's when I got it: When Steve had said *There must be some kind of way out of here said the joker to the thief*, he was talking about Woz and himself—the prankster and the guy who'd stolen the Xerox tech. Man, it felt good to figure that out. Who says I don't understand things? But this was no time to go there, so I continued. "Steve, didn't you tell me Woz used to operate a Dial-A-Joke phone line years ago?"

"Yeah, he did," Steve said. "But what's a Tom Swifty?"

"It's a statement," I explained pedantically, "made by teen genius inventor Tom Swift, delivered in a manner described by an adverb that's a punning commentary on the statement. '"I forgot what groceries to buy," said Tom listlessly.'"

" 'Don't you know who I am?' said Tom swiftly," Jim chimed in.

" 'Thanks for letting me borrow your cat,' said Tom petulantly," I exemplified.

" 'We'd love to smoke some reefer,' Steve and I said jointly," Jim added.

"Stop it," Steve whined.

"'Stop. It,' Steve said haltingly," Jim said.

Two-thirds of us laughed. We had a quorum and we had a majority vote. So, yeah, it was funny.

Chapter 13.2

We returned to Jim's place and took our seats back on the couches.

"Now what?" Steve demanded. The soup seemed to have had a healing, or at least energizing, effect on him, as he'd stopped reveling in self-pity and had returned to his usual bristly demeanor. "You bozos have done nothing but spend my money and give me the royal runaround," he growled. "You're shitheads who have your heads up your asses. I can't waste any more time on this shit. I have to be in Anaheim on May nineteenth—*four fucking weeks* from now—to unveil the Apple III at the National Computer Conference. And I'm gonna need to devote all my time until then handling a million details of the launch."

"So you're just going to ignore the hit AT&T put out on you?" I asked.

"I hear you've rented Disneyland for a private party after the Apple III launch," Jim said. "You should check the Haunted Mansion while you're there to see if they're accepting residency applications."

He was pissed. But I had a surprise. It was time to reveal my plan.

"Steve," I said, "if you recall, we've addressed two of your three requests. And I have a plan to handle the third—to get rid of the threat of AT&T altogether."

"Well then what the fuck is it?"

"Before I tell you, I need to ask you once again: Are you willing to do something that might not cast you in the most flattering light?"

"Absolutely. If it protects Apple and me, absolutely."

"OK, then," I said. "Prepare yourself. We're about to go down the rabbit hole. And we're taking them with us."

I told them my plan.

They listened quietly and interrupted only to clarify one or two points. I purposefully left out a couple of key details, like where we'd stage our engagement. That was for me to know and them to find out. Or be told.

And when I was done, they each passed judgment.

"That's devious," Jim giggled. "It's great!"

"It's insane!" Steve countered.

"It's insanely great!" I said.

"I think you might be brain-damaged," Steve growled.

"I am not brain damamaged," I said. "It's a mother beautiful plan, and it's going to work."

I let Steve ruminate over the details. He stared off into space for several minutes, probably reviewing the plan…and certainly looking for loopholes.

"No," he finally determined. "Your plan is shit. Here's what we should do…" And he proceeded to repeat my plan back to me, almost verbatim.

"That's brilliant, Steve," I said when he was done. I could allow his reality distortion field to have the win, if it got him on board.

"So when should we do this?" Steve asked.

"No time like the present," I said. "What's wrong with right now? This afternoon. If we start now we can be to the place I have in mind by four. Beat the rush hour traffic. But the main thing is if we act now we can get the drop on them. Right now, we're ahead of them. But we know they're poised to act, so this is our chance to stay ahead of them—to act instead of react."

"To level the playing field," Steve nodded.

"No," Jimmy said. "To own the playground."

"So we'll go right now," Steve said.

"No," I replied. "There are a few more dominoes we need to push over before we launch the plan. You shook your tail when we drove out here, for instance. The guys who're tailing you still think you're in your office, but we need them to pick up your trail again, so they can follow us—purposefully this time. And I have to go back to my office and get my gun."

"You're gonna need your gun?" Steve said skeptically. "Why? What do you think they're gonna do?"

"The answer, my friend," I said, "is pissin' in the wind. And you don't need a weatherman to know which way the wind blows." I assumed he'd be more on board if I explained things to him in a language he understood. Dylan-speak.

I stood up and pointed to each in turn, giving direction.

"Jim, you drive Steve back to Apple. Then you'll probably need to get started on the rest of your role. Steve, as soon as you sneak back into Apple, make a big show of leaving. Maybe walk around the parking lot like you're looking for your car or something. Make sure your tail sees you and stays with you. Then drive to my office and pick me up. They've already seen you do that to, uh, take me out to dinner, they think, so they won't question why you're picking me up. I'll meet you out on the street, on the corner my building is on. Everybody good?"

They nodded.

"Let's go kick the shit out of those assholes," Steve enthused.

"One question," Jim said. "Where would you guys like to be abducted?"

"I might know a place," I said.

Chapter 14.0

Once back in my office, I cleaned and reloaded my Beretta and put it in my pocket along with the compact. A few minutes later I went down to the sidewalk and waited at the corner until Steve drove up in his Mercedes. I hopped in while he was stopped at the red light.

"Where we going?" he said by way of greeting.

"Take a left here and the next left on University," I said. "Are you being followed?"

"Yep," he said. "They picked me up before I even left the parking lot."

"Same guys?" I said. "Could you tell?"

"I think so."

I opened my compact and looked through the looking-glass to check behind us. Yep. Same poop brown Cutlass. The game was afoot.

I guided us out of Los Gatos and had him take a right on Blossom Hill Road. We stayed on it for about 15 minutes, but we saw no hills, no blossoms. Valley Replacement Theory validated once again, damn it.

I checked frequently to make sure the Cutlass was behind us. It was.

"We're not going to IBM, are we?" Steve asked as we neared 101.

"No. Take 101 north about four miles, then east on Aborn."

"Where are we going?

"It's a surprise."

"The last time you told me that I ended up rooming with you on Gilligan's Island for the night."

"You'll like this place. No boating required."

Once we hit Aborn we were deep in southeast San Jose, at the base of the eastern foothills. Straight road, low speed, no traffic. Good place to spring my big surprise.

I took the Beretta out of my pocket and showed it to Steve.

"You, uh, think you might need that?" he asked.

"I brought it for Plan B," I said.

"We never discussed a Plan B," he said skeptically.

"Do I look like a guy who has no Plan B? It's always best to have a Plan B. And the reason we need a Plan B is this: We *think* we know who these guys that have been following you are. And we think we know what they want. But what if we're wrong?"

"How could we be wrong?"

"We were wrong about the IBM guys," I reminded him. "We thought they were a threat but they turned out to be an asset—a feature, not a bug. But Mad Hatter and White Rabbit were specifically ordered to try to get you on board before they take you out. So chances are that they'll just want to talk to you at this point, and we go with Plan A. But on the off chance they *are* out to get you, if they turn out to be a bug instead of a feature…if they physically *threaten* you…then you shoot me, wave the gun at them and run like hell."

"*What?* I *shoot* you?"

"Yeah," I said. I pointed the Beretta at him and fired off a round. The bang echoed in the car and in our ears. Steve nearly drove off the road before he got the car under control again.

"*Are you fucking insane?*" he screamed. "*Are you trying to fucking kill me?*"

"Are you fucking bleeding?" I inquired calmly. "Are you fucking hurt?"

He touched his ribs. He looked down at his shirt. No blood, no pain.

"No bullets," I said blankly. "Half charge. I essentially turned it into a starter's pistol." I lifted my T-shirt and showed him the blood packs and squibs I had taped to my chest. "You think they're gonna do business with a madman? A murderer? They have an image to protect. A wholesome rep to maintain. A rep they want the public to believe anyway, despite their insider rep for underhanded business techniques they've been getting away with for the last hundred years. So if they physically threaten you, you just point the gun at me and shoot. Then run. They'll report back to their corporate masters that you're an insane asshole and recommend they never do business with you." They'd be at least half right, at any rate.

"I dunno…" he balked.

"You wanna save your company?" I barked. "The Great Humanitarian? Take the gun."

I handed him the little pistol. He took it. Reluctantly. But he took it. In a checklist of dramatic rules, I could check off Chekov.

"That sounds a lot simpler than Plan A," he grumbled. "Why don't we just do the shooting blanks thing instead of the main plan?"

"Do you really want to spend the rest of your life dodging gossip, rumors, and allegations that you shot a guy? That you murdered a guy in cold blood? Could you live with that?"

"Well… no."

"Then think of both plans as just creating a different reality. A reality you want them to believe. A distortion where you define the terms. Reality is what you can get away with."

If anyone would understand that logic, it would certainly be Steve Jobs.

Chapter 14.1

"Pull in here," I said a few miles down Aborn.

"Mirassou Winery?" he said. "What the fuck?" It seems he'd fully recovered from the shock of being "shot."

"Yep. It's perfect for our purpose."

Steve parked. The little lot was empty. Good. We were alone aside from whatever staff and winery workers were around the grounds.

Once out of the car, we took a moment to soak in the view—rolling golden foothills, speckled and mottled with green foliage—then headed for the main building. It was an impressive, ivy-covered stone structure with an oddly-shaped roof—flat on top and angled on the sides. It looked like someone took a capital A and removed the sharp peak. The entire roof was covered with dull red half-moon terra cotta tiles in the California Spanish hacienda style.

"One of the oldest buildings in San Jose," I said to Steve. "The Peralta Adobe downtown is older. Dates back to when San Jose was the state capitol of California. Instead of just the capitol of Silicon Valley."

"Self-proclaimed capitol," Steve corrected me. "Cupertino is the capitol of Silicon Valley."

"Of course it is," I sighed resignedly.

We passed beneath a trellis of grape vines, entered, and approached a young woman standing at a podium in the small lobby. She was nondescript, but since nondescript is not a description, I'll put it this way: No one would ever use superlatives to describe her. She had the kind of face that requires two descriptions, because by the time you got to the end of the first one you'd already forgotten what she looked like. She was wearing a light blue dress and a white apron. Her blonde hair was pulled back in a ponytail tied with a black bow.

"Welcome to Mirassou," she said with a smile. "And you are…?"

"He's Charlie Brown," I said, "and I'm Charlie Dodgson. And *whooooo* are *youuu*?"

"I'm Alice," she replied.

Steve gave me a cocked eyebrow glance. *Alice?* he mouthed silently.

"I warned you," I whispered back.

"Are you here for the tour?" Alice asked.

"Sure," I said. "What time does it start?"

"Well, it's slow today. Matter of fact, you two are the only ones here, so we can do this anytime you're ready."

"Good, good," I said. "I was afraid I'd have to say I'm late, I'm late, for a very important date. Well, then, consider the starting gun fired." Steve shot me the stank eye. Too soon?

Alice led us down a hallway lined with photos of the buildings and the vineyards as well as several ancient, Matthew Brady-era shots of a stiff gentleman and lady.

"Pierre Pellier landed here from France in 1854," our guide recited, "and quickly discovered that this really was the Valley of Heart's Delight—a perfect climate to transplant his prize grape cuttings. Today, the company is still family owned and Mirrasou is the oldest winemaking family in the state."

She walked us through the bottling plant, where a dozen or so workers in lab coats oversaw the filling of the bottles as they shimmied along a series of silver rollers lined with guard rails and were corked by a machine. She explained the steps and the process, but I was distracted—keeping an eye behind us. I knew the tail had followed us here, but there was no telling when they'd choose to confront us. Besides, I'd been here before. That's how I knew it would be perfect. My ears did perk up, however, when Alice mentioned that "they filmed an episode of *Columbo* here in '73."

She walked us through a cavernous stone warehouse filled with row upon row of obese wooden barrels—dozens of enormous barrels of aging wine, each perhaps fifteen feet tall, each with a tiny sign denoting its type and testing dates. At least two of these vats were so large that I had the crazy idea of relocating one to a foothill and converting it into a round house. That would probably be expensive, however, and would most assuredly be, shall we say, abundantly aromatic.

The warehouse was quiet, and even better, cool. I made a mental note to bring Laurel out here some hot summer afternoon. Relief from the heat and free wine? What could be better?

The tour over, Alice brought us back to the main entrance and into the Tasting Room just off the lobby. The room was small, as befit the winery, but cozy. A short bar of polished wood separated three tables—two seating two, one seating four—from a back wall display of bottles of their wines. The entire room was decorated with curly wrought iron and grape vines.

Steve sat at the table for four. His back was to the wall, his eye on the entrance. We still hadn't seen our tail, but they'd be difficult to miss once they entered the lobby. If they entered the lobby. We could only hope.

Alice stepped behind the bar.

"What can I get for you gentlemen?" she said pleasantly. "We have a nice Chardonnay for starters…"

"Do you have any of the '74 Gamay Beaujolais?" I asked. "I discovered that a few years ago and it's the best wine I've ever tasted."

Her smile faded. "Oh, sorry, no."

"Well then, I'm glad I tracked down a dozen bottles back then," I chuckled. "I guess I'll have to dole them out one every few years for the rest of my life."

Her smile faded and she shook her head sadly.

"You shouldn't plan on that," she said. "Beaujolais is best when it's young. It doesn't age well. In a few years, all you're likely to have is a case of wine vinegar."

This information came as both a shock and a disappointment. I resolved to start opening my bottles as soon as I got back home. Maybe it wasn't yet too late to salvage a few of them from degenerating into salad dressing.

"We have a nice Pinot Noir," Alice suggested. "Very similar. Our Beaujolais is about seventy-five percent Pinot Noir."

"Worth a try, I suppose," I sighed. But all I could think was, *'74 Gamay Beaujolais: R.I.P.*

Chapter 14.2

She poured two wide bowl glasses. I took them to our table and sat next to Steve.

And no sooner had we swirled and sipped and begun to formulate some pretentious opinions about its nose and bouquet and *terroir* than Mad Hatter and White Rabbit—our AT&T shadows—entered the lobby. Caucasian, middle-aged, one about six feet, average build; the other, stocky and several inches shorter. They were wearing dark suits, white dress shirts, and skinny ties. It was 1980 and they had crew cuts.

They approached our table. We had nowhere to run and nowhere to hide. So far, so good. I just hoped Steve wasn't feeling too anxious or hemmed in, sitting in a corner with no escape, even though this was exactly what we'd planned.

"Excuse me," Mad Hatter, the taller of the two and clearly the alpha male, said. "Mr. Jobs?"

Show time.

Steve gave him his unblinking stare.

"Yes?"

"May we speak with you for a minute, please?"

"What can I do for you?" Steve said.

"May we have a seat?"

Steve gestured for them to sit. They sat. I sat stock still and quiet. This was Steve's show now, not mine. Everything required to set up our plan depended solely on him and how he dealt with these mugs. I could only hope he'd stick to the plan. If ever there was a time for him to curb his notoriously rude behavior, this would be it.

"So who the fuck are you guys?" Steve asked. My hopes were dashed.

"How about that?" Mad Hatter announced. "I forgot to introduce myself. My name is Smith." *Smith.* Yeah, sure. "This is my colleague, Mr. Jones."

Smith and Jones? I thought. *More like Smith and Wesson.*

Steve didn't bother to introduce me. Why should he? They didn't know who I was, or care. It wasn't rude. It was just Steve being Steve. So, yeah, maybe it was rude.

"We represent a potential major investor in your company," Smith continued, "and we'd like to talk to you about a possible mutually advantageous collaboration."

"Continue," Steve said, swirling his wine and sniffing the bouquet. Gotta hand it to him—he might be acting like an asshole, but at least he was keeping his cool.

Smith reached into his coat. I reached for my gun. But it wasn't in my pocket. It was in Steve's pocket. I nudged him and he put his hand in his pocket.

Smith didn't pull out a gun, however. Instead, he pulled out a badge—a photo ID for one "Thomas Smith" with his picture on it. Well fuck me—maybe his name really *was* Smith. At the top of the badge were the words "AT&T," and at the bottom, "Telephone Crime Lab." He displayed the badge and we scrutinized it.

"Oh my," Steve said in mock shock. "Are you here to bust me for building blue boxes?"

Smith cocked his head and furrowed his brow. But then he got it and smiled.

"No, sir, the past is the past. We, like you, are more interested in the future."

"Then how may I assist you?" Steve asked, apparently shifting gears to first-date behavior, bless his spikey little heart.

"Our company is very interested in cooperating with Apple in adding a modem to your next computer."

There it was. Verification, straight from the horse's ass.

Steve nodded slowly and furrowed his brow.

"We built a modem into our current product, the Apple II," he said.

Smith nodded. "We're aware of that. But then you removed it."

Steve nodded, more energetically this time. "I discovered it was a Trojan Horse," he said. "A couple of our, uh, less ethical employees tried to include a board that reproduced everything every illegal phone phreak device could accomplish. I made it very clear that we were a legitimate business and that that type of illegal shenanigans was off the table and would not be tolerated."

Smith nodded soberly. "Yes, sir, we're aware of that as well. But what would it take to get you to reconsider and add a *legal* modem into your products?"

"Well," Steve said, "we're launching the Apple III a few weeks from now. The engineering specs were frozen months ago —locked down so we could begin production. So there's zero chance of adding a modem to that model." He swirled his wine glass, sniffed the bowl once again, and took a small sip.

The son of a bitch! He was playing them—and loving it.

"But," he continued, "your timing could not be more propitious. Earlier this afternoon I attended a meeting to discuss upgrades to our next model. And we decided that adding a modem was not off the table. My vision is that someday—someday soon—personal computers will all be able to connect with large servers, and will need a large network of wiring and cables to accommodate this networking. Who better to partner with than the company that owns the world's largest communications network?"

Smith smiled. Jones did not. I knew which one would be trouble if it came to that. But it was beginning to look like it would not come to that. Steve was doing an admirable job of being Genial Steve—Steve the charming and charismatic cult leader—and suckering these guys into his reality distortion field.

"My superiors will be very happy to hear that," Smith said.

"Well, I'm very happy to hear that you're not out to kill me," Steve said with a shit-eating grin.

Oh no, he was going to blow it. *What is this arrogant asshole going to do next?,* I wondered. Is he going to ask them what kind of mileage they get in that Cutlass? Is he going to quote *Apocalypse Now* and rub their noses in the fact that we'd been eavesdropping on them? He was going to blow our cover and the deal. And when we were *that close*. I did not want to return home thinking *missed it by that much*.

To my surprise, Smith started, as if surprised, then furrowed his brow.

"Why on earth would we want to kill you?" he said. "We want to partner with you."

Steve just gave them his hypno-stare.

"We're mighty sorry about any trouble or inconvenience we might have caused you," Smith continued, "but I know once we've explained our problem, you'll understand."

"Why didn't you just come by the Apple office, or make an appointment? Why all the cloak and dagger?"

I was beginning to catch on. Regardless of his pathological inability to refrain from playing one-upmanship, Steve might actually be a more shrewd negotiator than I'd given him credit for. If not, we always had the gun.

"Are you aware of the FCC's 1968 agreement with AT&T?" Smith asked. "The so-called Carterfone agreement?"

Steve cocked his head and aimed his eyes at the ceiling, squinting as if chasing an ephemeral memory. "Hmm," he hummed. "No, sorry, doesn't ring a bell."

"That decision strictly prohibits us from entering into the computer business," Smith said, explaining what we already knew. "That's why we want to team up with you to connect your computers to our phone lines. The catch is we literally cannot be seen in public together. Any appointment we could make for a meeting would leave a paper trail that might connect us to you, and get us in hot water, legally. This meeting—and any future meetings—have to be entirely clandestine…for the time being, at least."

"Well," Steve said, faking a tone of deep concern, "as I mentioned, we can't engage in any activity that's illegal. We have a reputation to maintain."

"As do we," Smith agreed. "However, we have every reason to believe that the Carterfone restrictions might be reversed soon, and we want to be prepared."

We both knew he was lying, if Jim's conference room tap was accurate. But we were feigning ignorance and could hardly contradict them without tipping our hand.

"Consider this our lead time," Smith continued, "so we'll be ready for market at the first possible moment rather than waiting until the lawyers give us clearance and losing months of development and negotiation time. As long as we keep our collaboration off the books, so to speak, by not entering into any agreements or contracts, any association between our two companies, if discovered, could be considered merely a friendly exchange of information rather than a business agreement."

Corporate espionage. Again. Sigh.

"Well, yes," Steve said, slowly, nodding. "I completely understand the logic and the necessity for, uh, discretion under these circumstances." He took another sip of his wine, making them wait for him to apparently mull over their dilemma and come to a decision.

"Yes," he continued at length, nodding again. "I believe we can move forward without contracts or even an NDA. As long as we're clearly *not* doing business with one another, we might even be able to associate aboveboard, without all the cloak and dagger. But keeping our association clandestine seems like a wise precaution at this point. We can characterize our relationship as a friendly exchange of information rather than a business agreement, if it's ever noticed by any authorities, as you suggest, but discretion is clearly advisable."

Smith nodded. "I think we agree on that."

"Well then," Steve continued, "as long as we're in agreement, it might be worthwhile to have some of your executives come out and tour our manufacturing facility, to begin your due diligence. We can discuss future negotiations, quietly and without a paper trail—maybe come up with a general handshake deal, completely off the books, of course, then turn the details over to the lawyers to enact at such time as the—what did you call them? The Carterfone restrictions?—are repealed. Of course, as I said, I'm extremely busy at the moment, what with the launch of the Apple III, but if you could convince your guys to drop in soon, we can certainly get the ball rolling. The sooner the better."

Smith was beaming. His job just became easier, or completed. Jones remained stonefaced—possibly angered because now he'd never get to do his part of the job.

"I'll call them right now if there's a pay phone nearby," Smith offered.

"Oh, we can do better than that," Steve said and turned to the bar. "Alice, is there a phone we can use?"

She brought out the desk phone from behind the bar and set it on the counter.

"It doesn't have a wire long enough to reach the table," she said apologetically.

Smith stepped up to the bar and punched out a number he clearly knew by heart. It was answered almost immediately.

He turned his back to us and carried out his conversation quietly.

I sipped my wine. "You want a sample?" I said to Jones, cocking my head toward the bar.

"I'm a beer man, myself," he said.

"Amen, brother," I said.

Smith placed the handset on the bar and turned back to our table.

"Is this coming Monday good for you?" he asked Steve.

I looked at Jobs, wide-eyed. My back was to Smith, so he couldn't see my reaction. Next Monday? We had *one weekend* to arrange the details of our plan? Two days? Was that even possible?

Steve, bless his pointy little soul, remained calm and nonchalant. "Have your admin call my area associate later with the flight details. I'll send someone to pick them up from the airport," he said.

Smith repeated the message, hung up, and returned to the table. He didn't sit. Instead, Jones rose. Steve and Smith made their goodbyes. Jones and I didn't. Steve and Smith shook hands. Jones and I didn't. After all, they were the knights. We were just the squires.

And they left.

"OK, then," I said to Steve. "Two days."

He sniffed his wine and nodded.

"I guess I shouldn't spend any time drinking," Steve said soberly.

"Buddy," I said, "this is exactly the time when we *should* be drinking."

I tried to sip my wine, but all I could do was gulp. And return to the bar for another dose.

"More Pinot?" Alice asked.

"I'm gonna need something stronger."

"Cabernet Sauvignon?"

I nodded. "Make it a double. And leave the bottle."

Chapter 15

Monday, April 28, Noon

And that's how I found myself standing outside the Arrivals gate at San Francisco International Airport at noon the following Monday, wearing my best dark suit, a crisp white dress shirt, and a thin, dark, patternless tie. And a chauffeur's cap. Since Steve was busy setting up for our meeting and Jimmy had his hands full organizing behind the scenes, I was elected by default to be the humble chauffeur. I agreed to wear the hat solely to complete the image, because, as we all know, hats are stupid but image is everything.

I was holding a placard so our guests could identify their ride. If I were an actual livery driver I'd be holding a card that had their names on it, but since we didn't know who they'd be sending, I held a card with an outline of an apple missing a bite decorated with rainbow stripes. We were trying to do this meeting on the Q.T., and I was pretty certain no one would recognize what that symbol stood for.

I was surprised that our visitors were flying commercial. Surely AT&T had corporate jets for their execs. But it did make sense since we were trying to keep this meeting sub rosa. A private jet would have to file a flight plan, an itinerary, and a passenger list, which would leave a paper trail. But the execs could use fake names to board a commercial flight. Still, my guess is they flew first class. They could have saved an hour on the road by flying into San Jose Municipal Airport, but they were High Level Executives, Vice Presidents of Stuff and Junk, and making them land in Podunkistan was beneath their dignity and an insult to their stature.

Among the deplaning parade, I spotted a trio of businessmen walking down the Arrivals tunnel. Dark suits, conservative ties, hard, polished shoes. Two had slicked-back silver hair; one was bald. All three were schlepping black briefcases. They were all in their mid-50s, I guessed, but looked older; well-groomed but with tummy pouches and that typical East Coast pallor. Too long behind a desk, too many three-martini lunches.

It was pretty obvious these were my guys. It was also pretty clear what the pecking order was: The Head Honcho, a boxy silver-haired guy with a grim visage, walked a step ahead of the two who flanked him and trailed him.

I held my sign up and they approached me.

"Gentlemen," I announced. "Welcome to California."

"Is this Silicone Valley?" the Big Cheese barked.

"No sir, this is San Francisco," I replied, correcting only one of his mistakes. "Sili*con* Valley is south of here." Couldn't help myself.

"How long to this…" he checked a note in his hand, "Que-pertino?"

"About half an hour, sir," I said. "Shall we head down to Baggage Claim?"

"No luggage," the Big Man said. "Let's get on the road."

"Right away, sir," I said deferentially. I led them outside and asked them to wait while I brought the limo around. Their sour reaction made me believe they thought "Way Ting" was a Chinese name, and they no savvy Chinee.

I retrieved the stretch limo I'd rented for the big visit. They'd expect it, and Steve could afford it. I could have driven down 280, the scenic route, but decided to take 101 and 85 to shave a few minutes off the trip.

Once on the road, I looked over my shoulder and smiled at the boys.

"So I hear TWA is planning a merger with AT&T," I said. "But one of you is gonna have to change your initials."

My brilliant jest was met with stony silence, broken only when the Head Honcho growled, "Can you close the privacy window please?"

I hit the button and the smoked glass partition that separated the classes rolled into place.

Half an hour later I pulled into the Apple parking lot, empty but for a bus parked at the far end, and led the men to the front doors. Steve was waiting in the lobby to greet them. Given that his typical MO was to make people wait for him if only to show them his time was more valuable than theirs, I breathed a sigh of relief that he was committed to following through with our plan without any display of his typical atypical behavior.

He opened the door and greeted us as we entered. The lobby was empty save for the five of us. No wandering employees, no secretary—sorry, "area associate"—at the front desk. Good. Clearly, Steve had taken my suggestion and given his people the day off so we had the place to ourselves and could institute our plan without any interference.

The trio took turns shaking hands with Mr. Jobs and handing him their business cards.

"Mm-hm," he said, reading the cards. "Vice President of Western Electric. Vice President of Bell Labs. Wow. And a corporate lawyer. It speaks volumes about your interest that AT&T would send such high-level executives to our humble little company."

The Head Honcho actually smiled at that ego boo.

"You've met my assistant?" Steve said, nodding at me.

"Mac," I introduced myself. "Mac Macintosh." I held out my hand. Nobody shook it.

"Can I get you gentlemen anything?" Steve offered, ever the gracious host. "Water? Coffee?" He glanced at their belt lines. "A donut?"

Head Honcho shook his head. "We ate on the plane."

"Well then, let's not waste any more time," Steve announced. "Follow me and I'll give you the grand tour of our manufacturing facility."

He led us to the rear of the building.

"Apple has actually spread to several buildings," Steve informed, or bragged to, the tourists. "But this is the one you want to see. We have a fully operational manufacturing and assembly facility in the rear. We're in the process of moving to a much larger building, and are planning large-scale factories in Ireland and Texas."

He led us through a set of double doors onto the manufacturing floor. I spotted Jimmy, costumed as a security guard, leaning back in a folding chair in one corner.

The entire factory was painted white. The space was filled with carousels and bins and stacks of white shipping boxes. Rows of desk-like workbenches and workstations lined the walls. Several rows of horizontal silver rollers at waist height formed assembly lines where trays of various components were soldered, screwed, or snapped together. Each operator workstation was occupied. The place was busy but surprisingly quiet. Dozens of workers, all in white lab coats and hair nets, toiled away, all assiduously engaged in their tasks.

Steve looked over at Jimmy and gave him a nod. The Ferret clapped his hands twice, loudly. All activity ceased. The line workers all raised their heads. And we looked out over a sea of smiling Asian faces. The oldest was maybe twelve; the youngest, about six. The younger ones stood on wooden apple crates to reach their workstations.

All three VIP VPs froze. All three jaws dropped.

The lawyer was the first to regain his voice.

"Those..." he croaked, "those are..."

"Yeah, thank God for boat people, huh?" Steve chuckled. "Couldn't do it without 'em. Good thing for us there are so damn *many* of them."

"But..." the lawyer stammered, "but... those are... *children*."

"How do you think we keep our costs so low?" Steve laughed. "And these Vietnamese kids come with so many additional benefits! Their little hands are very nimble—great for soldering and assembling tiny components. They're used to working twelve or sixteen hours a day, so they don't complain. Heck, most of 'em barely speak English. And they've never even heard of the word 'union.'"

The executives stood stock still, clutching their briefcases literally and their pearls figuratively.

The lawyer among them whispered something urgent in The Boss's ear.

Without moving his immobile body, the Big Cheese rotated his head slowly to face Steve.

"Mr. Jobs," he growled in a gruff, gravelly voice, "our association is *over*."

"Awww, sorry to hear that, guys," Steve said, feigning disappointment. He quickly recovered his enthusiasm. "But, hey, it's a volatile industry, and those are the breaks, huh?"

The Big Kahuna looked at me. Wahoo, I existed!

"Take us back to the airport," Alpha Dog barked. *"Now!"*

The Three Stooges turned and marched away.

"I'll tell you what," Steve called after them. "If I ever get into the phone business, you'll be the first guys I call."

I followed the guests, but turned back to give Steve a thumbs-up. In return, he gave me a mile-wide smile…a trillion-dollar, shit-eating grin.

PART III:
AFTER

"The journey is the reward."
—Steve Jobs

Chapter 16.0

May 26, 1980

I was sitting in my office, disputing a long-distance charge with a live but idiotic robotic operator when Steve walked in.

"I'll call you back," I said and hung up the Snoopy phone.

He looked exactly as I'd seen him last: hair groomed, dress shirt untucked, slacks. No major image changes in the past month—a month during which I'd been unable to contact him despite my best efforts. I knew he was busy with the May 19 launch of his newest computer, so I didn't press the issue, or call a lawyer to sue him for non-payment, even though I'd sent him an itemized invoice for my services weeks earlier.

He sat down in my client chair. Do I need to mention uninvited? He was smiling—which, given it was him, was more of a smartass smirk. That meant trouble.

"Didn't expect to see you again," I said.

"I wanted to talk to you," he said. "And I certainly didn't want to call."

"It's safe," I said. "I had Jimmy do a thorough sweep. My line is free from taps, bugs, and holds."

He nodded. "I hired a guy to do the same at Apple. And my house. We're good. Looks like it's over."

"Well, it's not over until it's paid for," I said. "You got my invoice? The detailed expenses?"

"Yep," he said, pulling a manila envelope from his jacket pocket. It was folded over and wrapped with a thick blue rubber band, as though it contained a stack of bills. But he didn't hand it over.

"I have to tell you," he said, "I debated whether or not to pay it, seeing as how virtually everything you did was illegal."

"Everything *we* did. You're an accomplice. A co-conspirator."

He inspected his envelope.

"I can't write you a check," he said. "That would leave a paper trail."

"So you brought cash?"

"I thought about offering you one of our new Apple III computers as payment."

"Mmm," I said, as though I was actually considering it. "If it came out last week it's probably obsolete by now. I'll wait for the next one."

"Your loss," he sighed, slapping his palm softly with his envelope a few times.

"So what're you gonna do?" I drawled sarcastically, pointing to the package. "Pay me off with stock?"

He shrugged. "Haven't decided yet."

Once an asshole… I thought.

I reached into my top desk drawer and retrieved my own manila envelope—the one that brought us together in the first place.

"How about this?" I suggested. "I'll trade you envelopes. So if you ever get curious about who your birth parents are, you won't have to go through this process again and pay for it again. Just say you called the doctor who arranged your adoption and he left you a note on his deathbed." That was close enough to the truth that he might be able to pull the story off. He was an ace at self-mythologizing anyway, so he should have no trouble selling that version of his legend.

But he ignored my attempt at negotiation. My gut feeling is that he had his own agenda. Color me surprised!

"I have some questions about your methods," he said.

Since he didn't refer to my methods as shit, I saw a glimmer of truth in his question, and felt a glimmer of hope that I might be paid.

"Shoot," I said. Just to tease him.

"How did you know that would work?"

"Ha!" I laughed. "Oh, that's an easy one. W.C. Fields pegged it half a century ago: *You can't cheat an honest man.* I knew AT&T had larceny in their hearts, so they'd fall for our little flimflam. I gotta admit, though, you were good…so good you might have to change your first name to Con. Or Snow."

"Now do I know more than I did?" he challenged.

"OK," I sighed. If it was explanations he wanted, I had them. "I relied on the corporate psychology of AT&T. Even though they're ruthless bastards, they have a public image to maintain. Smith said as much himself. I counted on the execs to automatically retreat to their conservative values and their self-serving self-delusions as a default position when confronted with something that would damage their public image immeasurably if it was ever exposed. Employee abuse might be part of their corporate DNA, but active involvement in a third-world sweat-shop and child labor most definitely is not. If the public ever found out, AT&T would have a giant black eye that would never heal."

He said nothing. But he nodded. I took that as a green light to continue.

"I got the impression that AT&T was very old-fashioned," I said, "but I realized that was a sword that cut both ways. They used old Robber Baron techniques to attempt to subvert Apple, but I leveraged their other old-fashioned attitudes to *protect* you —their desire to appear publicly as God-fearing, flag-waving, upstanding citizens, no matter how ruthless and conniving and cutthroat they are in private. They simply couldn't risk tarnishing their image and public reputation any more than the last decade of scandals, strikes, and subversive and illegal activities had already done. I counted on the idea that if we gave Bell the impression that you're running a sweatshop—if we showed them how the sausage was made—they'd immediately realize what a PR nightmare that would be if it ever became public. They weren't about to take a bite of a poisoned apple."

"So you leveraged their own psychology against them," he said, nodding.

"Yup. Psychic judo, grasshopper. Good judo techniques use an attacker's strength against him. Never give a sucker an even break, or smarten up a chump, as they say."

He nodded again. He was satisfied with my logic, apparent-ly. I know I was. I think W.C. Fields would have been as well.

"How'd you know *I'd* go for it?"

"Again, pretty simple, Steve. You care deeply about your company...but you *don't* care what people think of *you.* And you especially don't care about the opinions of people you don't respect...like guys trying to subvert your company or kill you. I knew you wouldn't give two shits what the AT&T execs thought of you—especially if it meant they'd leave you alone."

"I still can't figure out how you came up with that plan," he said skeptically.

It was easy to read between those lines: *Just how did this chimp know to put the round peg in the round hole?*

Maybe it was time to open the kimono and set his mind at ease. Or maybe not. I could be as contrarian as the next guy, but in this case, the next guy was Steve Jobs, which greatly increased the level of difficulty of any contrarianism. Maybe it would take him down a peg to show him he was not always the smartest guy in the room. So I elected not to tell him that my inspiration came from a comic crime caper novel. I'll take full credit.

"I know you're used to being the smartest guy in the room," I said levelly. "But occasionally some of us mere shit-for-brains humans can be creative, too. Clever, at least."

"Well, I'll admit it was pretty clever of you to take us out for pho," he said. He might not have understood why AT&T could be tricked, but he knew when—and how—he was being set up.

I nodded and smiled. "I knew if we went there Jimmy couldn't resist telling you his story. And I knew you'd balk at my plan unless you had hard evidence that he could pull it off. So I just connected the dots and the solution was right in front of me."

"Couldn't you have connected the dots any sooner?"

I shook my head. "You can't connect the dots looking forward. You can only connect the dots looking backward."

He squirmed a little in his chair as though he was going to get up and leave. No such luck.

"One more thing…" he said.

I was getting irritated. I'd promised to take Laurel to dinner and I was already running late. I had to get rid of this bozo.

"Look," I said. "Rather than obsessing over what happened yesterday, why don't you go invent tomorrow? You are now free to create the future. To put a dent in the universe. But one tip of advice? Stay away from phones."

"I *am* thinking about the future," he protested. "Always. Apple is expanding. We're going public soon, for instance."

"When?"

"Well, I can't tell you that," he spat. "That's proprietary information. But soon."

Once an asshole...

"What I'm getting at is, would you be interested in heading up our Corporate Security department?"

I leaned back in my squeaky office chair, put my feet up on my desk, and laced my fingers behind my head.

Head of Corporate Security.

What did I have here? A shabby office. Unpredictable work. Cases that were mostly boring. Constant money troubles.

What would I have at Apple? A plush office. Stable employment. Regular hours. A steady paycheck.

OK, I reminded myself, it's a shabby office, but it's in a great location. The work is unpredictable, but I set my own hours. The cases are mostly boring, but every once in a while, *this*—an interesting case that pushed my envelope.

The money was the sticky point. If I went to Apple, I'd be well compensated, knowing this guy.

But, aye, there's the rub: I *did* know this guy. Maybe I didn't want to play Bud Barclay to his Tom Swift, or Watson to his Bell. Maybe I didn't want to place my fate in the hands of a possible madman. Maybe I'd rather live my own unconventional, unpredictable life as a White Knight than be a pawn in his *Through the Looking Glass* chess game.

"Nope."

He shook his head. "You're a fool."

"Yep. And I'm hungry. And I intend to stay hungry and foolish. That attitude got you out of your trouble, didn't it?"

"But that was only because of your insane ideas," he shot back. "You're a crazy one."

I nodded. "A misfit."

"A rebel," he accused.

"And you're a troublemaker. I'm a square peg and you're a round asshole. You have no regard for rules and no respect for the status quo—which is why you missed out on understanding how to deal with Bell. And you are monumentally arrogant. 'People will want what I tell them to want,'" I mocked him. "You're a disruptive influence. Don't expect me to glorify you."

He was getting a little steamed.

"You can quote me," he spat. "You can disagree with me. But you can't ignore me, because I change things. I'm gonna change fucking *humanity!*"

"Sure, sure," I waved him off. "How're you gonna push the human race forward when you barely qualify as human yourself? You're outta your fuckin' mind."

"You say crazy, I say genius."

"Why? Because you believe that people who are crazy enough to think that they can change the world are the ones who do? Maybe you're right. But you're still an arrogant, abrasive asshole. And that's just the A's."

He was on his feet now, hunched over, fists clenched, ranting rather than conversing.

"It's not my job to be nice to people," he growled. "It's my job to *push* people. To challenge them so they become better. It takes abrasion to polish a diamond. But clearly there's nothing I can do for you."

"Nice speech," I drawled sarcastically. "Just great."

"You're insane."

"Insanely great," I said. "But I must be insane to still admire you in spite of your massive catalog of faults."

I stood up and leaned over my desk, fists planted on the desktop.

"Mr. Jobs," I said in a gruff, gravelly voice, "our association is *over!*"

And then a miracle occurred. Steve Jobs shut up.

He unclenched his fists and relaxed his shoulders. He smiled. He chuckled. And then he laughed.

"We pranked them!" he laughed. "Biggest fucking company on the face of the earth, and we *pranked* them! Who'd ever think that a hundred billion dollar company could be defeated by three guys in blue jeans?"

"Well, you upset their applecart, that's for sure," I said, taking my seat.

"Might be the best prank I've ever pulled off," he enthused. "Even Woz would be proud…if I could just tell him. But I can't tell a single soul," he sighed.

" 'And I only am escaped alone to tell thee,'" I said.

"*Moby Dick*," he nodded. "Story of my life."

"The Book of Job, originally," I corrected. "Story of *my* life. But I can think of one person you can tell."

"Who?"

"Oaf Tobark."

We both broke out laughing.

And when we were done, when he'd realized I'd escaped the gravitational pull of his reality distortion field, and might even, God forbid, be immune to it, he placed his envelope on my desk and picked up mine. He held out his hand. I shook it. He turned toward the door.

"Best of luck, Steve," I said to his back. "Have a good life."

He was halfway out the door, half hunched over, when he stopped, looked over his shoulder, and shot me a crooked, Cheshire smile.

"Yeah," he said. "It's gonna be great."

I had no doubt that he meant insanely great.

And that was the last time I ever saw Steve Jobs.

This time, really.

Chapter 16.1

Two Years Later...

But that doesn't mean it was the last time I ever heard from him. Like a bad penny, he kept turning up…

As the tech reporter Malone had predicted, a couple of years later AT&T was busted up into several regional companies. Their long monopoly was finally over. One beneficial side effect for the "new" company was that the restrictions of the 1956 consent decree—the Carterfone agreement prohibiting their involvement in the computer industry—were eliminated. They were now free (in the words of AT&T's then-president and chairman, Charlie Brown, who oversaw the breakup) to "use the fruits of our own technology." I wonder what fruit he had in mind.

Not that this did them any good, really—by the time they could legally compete, IBM and Apple had already sown up both the business and the home computer markets. AT&T was just too late to the party. Even Xerox, from which Apple had cribbed many of its best ideas, flopped miserably in their attempt to market a personal computer.

And, as Steve himself had mentioned, Apple did indeed go public later that year, in December 1980. By the end of the trading day, the company was valued at $1.778 billion, and Steve himself was now worth $200 million overnight. He'd been promoted from the millionaire I knew to the status of multi-millionaire.

It took me a while to figure out just how I escaped his fabled "reality distortion field." But I had an intuitive feeling that Steve respected people who stood up to him—people who passionately defended their own point of view, knew what they were talking about, and refused to back down. I saw it happen in his negotiations with Jimmy. And I guess I qualified in at least one of those categories.

If I learned one thing about Steve Jobs from the short time I spent with him, it's that he was a genius and a visionary. OK, two things. And an asshole. OK, three things. But who's counting? Start listing Steve's character traits and you could end up counting to infinity. Twice.

Against all odds, I even learned a few things *from* him as well as about him. I learned I'm foolish. And I'm hungry. Becoming less foolish was the work of a lifetime. But hunger? I could solve that problem with a good steak, or a hamburger, or a pizza, or, if absolutely necessary, a healthy snack. A banana, for instance. Or some other fruit. A pomegranate, maybe. Or a pine— Ah, forget it.

And I learned—if only by negative example—the importance of keeping the people close to me happy, so I did attempt to make up for the days I spent with Steve by spiriting Laurel away for a romantic weekend at the East Brother B&B a few months later.

I didn't count on the hostess remembering me and greeting me by name. Laurel scowled at me suspiciously.

"I had a life before we got together," I said.

"Yeah, but you never had money enough for this," she accused.

We weren't a San Francisco couple. We weren't even a Silicon Valley couple. We were a couple from the rapidly evaporating Valley of Heart's Delight.

As we were leaving, the hostess looked and me and said, "Bye." Or maybe it was "bi." I don't know. I don't want to know.

While Steve was undoubtedly a royal pain in the ass, I don't regret my time with him. What good does regret do? As Adam discovered, you can't unbite that apple. I had no doubt that Steve would invent the future. He'd put a dent in the universe. As I mentioned, I saw firsthand that he's a visionary and a genius. Me, I'm neither. He's *The Jetsons*; I'm *The Flintstones*. I'll never influence the future or contribute a damn thing to it. I'm a vacuum tube in a microchip world, stuck in a film noir from the '40s or, at best, a *Rockford Files* episode from the '70s. I'd never predict a thing as long as I had my eyes on the past and my back to the future.

EPILOG

"One more thing..."

July 9, 1982

I was sitting in my office, feet up on my desk, sipping some 1974 Mirassou Gamay Beaujolais from the last viable bottle in my stash and reading the funny pages in the day's newspaper. In *Peanuts*, Charlie Brown's little sister informs him that his dog is at the door, crying. "That's not unusual," the ol' blockhead says. "Lots of dogs stand at the door and cry." In the last panel, Sally is looking at Snoopy on the doorstep. "With a handkerchief?" she asks as the dog dabs his eyes. What a crybaby.

I lowered the paper and found myself contemplating the Snoopy phone on my desk. And for some reason, I started thinking of Steve Jobs. That's when it hit me: Steve *is* Snoopy: brilliant, imaginative, independent, self-centered. And no Charlie Brown could ever control him.

I was ready to move on to *Garfield* when my reverie was interrupted by a knock on the door. I yelled enter, and a young guy wearing some kind of delivery man uniform walked in. He was so nondescript that no one would ever pick him out of a police lineup.

He was carrying a manila envelope. He looked at the label.

"Are you Mac Macintosh?"

I said I was. And I knew this was trouble.

I signed for the delivery. He left.

I opened the envelope and removed a certificate. A certificate for 5,000 shares of Apple stock.

I rummaged around the loose newspaper sections until I found the Business pages and looked up the price of Apple stock.

It had closed the previous evening at four cents a share.

Four cents a share.

Was this Steve pranking me? If it was, I'd show him, goddamn it: I'd hang onto that stock until it was actually worth something, no matter how long it took. In the meanwhile, I'd take the certificate home, show it to Laurel, and tell her I was ready to buy that dreamhouse she'd always wanted—as long as Barbie wasn't still living in it.

I was about to toss the sheet into a drawer when I noticed a Post-it stuck to the back. It was a note, in spindley handwriting.

A little bonus for doing work that was not shit, it read, and was signed "Oaf Tobark."

Beneath that was a second note:

One more thing... I'll call to follow up. I might have a job of work for you.

I got up from my desk to go home. Just as I reached the door, the phone rang.

I let it.

The End

"It's not the intention or the policy of The Phone Company to deal harshly with anyone. However, there are circumstances…"
—Phone Company Representative, *The President's Analyst*

"The pumps don't work 'cause the vandals took the handles."
—Bob Dylan, *Subterranean Homesick Blues*

Also Available from The Impermanent Press

All titles are available in both ebook and print formats

Also Available From The Impermanent Press

The Uncertainty Principle?

by D. Scott Apel

Alec Smart Comic Mystery #1

"Reads like a mashup of Raymond Chandler, Jorge Luis Borges and Donald E. Westlake."
—ComiCaper

When a small-town private eye is hired by a big name science fiction writer to find out why everything he writes comes true, the metaphysical assignment leads the young detective into a labyrinth of bizarre and life-threatening incidents, any one of which could be either incredible coincidence or part of a complex, carefully orchestrated conspiracy. He risks losing his client, his mind and even his life as he walks this razor's edge between coincidence and conspiracy to its unexpected resolution.

This period piece, set in the San Francisco Bay Area in the late 1970s, captures the offbeat atmosphere of the underground of the era: a playground of science fiction writers, religious cultists and dangerous psychotics. *The Uncertainty Principle?* combines comic capers with a novel mystery to create a mystery novel that is, in fact, novel.

"Brilliant, original, and damned funny as well!"
—Robert Anton Wilson,
co-author of the *Illuminatus!* trilogy and *The Cosmic Trigger*

Also Available From The Impermanent Press

The Infinite Mistress

by D. Scott Apel

Alec Smart Comic Mystery #2

"Fans of Donald E. Westlake's comic crime novels will love The Infinite Mistress."
—ComiCaper

When a bubble-headed North Beach topless dancer hires a young Silicon Valley private eye to investigate the authenticity of her "past life memories," little does he suspect that he's about to become entangled in a plot that has repeated itself through several lifetimes—and always ends tragically for the dancer.

Or is it all just coincidence? The real question is, can he piece together the past-life clues he uncovers in time to dodge the juggernaut of karma and avoid the fated fatal finale? It's taken several lifetimes, but this time around, time is running out. *The Infinite Mistress* is a fast, funny, and original twist on the mystery novel.

Also Available From The Impermanent Press

Detective, Comics

by D. Scott Apel

Alec Smart Comic Mystery #3

"The heir apparent to Donald E. Westlake's comic caper novels."
—ComiCaper

When a teenage comic book magnate has a valuable book stolen from his collection, he turns to small town private eye Alec Smart to find his Batman book...and justice.

But the path to justice is a rocky road, as Alec discovers when he's forced to deal with a corrupt comic book store owner as well as the kid's estranged parents, one of whom wants him dead and one of whom wants him in bed. Not to mention his own relationship crisis: If his beloved girlfriend leaves him, will he have the fortitude to assist the kid?

The third entry in the Alec Smart comic mystery series features high stakes and low comedy, quirky characters, odd plot twists and droll dialog, as well as action, insanity...and adults running around in rented superhero costumes, trapped in a giant videogame. Yeah, you read that right.

Detective, Comics is a fresh, fast-paced and fun-filled twist on the standard detective novel formula...because formula is for babies.

Also Available From The Impermanent Press

Escape from 50sville

by Casey Bragg

Edited by D. Scott Apel

The legendary, long-lost comic mystery novel by acclaimed mystery writer Casey Bragg is now available!

OK, Boomers! Looking for a unique vacation getaway? Escape to Sunnyville, where the '50s never ended! In this unique, full immersion theme park, your past is their present. Spend a week reliving the idyllic, carefree existence of your youth...just don't look beneath the serene surface, where corruption fills the utilidors. And don't go looking for trouble, because if you do, you are *definitely* going to find it...just like the web of depravity, conspiracy and deadly deception the town Sheriff stumbles into.

Is *Escape* a contemporary satire? A parable of the '50s? A quirky romance? A fond, nostalgic tribute to the days when both ethics and TV were black and white? A cautionary tale of the abuse of surveillance? Answer: Yes! And so much more! As Mark Twain said, "History doesn't repeat itself, but it often rhymes."

Casey Bragg's legendary mystery has been edited, abridged and is introduced by D. Scott Apel (author of the Alex Smart comic mystery series).

Also Available From The Impermanent Press

Killer B's:
The 237 Best Movies on Video You've (Probably) Never Seen

by D. Scott Apel

The iTunes Movie Guru (Emeritus) shares his selection of the best unknown movies available on demand.

We live in an age of unprecedented access to movies. Too bad most of them suck.

Netflix, Amazon Prime, anything with a "+" ... Thousands and thousands of movies are available at your fingertips. But with so many titles, the big question remains: How do you find a *good* movie?

The answer: *Killer B's: The 237 Best Movies on Video You've (Probably) Never Seen. Killer B's* makes full use of the on-demand advantage: easy access to lesser-known films. It's just as easy to find a hidden gem as a recent blockbuster...if you know what you're looking for. *Killer B's* lets you know what to look for.

Whatever you call them—buried treasures, sleepers, word of mouth movies, or "killer" B movies—these are great little films that never got the publicity, distribution or attention they needed to allow their audience to find them. Killer B's are terrific but little-known films, designed with a general audience in mind—no "cult classics," no "forgotten favorites," no "so bad they're good" flicks, just the delight of discovery.

Life's too short to watch bad films. Don't be stung by bad movies —put *Killer B's* to work for you, and find a few good movies you've (possibly) never heard of and (probably) never seen!

Also Available From The Impermanent Press

Science Fiction: An Oral History

Dialogs with Prominent Authors of the Golden Age (1930-1960) and New Wave (1960-1980)

Edited by D. Scott Apel

Science Fiction: An Oral History features in-depth interviews with Philip K. Dick, Theodore Sturgeon, Fritz Leiber, Roger Zelazny, C.L. Moore, Leigh Brackett, Norman Spinrad and Robert Anton Wilson. Through these interviews with some of the most highly-regarded figures in the field, we get first-hand insight into the changes in style, subject and society that shaped the evolution of the genre over its first half-century.

Topics covered include their influences and working habits, analysis of their major works, discussions of science fiction as the modern mythology and its differences from mainstream fiction, as well as numerous anecdotes from their professional and personal lives. Far from a dry history of a dynamic subject, the interview format captures the spontaneity, enthusiasm and humor of spending a couple hours in good conversation with an old friend.

Also Available From The Impermanent Press

Fourplay
A Theatrical Quartet

by D. Scott Apel

A Comedy Tonight! Treat yourself to a quartet of comic plays you'll never see on stage (unless you attended an early performance). "Fourplay" collects scripts for two three-act comedies and two one-act farces ("A Pair of Shorts") first staged by San Jose's famous Stage One performance company in the early '90s. Bonus material includes the script for a never-performed fifth play—a one-act farce to be staged in the theater of your mind.

If you're a fan of The Marx Brothers, you'll love "A Night in the Graveyard," an original homage to the films of the boys' early years. And if you hate PBS pledge breaks, you'll love "Pledge Night!" which reveals what might be going on behind the scenes and off-screen. "Fourplay" also includes introductions and numerous production photos. Uh-oh...the curtain's going up on these lively reads—better get a copy and take your seat!

Also Available From The Impermanent Press

Philip K. Dick:
The Dream Connection

Edited by D. Scott Apel

"A very impressive must-read for serious PKD readers... I literally could not put this book down. Reading the interview, you get the uncanny sensation that you're sitting in the room rapping with PKD himself."
—*Science Fiction Chronicle*

This exceptional anthology includes over eight hours of interviews with noted science fiction author Philip K. Dick, including the most complete and personal account of his March, 1974, "mystical experiences," plus numerous supplementary essays, including Robert Anton Wilson on PKD's mystical experiences, R. Faraday Nelson on collaborating with PKD, a rarely-seen short story in which PKD fictionalizes his mystical experiences, and much more.

"Hands down the most joyous and entertaining book on Philip K. Dick."
—Lawrence Sutin, author of
Divine Invasions: A Life of Philip K. Dick.

Also Available From The Impermanent Press

NO PLAN B

The Adventures of a Carbon Unit in Silicon Valley, or How I Made a Million Dollars in Hi-Tech Startups Basically by Just Showing Up (Don't Try This at Home)

by D. Scott Apel

Ever wonder what it was like to participate in the Silicon Valley hi-tech revolution? To work at a startup struggling for survival? To be deeply embedded in a major company like Apple? This worklife memoir gets you in on the ground floor...and like its author, you'll never rise any higher.

NO PLAN B is not a history of Silicon Valley. It is not the story of a struggling startup that went on to rule the world. It is the far more common story of a few startups that tried but tanked, as witnessed by a cubicle dweller who went down with those ships, often without a life preserver.

NO PLAN B is not a Silicon Valley overview. It is an *under*view. It is a memo sent from the trenches—notes from the break room, not the boardroom. *NO PLAN B* is not a business book, it's a *work* book.

There are more than enough books about Silicon Valley that concentrate on The Big Picture: the epic struggles of a startup to survive, and the outrageous and outsized egos of their larger-than-life founders. But for every successful startup there are a hundred that go belly-up, and for every Steve Jobs or Mark Zuckerberg there are 10,000 nameless, faceless workers who toil in obscurity to make the vision of these visionaries a success...if only just to hold on to their jobs.

Nobody tells their stories. *NO PLAN B* is one...

Also Available From The Impermanent Press

Killer B's 2:
Son of a Killer B
237 MORE Great Movies on Demand You've (Probably) Never Seen

by D. Scott Apel

The iTunes Movie Guru (Emeritus) shares his selection of the best unknown movies available on demand.

The original *Killer B's* covered great but little-known movies released between 1980 and 1995. This sequel volume picks up where Vol. 1 left off, and includes buried treasures released between 1996 and 2016—an additional 237 superb but overlooked movies (as well as a few bingeable, overlooked TV series).

We live in an age of unprecedented access to movies. Too bad most of them suck. With instant access to so many titles, the question remains: How do you find a *good* movie?

The answer: the *Killer B's* film guides, which make full use of the on-demand advantage: easy access to lesser-known films. It's just as easy to find a hidden gem as a recent blockbuster...if you know what you're looking for. *Killer B's* lets you know what to look for.

Whatever you call them—buried treasures, sleepers, word of mouth movies, or "killer" B movies—these are great little films that never got the publicity, distribution or attention they needed to allow their audience to find them. Killer B's are terrific but little-known films, designed with a general audience in mind—no "cult classics," no "forgotten favorites," no "so bad they're good" flicks, just the delight of discovery.

Life's too short to watch bad films. Don't be stung by bad movies —put *Killer B's* to work for you, and find a few good movies you've (possibly) never heard of and (probably) never seen!

Also Available From The Impermanent Press

Killer B's: The Hive
The 487 Best Movies* On Demand You've (Probably) Never Seen

**and a few TV Shows*

by D. Scott Apel

The iTunes Movie Guru (Emeritus) shares his selection of the best unknown movies available on demand.

The Hive is where the honey is! This handy guide to the great but underseen movies available on demand brings together the complete contents of *Killer B's, Volume 1 (1980-1995)* and *Killer B's, Volume 2 (1996-2016),* complete in one volume.

Whatever you call these flicks—buried treasures, sleepers, word of mouth movies, or "killer" B movies—these are great little films that never got the publicity, distribution or attention they needed to allow their audience to find them.

Life's too short to watch bad films. Don't be stung by bad movies—put *Killer B's* to work for you, and find a few good movies you've (possibly) never heard of and (probably) never seen!

Note: *Killer B's: The Hive* is available only as an ebook—it's just *too damn big* to fit into a print volume!

Also Available From The Impermanent Press

Famedroppings

by D. Scott Apel

We swim in a sea of celebrity—a sea that's both shallow and surprisingly wide. There are few people who don't have a "brush with fame" story in their repertoire of personal anecdotes. I've got 100...and then some.

This book of short, amusing anecdotes details my "close encounters" with the famous folk I've run across, interviewed, or even occasionally befriended, including Actors (Robin Williams, Meg Ryan), Directors (Robert Wise), *Star Trek* cast (and creator Gene Roddenberry), Cultural Icons (Joseph Campbell; Tim Leary), Musicians (Grace Slick), and Writers (Philip K. Dick, Norman Mailer)...not to mention *Playboy* Playmates, Astronauts, Scientists and Billionaires (Steve Jobs was my boss!).

These are the backstage stories and candid moments that happen when the tape recorder is turned off, or when Mary Tyler Moore steps on your foot.

Also Available From The Impermanent Press

Exemplary Lives of Impossible Men

by D. Scott Apel

Borges. Nabokov. Vonnegut. Joyce. If they were still alive, they'd all want the author of this book dead. (As would Pynchon, Barthelme, Auster, Wallace, Heller, Barth, Beckett, Calvino, Lem and DeLillo. Among others.) Why? Because *Exemplary Lives of Impossible Men* is the apex of the postmodern novel—the apogee and apotheosis, the capstone and culmination of the literary style they pioneered…written by a hack who appropriated and executed all their favorite literary tricks.

Exemplary Lives is the last postmodern novel—the final nail in the coffin of the literary form—and it's the only postmodern novel you ever need to read. It's funny. It's heartbreaking. (But mostly it's funny.) And it's the only novel ever written that analyzes itself. What more could you ask of a satiric metabiography that details the lives, careers and *oeuvres* of eight epically failed writers while simultaneously mocking both pretentious literary styles and skewering pompous literary criticism?

Is this book alternate multiverse science fiction? Yes and no. Is it literary fiction? Mmm…yes. And no. Is it a mystery? Oh, absolutely, and on every possible level. Is it a complicated word game full of intricate interconnections and a final surprise revelation? Is this a rhetorical question?

Also Available From The Impermanent Press

Mein Summer Kampf

by D. Scott Apel

The most common response I get to that title is: "You think that's funny?" The answer I'd really like to give you is the Joe Pesci answer: "Funny how? I mean, funny like I'm a clown, I amuse you?" But the answer I will give you (and Joe) is: Yes, I do, or I wouldn't have made it the title of this collection of short humorous essays, ludicrous lists, satirical stories and even (shudder) a couple parodic poems. Yes, the answer is Yes.

There is only one other word I'd like to say about this collection: *subtle*. And that is the last time you will ever hear that word used in connection with this material. An ex-girlfriend once told me that I was like a 1,000 watt light bulb: very bright, but a little obnoxious. And I've been informed that my humor has a certain "je ne sais merde." I prefer to believe, however, that, like the blind man whose other senses are heightened to compensate for his lack of sight, my total lack of common sense or any sense of common decency has allowed my sense of to humor expand...occasionally so far as to exceed the boundaries of comprehension by those poor souls born without a humor gland.

But that is not you, of course, despite what they all say about you behind your back. So what the hell. Take a chance. Prove them wrong. You might just LYAO. I mean, it's FREE, for chrissake. (Except on Amazon. They won't let me give it away free. WTF?) What have you got to lose? I'll answer that question, too: You know that old adage, "You get what you pay for"? This book proves it wrong: Even though it's free, you're still getting far less than you paid for.

Hm. That hardly sounds like a successful sales pitch, now does it? OK, try this old adage: "Ya pays yer money and ya takes yer chances." Well, you're not paying anything, so there's a chance you might just get some laughs out of this collection. As a matter of fact, I guarantee you will, or your money will be cheerfully refunded. As long as you got the free version, anyway. If they made you pay 99 cents for this, we'll have to fall back on the new adage for internet commerce: "99 cents is the new free."

Made in the USA
Las Vegas, NV
09 June 2023